Emily

Emily

christine lawrence

Christine Lawrence

Emily

By
Christine Lawrence

Also by Christine Lawrence

Novels

Caught in the Web
Payback
Don't Step on the Cracks

Short story collections

Moments of Darkness
More Moments of Darkness

This novel is entirely a work of fiction
inspired by the real-life stories of those who lived and worked
in the Portsmouth Borough Asylum during World War 1.
Any resemblance to actual person, living or dead, is entirely
coincidental.

Cover photograph © Rollo Rawlings.

The Research

Funded by the Heritage Lottery, a group of research volunteers, working with the Good Mental Health Co-operative in 2021, looked at original patient records and hospital reports from the Borough of Portsmouth Lunatic Asylum, exploring books, articles and other research linked to the Portsmouth and Hampshire area. The group partnered with other local projects looking at life during that period and remembering the sacrifices made during the Great War. The outcome of this research was a pamphlet and online hub which contains more information and source materials. The aim of the project was to raise awareness generally about the social history of mental health care, to help reduce stigma and discrimination today. (Copyright © The Good Mental Health Co-operative 2021).

https://my.creative-learning.net/bundles/heritage-ww1

The author was privileged to be a part of this research group and during the process wrote several monologues based on the lives of those who were patients in the asylum at the time. Once the project was completed she decided to continue with developing one of the monologues into a novel. *Emily* is a fictional character but she could have been one of those women treated in the asylum in 1918. Her story is typical of the time but is purely fictional.

Christine would like to thank the Good Mental Health Co-operative for the opportunity to take part in this project.

About the author

Christine's career as a psychiatric nurse led to her working with those with drug and alcohol issues, as well as in many fields of mental health. During her career she successfully completed an MSc in Addictive Behaviour. Following her early retirement, she went back to studying and achieved a BA hons in English Literature and Creative Arts, followed by an MA in Creative Writing at Portsmouth University. She was one of the *2012 Writers to Watch* in the Portsmouth BookFest of that year and has short stories published in *Portsmouth Fairy Tales for Grown Ups, Pompey Writes, Star and Crescent* and *Day of the Dead*. She has written and performed for events including the *Victorious Festival, St. Valentine's Massacre, Portsmouth BookFest, Portsmouth DarkFest, Day of the Dead, Holmes Fest,* at several venues in Portsmouth, including The Guildhall, Portsmouth Historical Dockyard, The Kings Theatre, the Square Tower and the New Theatre Royal.

In 2017 Christine was one of the writers who took part in the *Writing Edward King* project at Portsmouth City Museum which received Arts Council Funding. She performed her writing for this project in several venues across the city. In 2018 she was one of the founders of Portsmouth's spoken word group,

T'Articulation, and is a Director of the Portsmouth Writer's Hub. In 2019 she was a co-writer for *Cursed City - Dark Tides,* a trans-media production for DarkFest. In 2021, Christine was appointed to lead workshops on the BBC/National Libraries, *Novels that Shaped our World* project, using Andrea Levy's *Small Island* as the novel to work with.

Christine's novels, *Caught in the Web, Payback* and *Don't Step on the Cracks,* and her collections of short stories, *Moments of Darkness* and *More Moments of Darkness,* are all available from The Book Shop at Lee-on-the-Solent, direct from the author at christinelawrence14@btinternet, or from Amazon. She is a member of the Portsmouth Authors' Collective and her books can be found on the table at many of the Authors' Collective's events.

Christine's Facebook page is https://www.facebook.com/Novelist2021

Portsmouth Authors' Collective website: https://www.portsmouthauthors.wordpress.com

Thanks as always to my husband Mark, for all his patience and feedback.

Thanks to my writing community:

Jackie Green, Eileen Phyall, Margaret Jennings, Lynne Stone, Will Sutton, Helen and Richard Salsbury, Alison Habens, Tom Sykes, Annie Kirby, Loree Westron, Pete Adams, all at the *Portsmouth Writers' Hub, Springwood Writers, Tea Tray Creatives,*

Will Sutton's *Edit Club, Scribblers Salon* and *Write your Novel* group members,

for the help, critiquing and support from you all.

Thanks also to the *Good Mental Health Co-operative,* especially Carolyn Barber and Sarah Haskett, and to Rollo Rawlings (King Rollo) for the film *Emily* and thanks for the use of his photograph for the cover.

Emily

by
Christine Lawrence

Prologue

Emily

When she opened her eyes she was back in her room. Feeling trapped, the walls closed in, the stain on the ceiling in the shape of a crib, mocking her. She closed her eyes again, trying to shut out the pain. It was still there, deep in her core.

Noises roused her again. It was nurse Paxton. Maud was her name although Emily knew her as Paxton. Briefly a thought brought a giggle to Emily's throat, 'take out the letter u and she would be Mad the same as me.' Turning to face her, Emily wondered why she was beside the bed and not out in the ward doing her duties. Tall and smartly dressed in her uniform, a grey dress reaching to her ankles with a crisp white apron and her hair caught up in the cotton cap which covered the whole of her head. She was smiling, something Emily always felt uneasy about. It usually meant something bad was about to happen when they smiled at you.

Emily didn't want to talk to her; the least you talk the better, she'd learnt. But when Nurse Paxton reached for her hand something shifted. The hard lump of ice around Emily's heart melted just for that moment, but long enough to let her in.

'Emily, it's alright, you're safe.'

Those few words were all it took to release the flow of tears and Emily's story. The nurse handed her a linen handkerchief to mop her face as she spoke about her plight and how she came to be in the asylum.

Chapter One

Emily

At the start of the war, The Great War, they called it now, there had been a feeling across Portsmouth of determination, patriotism, a belief that it would be a wonderful thing to take part in. Surely it would be all over in a flash. The young men wanted to rush in and be a part of it, their biggest fear that they would miss the fun, the adventure of a lifetime. The older men weren't so enthusiastic, knowing the hardships to come but the women were swept along with it all and pushed their young men to go.

Emily's two elder brothers Harry and Edward went, first one and then the other. Her younger brother Percy was still at school and she thanked heaven for that. The house was quiet enough without the elder two filling every space with their loud voices and heavy boots.

Ma kept house and was always there, holding the family together. Pa kept the butcher shop in Buckland which had always been busy with enough work for the two eldest boys before the war. All the same, Emily was grateful that her sweetheart, Billy Anderson, worked in the dockyard and had not gone with the others. She had not been like other women, encouraging their loved ones to war. But time brings changes to all lives whether we want it or not.

Southsea - September 1917

The sun had gone down beyond the horizon, turning the burning sea to a dull black.

It was the first time she had ever let him go this far. Afterwards she wondered what it had been about the evening that had led to this. Before, she had always been proud to have self-control, was better than any of her girlfriends who had spoken to her of things they'd done with their sweethearts. Now it was done and she wondered what all the fuss had been about. Suddenly she felt trapped. Pushing away the fear, she told herself she would be safe this time. It wouldn't happen again. She would never be that stupid.

Billy held her hand in his. She sensed he was building himself up to ask her. Emily suppressed a giggle.

'What is it, Billy?' she whispered.

'Emily, I...'

'What?'

'You know how I feel about you, Emily.' He took a breath and looked at her. His eyes were dark like his hair, his long legs stretched out before him on the shingle. She could almost hear his heartbeat before he went on. 'I can't wait to marry you.'

Emily took her hand from his. 'I know and I love you too. I'm not ready to settle down yet. I mean, I don't want to get married until I've lived life a little. I don't want to be worn out like my Ma, with babies and hard work every day. I want more than that.'

'I know you want more Emily, but I thought after tonight you would feel differently. You are mine now, you know that.'

Shaking her head, Emily laughed.

'Why are you laughing?'

Seeing the hurt look on his face, she paused.

'Well?'

'I do love you Billy, I've already said that. But I am not yours, nor anyone else's either. I am my own person and I'm not ready to marry yet. When I am, you will be my first choice.'

'But you let me do it.'

'Billy, I know what we have just done together. I wanted it too. I didn't just let you. To be truthful, I don't know what came over me. Maybe it was the sun setting, I don't know. I have strong feelings for you but I don't want to marry you yet.'

'What if I go to war? I might be gone a long time.'

Emily felt the chill coming from the sea. 'You won't though. They need you in the dockyard.'

'All my mates are going. I can't stay here and not be a part of it.'

'You'd better go then. Ask me again when you get back.'

They walked back through the streets to Emily's home in silence. Billy still held her hand but once they'd reached her front door, she gave him a quick peck on the cheek and entered the house with just a quiet, 'Goodnight,' leaving him in the street as the door slammed shut.

Emily's Ma was waiting in the kitchen, sitting beside the range. She looked at Emily as she entered the room.

'You're late home. Was that Billy you were with in the street?'

'Sorry Ma, I didn't think you'd still be up. We walked back from Southsea. We were watching the sun set over the sea.'

'Very romantic, I'm sure. Billy is a good lad.'

'He is.' Emily moved to the scullery door. 'I'm in love with him, Ma.'

'You're at the age when you think you're in love with every young man who says a kind word to you.' She smiled wistfully. 'I well remember those times.'

'I know Ma. I'm too young to settle down, but Billy wants to marry me. I told him I'm not ready.'

'You will be careful? Don't let him get too close.'

Emily blushed. 'I'm not stupid, Ma.'

'Emily, I know you think I'm old and past it but I know how hard it can be to say no. You have your whole life before you. I just don't want you to throw away your chance to have a good life by getting married too young. There's plenty of time for all that. There, I've said my piece.'

'Oh, Ma, I love you. I will be careful, don't you worry about that. I'll hold Billy at arm's length until I'm quite ready.' She gave her Ma a hug.

Once in her own room, Emily took off her only good dress and carefully hung it on the hook behind the door.

She looked at the blue of the wool which complemented her own blue eyes, thinking as she did that she would always remember this dress as the one she was wearing this night. Brushing her hair, she wondered how anyone could think this dull brown colour could be considered beautiful as Billy did. 'Love is blind,' she laughed at herself, plaited her hair and got into bed.

Lying awake for hours, she couldn't stop thinking about what had happened on the beach with Billy, flitting across things that had been said and things they'd done. She was confused. It was wrong. But it had felt so right at the time. And why afterwards had she needed to hold back, to push him away? She only knew she was afraid of being tied down to the drudgery of being a wife and mother. Maybe she didn't love him enough. Maybe she was just selfish, wanting something that was beyond a mere woman's dreams. She didn't really know what she wanted from her life, not yet, only that it wasn't that.

Chapter Two

Emily

Autumn evenings had set in and It was dark by the time she'd finished her day's work at Mrs. Cartwright's house. Working as a general house-maid was hard, the hours were long and there was little time for chatting and no-one to chat to anyway. Emily's friends had started to get jobs that the men had always done before the war started. Her friend Mabel worked in the post office now, sorting the mail, and Maureen, her old schoolfriend, was working in the dockyard. She remembered only a short time ago when Billy had told her he might be leaving the dockyard to join the Army. Was it just a threat to make her want to get married sooner? It didn't matter, she wasn't going to be pressured into doing something she wasn't ready for, whatever he did or didn't do.

Thinking of Billy gave her a warm feeling. She thought about the times they'd been together over the past few weeks. Despite her intentions, they had found moments to get close again. It was hard to resist, when you were in the arms of such a sweet man, not to let yourself get carried away with making love. Of course Emily knew she was taking a risk, and every time it happened, Billy persevered with his wishes to marry sooner rather than later. But Emily still wasn't ready for that. So he would go off to war and she would wait for him. She had made that perfectly clear to him.

Pa was in the kitchen, sitting in Ma's place beside the range. His butcher's overall was draped on the chair he usually sat in and the air smelt of raw meat. Pa's face was drawn and there were splatterings of dried blood in his grey hair. Emily pushed aside feelings of nausea and annoyance. 'Where's Ma?' she asked.

'Ma's unwell. She's lying down upstairs. You'll have to get our tea.'

'What's the matter with her?' Emily moved to the stairs.

'Got a fever. And she's been sick.' He stood up. 'She'll be alright tomorrow. Just needs to rest.'

'She's not pregnant?' Emily felt a coldness run through her.

'No! Well, I don't know. But I don't think so. It looks worse than that. But hopefully just a chill.'

Emily climbed the stairs, fearfully remembering the fevers that were spreading throughout the city.

Ma lay on the bed, covers thrown back. Standing for a moment, not knowing what to do, Emily swallowed down her fear and gently touched her Ma's hand. Her skin was clammy to touch and the sheets were damp. Her hair was loose and tangled, strands stuck to her neck.Opening her eyes, Ma seemed unable to focus on Emily. 'Harold, is that you?' She whispered.

'It's me, Ma. Emily. Should I fetch the doctor?'

'No need. I'll be fine with a bit of rest.' She gripped Emily's hand with a surprising strength. 'Look after Pa and the boy. Get the tea, won't you.'

'Of course. I'll bring you up some broth in a while. Do you need anything else?'

Ma shook her head. 'So tired,' she said. 'I'll just sleep for a bit.'

Emily moved to the door, turned to look back at her Ma who had already closed her eyes again. Standing there for a moment until she could see the rise and fall of Ma's chest, Emily quietly opened the bedroom door and closing it behind her, made her way back down the dark stairs to the kitchen below. Her Pa looked up as she entered the room. She thought he'd been crying. Pa never cried. Emily moved across the room as he stood up.

'It's alright Pa, Ma will be alright, won't she?'

He sniffed and wiped the back of his hand across his face. 'Course she will. I'm being daft. My Rose is a strong woman, she always was. Here, give me a hug girl.'

She stepped into his arms, always strong, always the same. But inside she was afraid. What would they do without Ma? So many people in town were dying of the fever. You never knew when or where it would strike. And she would be the only woman left in the house if anything happened and Ma was lost.

'Yes, Pa, she will be alright. I'm going to get our tea and make Ma some broth as well. Where is Percy?'

But she hadn't been alright. Ma got worse and Pa didn't know how to cope with any of it. Emily went to work each morning with a lump in her throat as she tried not to let the fear of losing Ma overcome her. Working hard all day was a way of not facing what was sure to happen. She'd seen it so many times before in the people living nearby. Whenever an illness spread through the community, people died. She knew this.

A few days later she woke suddenly, feeling so cold. It was too quiet, almost as if the house itself had stopped breathing. Creeping down the dark stairs into the kitchen below to light the fire, her Pa was sitting there again, with his head in his hands. He looked up as she entered the room. Even before he'd said anything she knew.

'Ma's gone,' was all he said. His eyes were dry but his hands shook as he stared into nothingness.

'Oh, Pa,' Emily knelt beside him and held his hands. 'What are we going to do without her?'

Pa shook his head and said nothing.

Wiping away the tears that had somehow started to flow, Emily stood and looked about the room. She shivered. 'The fire needs lighting,' she said. 'You'll need to light it and I'll get the breakfast ready. I'll be back down in a minute.'

She turned and went up the stairs to see her Ma for the last time. The room was cold, the curtains drawn tightly across the window. Emily opened them to let a little light in and moved to the bed. Her ma looked so pale and her stillness cut Emily to the heart. Her once vital and lively Ma was gone and in her place was this shell of nothing. It was all wrong. And there was a rotten smell in the room, the smell of death. Emily gagged and went back to the window. She pulled the curtains apart and opened the window wide. The fresh gust of an autumn wind blew the curtains in as the air in the room was refreshed. Emily went back downstairs for hot water to wash her Ma.

Pa hadn't moved. Emily's head was spinning with all that needed to be done. She shook her head.

'Light the fire, Pa,' she said. 'I'm going next door to ask for help with Ma and you'll need to send for the doctor for the death certificate. Ma will need to be cleaned and dressed ready for the undertaker. And wake up Percy. He will need to be fed and then go to school.'

Ma's funeral was a small affair, held in the nearby church of St. Marys. She was buried in the cemetery behind the prison, in New Road. Before, it had always been a place that Emily had loved to walk, amongst the trees with its meadow flowers. There were always squirrels and the sound of birdsong. It was a lovely place to spend quiet moments. Now, and forever more, it would be a place to come to talk to her Ma.

Chapter Three

Emily

Ma was sorely missed by Emily, the only girl. Working as a skivvy in the big house was hard but made even harder when she had to start all over again when she got home at night. Death had taken Ma away and Emily wanted to follow her.

It was hard to keep the three of them fed and the house cleaned when Emily was working six days a week as house-maid. She should have given up the job but the thought of being nothing but a house-wife replacement for Ma was too much. Even the butcher's shop was flagging, and Pa was struggling to make a living any more.

Billy was holding Emily's hand when he told her.

'I've signed up. I had to do it Emily. I got one of those letters put through the door.' He blushed and looked away.

Emily shivered. 'What do you mean, one of those letters?'

'A white feather.'

She said nothing.

'I know I said I wouldn't go but don't think I've got a choice any more. You have to see that, Emily. So many of the lads have gone from the dockyard. There's only old men left and now there's more and more women working there. It shames me knowing I'm the only youngster. Or I will be before long.'

They were walking across the common. The wind whipped against their faces as Emily tried to gather her thoughts. It was wrong, this war, so wrong. Three years had passed and it was only luck that her two brothers were still alive, although God only knew where and how they were surviving. She'd heard all the stories and seen what it could do to a man. Those that had returned on short leave weren't like young men any more. They had turned into old men. Each one of them had a crazed look in their eyes, or were angry, changed beyond all recognition. She'd been glad not to have seen Harry or Edward during these past years. Rather not see them at all than to have seen the changes in them.

'I don't want you to go, Billy. I don't care what people say about you. Your work in the docks is important. Someone has to keep the ships repaired and seaworthy. You've said that yourself, haven't you?'

'I did, of course I did, but I think I was wrong now. I'm starting to feel ashamed of myself and can't live with it anymore. I have to do the right thing, Emily.'

They walked in silence for a while longer and soon were at the pier. Her hand was still in his but she could already feel the distance between them stretching out into the future.

'Come on, let's have a cup of tea.'

Billy opened the door to the tea room and in they went, into the warmth, the steam of the tea urn and the people's chatter clouding the windows facing the Solent. Billy wiped the condensation away with a sweep of his arm and they both looked out at the choppy sea before he turned to face her.

'I'll be going away on training in a few days time and I know you're going to say no again, but I can't go without asking you once more. Emily, why won't you marry me before I go? We can have a quick ceremony and plan a big party for when this is all over. It would mean the world to me.'

Emily was unable to bring herself to look at him. Her answer would hurt his feelings yet she knew it was the right thing to do.

'Emily?' he reached across and touched her arm.

'I'm not going to marry you, Billy. I don't want you to go to war, of course I don't. I'm scared to death that I'll lose you, that I won't see you again, or if I do, you'll be changed. But I can't marry you yet. I'm just not ready for marriage. I've told you before and nothing's changed since then. If—when we survive this terrible war, ask me again. There won't be anyone else for me. Not ever.'

The look on his face almost made her change her mind. Her stubborn streak stopped her even as she wondered that maybe she should have relented and agreed to marry him before he went.

The awkwardness of being in such a bustling room full of people after such a conversation made the hour drag out. Finally it was time to leave. Billy stood and held her chair for her, helped her on with her coat and they left.

The journey on the bus had seemed to take an age but once they were outside Emily's gate it was with relief that they said their final goodbye.

'Please don't be sad,' Emily said. 'I don't want us to part like this.'

Billy had his hand on the gate. He looked at her and smiled. 'I will be sad, but once I've gone, I'll be busy and can try and forget the sadness. I'm not giving up, Emily. I will keep asking you until you agree.'

'That's the spirit. Now I must go in. It's late. Goodbye Billy,' and she reached up to kiss him before she turned and went into the house.

Chapter Four

Emily

The town seemed to be even more quiet once Billy was gone, Emily hadn't realised how much she would miss him. They'd only seen each other once a week and yet it was something to look forward to. The house was too quiet without Ma. Pa spent more and more time at the butcher shop, coming home late. She wondered what he could be doing there and whether he went somewhere else each evening whilst she sat indoors watching his supper growing cold. Percy missed Ma too and would sit with Emily in Pa's chair most nights, his young face with a worried look that broke Emily's heart.

'Is Pa in the pub? Why don't he come home anymore?'

'A man needs company,' Emily would say. But Pa didn't come home stinking of beer and one evening Emily had walked down to The Stag just around the corner to look for herself. Hesitating to walk into the bar, a woman alone, she peered through the window. He wasn't there as far as she could see and when old Albert from three doors down stepped out through the door, she called him over.

'Have you seen my Pa?'

'Not seen Harold in a week or more,' was the reply as Albert stumbled away down the street.

Emily wondered if he'd found another local to drink in. In the past he'd not been one to spend time in the pub, preferring to sit by the fireside with Ma beside him. 'How things had changed since she had died', Emily thought as she walked home.

Emily plodded on through the days and long nights, working and doing her best to keep the family fed and the house clean. Time seemed to stand still with each day the same as the last. Each morning she woke up feeling so heavy and tired. One morning she had to dash to the outhouse where she was violently sick. She wondered with fear whether she'd got the fever and was going the way of her Ma. Everything seemed to be going wrong in her life since Ma died. There was no-one to talk to about anything anymore. Her old friends were so busy with their own lives and she'd seemed to have lost touch with them. Time for herself was so little these days and without Billy to meet, Emily was feeling quite lost.

One afternoon, she left work earlier than usual. Mrs.Cartwright had taken pity on her saying she looked like death itself and should go home and rest. 'You should go straight to bed when you get home,' she'd said.

Emily thanked her knowing that going straight to bed would be very unlikely as she mentally listed the jobs that needed doing. Expecting the house to be silent and cold, Emily opened the door and was surprised to hear someone was already home.

'Percy? Is that you?' She walked down the passage to the kitchen. 'What are you doing home so early?'

'It's me. Pa. Not Percy.'

As she entered the room and looked at her Pa she realised that he looked different. She hadn't seen much of him lately as she'd gone to bed most nights before he even got in. His hair was brushed, he was newly shaved and had on his best white shirt. Sitting in his chair beside the range, he was buffing his best black shoes.

'You'll get boot polish on that shirt,' she said.

He shrugged his shoulders. 'I'm being careful.'

'Why are you wearing your best shirt anyway?'

'Nothing wrong in making an effort.'

'No. But Pa, you haven't worn that shirt since Ma's funeral. Do you have something to tell me?'

He said nothing for a while. His head was down as he furiously worked at polishing his shoes.

'Pa?'

'A man needs a woman in his life, Emily. You might not understand, you being so young.' He put his shoes down near the fireside and looked around the room. 'I know it's been hard for you having to take Ma's place, doing all the cleaning and everything. And with the two eldest boys away I've been lonely. I've got a lady friend. It's Kate. You know Kate; she was Ma's childhood friend. It was always Rose and Kate when they were youngsters. Kate used to pop in to see Ma all the time. Her husband died a few years ago and she's been lonely too.'

Emily looked at the net curtain at the window and noticed that the sun shining through showed up a cobweb, the spider sitting there in the centre, waiting for its prey. Resisting to reach up and sweep it away, she sat down in Ma's chair.

'You've been courting her. We wondered where you were going all these evenings.' The pain Emily felt was dull and deep. Her Pa was courting another woman. And Ma only gone a few weeks. 'How long?'

'Only since Ma went. It hit me hard, losing her and Kate has been kind to me. I think she'll be good for me and for all of us. Percy needs a Ma, and it'll take some of the weight off you.'

'What do you mean, Percy needs a Ma? And take the weight off me? Please don't say you're planning to propose to her?'

'I have already and she said yes. I had hoped you'd be happy and I'm sure you will be in time. Kate will be good for you too. You need a woman to talk to.' He paused. 'Kate wants you to call her Ma.'

Emily took up the kettle from the range and shook it angrily before slamming it back down on the hot plate. She spun round to face her Pa.

'She'll never be my Ma. My Ma is dead. I'm ashamed of you, Pa, thinking that anyone could take Ma's place. And what about her own two?'

Pa shook his head and looked at her. 'Jimmy and Eddy are at the front, same as our boys, but when they come on leave they'll stay here I suppose.'

'And what about when our boys come home?'

'We'll fit them all in somehow. They'll be bringing in a wage each as well so that should help. You know the shop's not doing so well now. People can't find the money for meat and anyway it's scarce these days.' He reached for Emily. 'Come on love, be happy for me.'

'I wish I could, Pa. But it hurts too much, missing Ma, and now this.' She turned and went into the back yard, slamming the door as she went.

They got married within three weeks. Pa said it would make Emily's life easier but it didn't. Things changed from the day Kate moved in. It was worse. Although she wasn't very tall, there was a presence about her that took over every room she entered. Her grey hair was coarse like wire wool which seemed to suit her character and although she'd complained of lack of money before marrying Pa, her rounded figure denied she'd ever had to go hungry. Sly, she was sweet to Emily in front of Pa but it was all for show.

Emily arrived home from work and Pa was out. He'd taken to playing darts some evenings since the wedding. Kate was waiting for Emily and as soon as she entered the house, Kate called her through to the kitchen.

'At last you're home. My poor old feet are killing me. The washing needs sorting.'

Emily wondered what Kate had been doing to make her feet hurt so. She looked around the kitchen. The cobwebs that had been there before were still there, a thick layer of dust coated the dresser and the floor was dirty.

'I'm tired, Kate. It's been a hard day. But I will help with the washing as soon as I've had a cup of tea.'

'No. You will do it now. The sheets need wringing out. You think you're a little princess don't you? You won't have any tea until the jobs are done. And when you've done that you can scrub the floor. It's disgusting.'

Emily sighed.

'Don't sigh at me you little madam. Get on with it.' She picked up the poker and turned to face Emily. 'You might as well get used to pulling your weight, or you'll feel this on your backside.'

She pushed Emily into the scullery.

When Pa returned two hours later, Emily was sitting in the kitchen, just finishing off her now-dried supper. Her Pa looked at her as he entered the room and smiled. 'You look tired, girl. Been overdoing it have you?'

'No, Pa. I'm alright, really.'

Kate had been seated by the fire. She stood and gave Pa a hug. 'We've been having a lovely evening, haven't we, Emily, dear?'

Emily shook her head. 'Pa, I can't...' She noticed Kate was glaring at her. 'Never mind. I'm just a bit tired. I think I'll have an early night.' Kissing her Pa on the cheek. She took her plate to the scullery, washed up the supper things and made her way up to bed.

This was the pattern of life after that. Sometimes Kate would pinch Emily if she didn't work hard enough and more than once she'd hit Emily across the back with the poker.

You'd have thought Pa would have noticed Emily was unhappy, only he was so caught up in his own happiness he couldn't see what he didn't want to see.

And Emily soon had more of her own troubles to deal with.

Chapter Five

Emily

The sickness she'd suffered a few weeks before gradually faded and Emily was working as hard as ever at Mrs. Cartwright's during the day and then back in her own home every evening. It no longer felt like a home and as she got stronger, Emily started to plan how she could leave, and maybe even find a job somewhere else, perhaps move away from Portsmouth to make a new life for herself altogether.

She met up with her old friend Mabel. It was a rare occasion that they both had the same day free. Mabel's job in the post office only gave her time off once a fortnight and it was rarely the same day as Emily's. They sat together in the tea room near the pier. Emily felt a sadness wash over her as she remembered this was the last place she'd spent time with Billy.

'Blimey, Emily, cheer up for God's sake. Come on I'll treat you to one of those currant buns they do in here.'

'Sorry, I was miles away.' Emily was staring out at the waves, wondering where Billy might be.

'You do look a bit peaky, I must say. You been alright?'

'Of course, I'm just tired that's all.'

The waitress had arrived at the table to take their order. When she had gone, Mabel spoke again.

'Come on then, tell me the latest news.' Mabel leaned across the table to Emily. 'Are you engaged yet?'

'No, I'm not and probably never will be.'

'Why's that? You're still with Billy aren't you?'

'I haven't heard from him since he went to the front and that was several weeks ago. He wanted us to get engaged before he left but I wouldn't have any of it. Don't shake your head, Mabel. I'm not ready to get tied to a man yet. I've seen what it can do to a woman. Getting married seems romantic before it happens, then you have the babies, one after another, until you're worn down and life is just a drudge. I've seen it with my Ma. I don't want that. Not yet anyway.'

'Hmm, you make it sound like a miserable future for all of us women. I can't believe it's like that for everyone. And what else is there for a girl? You can't go through life without a man to support you, to look after you, can you?'

'Can't you? I can't see why we always have to rely on having a man in our lives.'

'Well there's the laws aren't there. They all go against us. You can't be independent that easily without a man to sign papers for you. Can't have your own bank account, can't buy your own home. Not that the likes of us would ever be able to afford to do that. It's all very well us doing the men's jobs whilst the war is on and they're all away fighting for the country, but when they come back, those that do'll want their jobs back. I for one, will be out of work and then what's left? Going into service as a maid, or working cleaning floors somewhere. Sorry, I know that's what you're already doing.'

'There must be more for us.' Emily said. 'Things have started to change and they can only get better. They can't be worse than how it is at the moment anyway. I've got to find some way out of this. My Pa remarried and I don't get on with his new wife. Her name's Kate. I don't think I can bear living in the same house as that woman any more. I was thinking of looking for work somewhere not so near to home. Somewhere I can have a room and be independent. I'd try anything. I just need to get away.'

'Well good luck with that,' Mabel sighed and shook her head. 'You always were like this, full of fancy ideas.' She stopped as the waitress returned with their tea and two buns, 'Let's just enjoy our tea, eh? I'll be able to think clearer after a cup of tea.'

Half way through the bun, Emily felt faint. She sipped at the tea, hoping that a drink would make her feel better.

Mabel stopped eating and looked up at Emily, her mouth still full. 'What is it? You look awful.'

'Thanks,' Emily took another sip of her tea. 'I think it's the bun. Too much sugar or something, making me feel sick.'

'Well if you don't want it, I'll eat it. It's a real treat it is.'

Emily pushed her plate across the table. 'Here you are then. I don't know what's the matter with me lately to be honest. I used to love a currant bun.'

'You're not pregnant are you? You're just like my Ma was when she was expecting.' She glared at Emily. 'Oh, God, you're not are you?'

'No. At least I hope not.' Emily looked across the room at all the faces which seemed to blur into a pattern. 'I can't be, can I?'

'Don't ask me. I don't know what you've been up to. When was the last time you saw Billy? Did you, you know, do it with him?'

'Stop it, Mabel. I can't talk about it in here.'

'So that's a yes then. What are you going to do about it?'

'I need to get out of here.' Emily stood.

'Oi, let me finish my bun first. What's the rush?'

'Sorry.' Emily sat down again.

'No. I'm sorry. It's not something that you wanted is it? But it looks like you might be expecting. There's no need to feel ashamed about it. It's this war, leading so many young people into doing things they might not have done. Will you tell Billy? He will marry you, you already said that's what he wants, so maybe it's not such a bad thing. If you are pregnant I mean.'

Emily cast her mind back over the past weeks. 'It looks like I probably am. I still don't want to marry Billy yet but it seems like I've got no choice.'

'You'd better be writing to him then.'

Emily posted the letter the next day. She hadn't told anyone else about the baby. Mabel had promised to say nothing. It had taken a while for Emily to believe herself what was happening to her. The changes in her body were uncomfortable and she was afraid but telling no one about it kept it unreal. She wondered what Billy would say when he got her letter and hoped he'd still want to marry her. She couldn't bear to think otherwise.

Chapter Six

Emily

Christmas came and went, a quiet affair, the first one since Ma had died. Pa tried to make it special, bringing home a piece of beef that he'd managed to save but Kate was no cook and it shrivelled in the oven so there was little to go around. They exchanged presents. Percy had made Emily a card, something she treasured, and she gave him a scarf that she'd knitted herself, but there was nothing from Kate and Pa was drunk from early in the morning until late in the afternoon when he fell asleep in his chair. Emily was on edge, waiting to hear from Billy and wondering why she'd not had news from him before Christmas.

It was a few days into the New Year that she got her answer. Billy's Ma was at the front door. A tall and elegant woman, her hair in a tight bun. Still she seemed different, her coat cuffs frayed and she looked like she'd thrown on the first garment she'd found. Emily remembered seeing Mrs. Anderson wearing this coat in the garden when she was working. She'd obviously come out in a hurry with little thought. Emily knew it was bad news as soon as she saw the pinched look on the woman's face. They stood for a while, neither saying anything, normal evening family sounds coming from inside the house. Then Emily remembered her manners.

'Mrs. Anderson. Come in, please.' She stood aside and ushered the older woman into the hallway. 'It's warmer in the kitchen but the parlour is quieter. Please, sit down. I'll get you a cup of tea.'

The chill of the front parlour seemed to match the iciness of Billy's Ma.

'No need for that. I won't be stopping.' She still hadn't looked at Emily, rather her eyes glanced around the room as if she were judging the furniture and Emily's Ma's own taste in decor.

'Are you going to tell me why you've come? Has Billy written to you? Is he well?'

'Billy is dead.'

The room seemed to be shrinking as Emily's legs lost all their strength. She sat down heavily on the sofa. 'Dead? Are you sure? He can't be.'

'Of course I'm sure! Telegrams do not lie.'

'I'm sorry.'

'Please don't start crying over him. It's your fault. If you hadn't led him on and then turned him down, he'd still be here now. He only joined up because of you. So now you've sent him to his death, you start crying? Pretending to care when you're so hard-hearted. I see through you.'

Emily didn't notice the woman had left. It was some time

later that Pa came into the room, wondering who had been at the door. Emily shook herself to the present.

'Who was that?' Pa asked. 'I heard the knock and then nothing. Who could be calling at this time and why didn't you bring your guest through to say hello?' 'It was Mrs. Anderson. She's just told me Billy's dead. She didn't want to come through. I don't know what to do, Pa.' She stood up and wiped the tears from her face.

'Come here my girl.' He opened his arms and she fell into the safety of his embrace.

Emily found it hard to believe he was gone. He couldn't die, not now he was going to be a father. Still she didn't tell anyone else she was with-child. She could go through each day and try not think about what would happen to her. She kept her secret, feeling it grow gradually into a real person inside her - Billy's little baby - and it must be a boy, it must. She could see him running on the beach, a tiny replica of Billy, his hair, his smile, his laugh.

Chapter Seven

Emily

Mrs. Cartwright let her go when she got too big and could no longer hide her belly.

Pa was a good man - he could have thrown her out - any other man would have. He held Emily's hand and told her what a fool she was. 'You're a bloody foolish girl,' he'd said and then had walked down the garden, lighting his pipe to talk to his dead wife. Later he told Kate. She looked at Emily in disgust behind his back.

'We'll look after you, girl,' Pa smiled and nodded to Kate.

'Of course,' she replied.

It was difficult being in the house all day with Kate. Living with the disapproval of all she did was dragging the strength out of Emily. Kate was demanding, expecting Emily still to take her "fair share" of the work, saying that Kate wasn't going to think she was in for an easy time just because she was pregnant. Emily wished again and again that her own Ma was still alive. Sometimes it seemed as though she was going mad with grief for her Ma and for Billy too. She hadn't wanted to marry, had wanted to keep her freedom by not being married and yet, here she was, struggling on her own, with no happy future ahead. And she did love Billy, of course she did. She had been so stupid, taken too many chances thinking she was invincible when really she was no different from any other young woman.

She only had Percy, now thirteen and longing to go to war himself. He spent a lot of his time out playing football on the street with his pals and anyway he wasn't someone Emily could have a proper grown up conversation with. Kate seemed to fill the house and when Pa was at home, she was always there beside him so there was never any time that Emily could spend alone with her Pa.

Letters came from Edward and Harry. Short and full of talk about the weather and the mud and wishing they could come home on leave soon. Nothing about Billy.

When Emily got so big that she could hardly walk to the corner shop, Kate still made her do the heavy work. Emily could see the pain in her Pa's face every time he looked at her - the shame in his eyes cut through her. She tried to tell him that it would have been different if the war hadn't come but she couldn't find the words.

Emily's time was only a few weeks away when she fell. The floor in the scullery was wet from the washing. She slipped and down she went. It happened when her Pa was at work and Kate took it upon herself to get the neighbours to help Emily onto the cart and pushed her all the way to the Workhouse Infirmary.

Emily shuddered the day they entered those gates, the building red-bricked and sullen, its blank windows gazing at her in judgement.

Kate said goodbye to her before she left her alone in the ward. 'Now, Emily, listen to me. You know this child will not be coming home with you. It just would not work. You will have to accept that it's for the best. A girl like you cannot bring up a child on your own.'

'No, Pa said I could keep my baby. He promised.'

'Don't be ridiculous, girl. He didn't mean it. You have to wake up.' She turned and walked down the length of the ward and out of the door without looking back.

Pain was pulling Emily down, like she was sinking into some sort of hell. 'This can't be real', she remembered thinking. She couldn't describe the pain, not really, just that pulling sensation. They say you don't ever remember labour pains but she would never forget them even though there were no words to describe them.

She would have gone through it all over again to hold her child, if only for a moment, to smell his warm, baby-born skin, to kiss his tiny fingers. The pain that ripped her apart when they took him away from her was deeper by far than the physical pain of his birth.

The attendant was kind. Looking back, her kindness was only a mask she wore to make Emily feel at ease. She remembered being in a haze of love, floating above her truckle bed, dreaming of her with her baby boy, running along the shore together. His cries brought her to her senses. She felt the tugging of her now empty womb as she opened her eyes in time to see the back of the attendant disappear through the door at the end of the long row of beds, the child in her arms.

Emily's scream was endless.

Chapter Eight

Kate

Harold had been married to Rose. She was Kate's friend, her best friend once. Kate knew Harold long before they got married and once he'd been sweet on her. Then she'd met William and he'd swept her off her feet. Their first boy came just seven months later so it was just as well they married when they did. She was soon back down to earth after the wedding. William was a cruel man but she had to stick it out somehow. There was no alternative was there?

Another child later and she'd had enough of his demands. She'd started planning how she could get rid of him. She knew it was madness. How would she manage without his wage for a start? She'd spent a lot of time working out how it could be done without being caught, saving up weedkiller and hiding it in the back of the wardrobe, determined to use it on him the next time he came home drunk, fists flying.

In the end she didn't have the courage to do it, but hadn't needed to. He had a stroke and that was the end of him. There was a small pension, only enough to bury him decently and little left to feed and clothe the boys. Kate had to work and it wasn't easy. She did shifts in the laundry, long hours with only a few shillings to take home. But she managed somehow, and she didn't want to share how.

Kate prayed a lot and one day her prayers were answered.

When Rose got the fever and died, Kate was relieved. She could see this would be the way out for her. Harold had the shop and his family had never been short of fresh meat. Rose's boys had new clothes, and Emily did too. Kate thought they were spoilt. Now it could be her turn to have all she'd dreamed of and her turn to spoil her boys, and herself. It hadn't been hard to persuade Harold that they should marry.

It was difficult being in the same house as Emily, now grown to a young woman herself. She'd been working in the big house but that didn't mean she could get out of helping Kate around the home. The boys had all gone to war. They couldn't join up quick enough. Only the youngest boy of Harold's left, and Emily of course. Life should have been easier but gradually a blackness seemed to descend on the house. Harold came home later and later and always looked disappointed. Emily had stopped doing what Kate asked, saying she was tired and working in the big house was too much. Kate had to admit she'd lost her temper with Emily more than once.

She'd realised Emily was with child one day when she was leaning over the copper in the scullery, her clothes clinging to her, showing off her belly. Kate said nothing at the time but was trying to work out what should be done. Then the girl had told Harold. Without even discussing it with Kate he'd told her he'd stand by her and she could bring the child up at home. Kate would never forget the way he'd looked at her that day. It was like he was pushing her away. She'd pretended she'd agree to anything but Kate couldn't get it out of her head that he'd put Emily first.

The anger overwhelmed Kate, all the memories of her own past pushing away any feelings of kindness towards the girl. She kept it in as long as she could but when he left for work the next day and Emily sat there at the kitchen table, looking so full of herself, it was too much. Of course, Kate knew that she couldn't keep the child.

Rose had known about Kate's own distant past, but they'd never talked about it afterwards. It had happened long before Kate had married William and if he knew about it he never said. Kate had tried not to think about the night of dark fumbling in the alley nor the boy that got her pregnant.

She'd tried her best to keep her baby - a little girl she was. Kitty. Kate would have done anything if only she could have kept her. When her Ma took her away she was nearly six months old. They'd bonded of course by then, but there was no money coming in, not enough food for the family, so when the milk dried up Kate was forced to let her go. Someone had paid her Ma for the child and Kate had remembered the pain like it was yesterday. It stabbed through her like a sword through a stone. She'd had no chance to keep her even though she'd tried to run away with her. After two nights of sleeping in the cold streets with no food for her and the baby starving, she'd had to go back.

Whatever Kate thought of Emily, she didn't want her to go through that. So she'd had to take the babe from Emily before they'd bonded. It was for the best - the same words that were said to her so long ago. She found a loving couple who were childless. They lived away from the city, in a small village in Hampshire. The wife came to see Kate and said that her husband was a doctor and away at war. Kate hadn't wanted money, only the promise to give the boy a good life in a wealthy home. He'd be educated and well fed and be far enough away from Emily. She would never know where he was, Kate would make sure of that.

How was she to know Emily'd be unstable and weak and let the madness take over. It had happened to Kate and she'd survived, hadn't she? Maybe it didn't seem like it but everything she'd done was for Emily's good. She knew what it was like to suffer after all.

Chapter Nine

Emily

Pa visited Emily in the workhouse infirmary the next day. He couldn't look at his daughter but spoke to the window high up in the wall behind where she lay. His reach for her was tentative, his fingers not quite touching her hand. There was a tear in his eye when he told her that the child had been sent away for adoption.

'It's for the best,' he said. 'You will get strong again, come home and have a fresh start.'

The words came from his mouth but Emily only heard Kate's voice saying them.

The black cloud in Emily's head and heart weighed her down so heavily she could not even look at him. Closing her eyes, she turned away from this man who had loved her more than life itself when she was little. Or so he'd said. 'How things change', she thought. Now he had torn her life apart.

The following days were times of confusion, of fever and nightmares which seemed to continue whether she was awake or asleep. Her breasts were sore, echoing the pain she knew she would carry with her for the rest of her life. The attendants fed her broth, a thin watery concoction, tasteless and tepid and when she was restless they gave her laudanum so she would sleep. But nothing could ease what she was feeling.

It was on the fourth day when Kate came to visit. 'Time to pull yourself out of this self-pitying state,' she said. 'Life has to go on and you need to get home and back to work. I can't be expected to run the house on my own.'

Emily glared at her. 'I've only just given birth, and had my child taken away against my wishes,' she said. 'Have you no pity?'

'The least said about that the better,' Kate replied. 'I've signed your discharge papers and you're coming home.' She placed a holdall on the bed. 'Now, get yourself up and dressed.'

Emily looked about the ward, hoping for some way she could make all of this go away, for the past year to have been different, for Billy to be here, for her Pa to still love her like he had in the past. She struggled to sit up, pushed the thin covers from herself and swung her legs over the edge of the bed. A blackness descended.

Waking a few hours later, and realising she was still in the workhouse, Emily struggled to sit up. An attendant was by her side.

'You passed out,' the woman said. 'You have to rest, to stay another night.'

'Where did Kate go?'

'She wanted to take you home but it was too soon. She'll come back tomorrow to take you if your strength has returned. No point in you being sent home until you are well enough to walk on your own.'

Emily sighed. 'Thank you,' she said.

'Now, I'll fetch you some tea, and maybe you could try some bread and dripping? I know there's some in the pantry.' She smiled. 'It'll perk you up.'

Emily's stomach heaved at the thought but with persuasion she managed to eat a small heel of bread, smeared with thick beef dripping which had been smothered with salt. The tea she washed it down with was most welcome. Emily hadn't realised how hungry and thirsty she'd been.

Once the attendant had left her alone, she looked around the ward. The beds were set along the walls, facing each other across a centre row of more beds. So many sick people. The room was noisy with sounds of crying, the clatter of metal trolleys and instruments, nurses and attendants calling to each other and speaking to the other patients in raised voices. It crossed Emily's mind that this was what it would be like in that place called Bedlam, where all the mad people were locked up. She shuddered at the thought. Despite all of the clamour, Emily soon felt her eyes growing heavy. She sank down onto the thin pillow and fell into a troubled sleep.

Waking again, suddenly, at the sound of a crash, Emily immediately wondered where she was. Then it all came back - the birth of her child, seeing him being taken away, her Pa telling her it was for the best, and Kate. She knew in that moment that she would never go home again. She needed to get out of this noisy place, find somewhere to go away from the workhouse, away from her old home - a place that no longer felt safe.

The attendants were busy with a patient. The crash had come from the far end of the ward. Emily pulled herself up slowly, not wishing to faint again, then got herself out of the bed. Her clothes were still in the holdall beneath. She pulled the bag out and dragged her dress on over the top of the night-shirt she was wearing. Rummaging in the bag, she saw her boots were missing. 'What had Kate been thinking?' She wondered.

Afraid that she would be stopped before she could leave, Emily made her way slowly to the door. Luckily her bed was beside the exit, a door which was little used, the main one being at the other end where all the hullabaloo was coming from. No-one noticed her slip out into the yard. It was only a short distance from there to the side gate out into St. Mary's Road.

Once outside, feeling stronger, despite the unusual heat of the late Spring day, she found herself making her way past the prison and towards the cemetery. How she loved this green place with its trees and squirrels, rabbits, and the flowers, those on the graves and the ones planted there also. It only took a moment to find Ma's grave. She knelt and gently removed the posy that she'd placed there only a few weeks ago. It seemed like another world now. Everything was different.

'You would have understood what I feel, Ma,' she said. 'If only you hadn't died, I would still have my little one and Pa would be happy too.'

Emily stood and looked down at the grave. 'Well, Ma, you're not here so there's no point now, is there? You left us and that's that.' She turned away and walked, dashing away the tears. 'No more self-pity,' she told herself.

Chapter Ten

Emily

Her feet were sore, her hatless head was hot under the midday sun, but still she walked, finding herself wandering towards the sea. In her mind, she had a small glimmer of hope that the sea would be the answer, would heal her, and help her find a new way forward. She would leave all the past behind - Kate and her boys, her own brothers, the loss of Ma, Billy, her baby, and even her Pa. Everything and everyone from before was poison to her now.

When she arrived finally at the shingle beach, the sea breeze seemed to briefly help, to gently blow away some of the pain, but it wasn't enough.

She turned to the west and stumbling on the pebbles, her bare feet now bleeding, bore the pain. It was as though she was deserving of the cuts and the pain as a punishment for all that she had done.

Reaching the ramparts in Old Portsmouth was quite a relief. Standing on the pier, she looked out at the shores of Gosport and then in the further distance, the Isle-of-Wight, remembering days she'd gone on boat trips with her Ma and Pa when she and her brothers were all small and innocent. How she longed for those days.

Berating herself, she trudged inland towards the Cathedral which was tucked behind the row of shops and terraced houses in the High Street. Longing for somewhere safe to stop, to seek sanctuary and to rest, she made her way to the doors of the Cathedral and slipped into the cool darkness of the building. She sat on the nearest pew and tried to pray to a God she no longer believed in.

She may have slept. If she had it was a dreamless sleep, much needed. Waking, she wondered for that instant where she was and how she'd got to this place. There was a chill in the air but a kind of peace had descended upon her.

Outside again, she could smell rain in the air; clouds had formed, black and heavy. Over her shoulder loomed the Cathedral. Now, in the shadows of the angry sky, it seemed threatening somehow, no longer a place of sanctuary.

Stepping away from the porch, her bare feet flinched from contact with the still-scorched dirt track that led away through the avenue of trees to the town beyond. She hesitated, but only for a moment. Should she go forward to her future or remain hidden until the storm had passed? But the storm was within her again, raging at her guilt for what she'd done. She knew the time had come to face it.

A flash of lightning spurred her forward. Running, she heard the sound of thunder burst and roll in the distance. The wind roared, the trees seeming to lean towards her, the sound of their leaves like a mountain torrent to her ears, shouting at her to run, run, run. The taste of fear was bitter, mixed with salt from the tears that ran from her eyes onto her lips. Never before had the Cathedral Close seemed so vast.

The rain pierced her skin with sharp needles of ice. Welcome at first, soon painful, heavy, vicious. The earth beneath her feet turned to mud, deeper as she

staggered, falling to her knees, her face slapped into what was now an unwelcome mire. She longed for it to stop, she longed to go back in time to before when all was safe and the world was easy to live in.

They found her there some time later, her mud-caked hair now dried after the storm had passed. It was the gentleman who stopped and looked; his wife had shuddered at the sight and tried to hurry on.

'She's only a youngster,' he said, leaning over her.

'You might catch a disease,' his wife stood behind him, not wanting to look.

'Poor child, she looks hungry.' He touched Emily's shoulder gently. 'Are you all right?' he asked.

When Emily opened her eyes, her first emotion was shame. Shame that she'd been laying in the street like a vagrant, and shame at the state of herself. Then she re-membered what had happened in the past week: losing her child, her home, her Pa and now her mind. Trying to get up, she shook off the helping hands of the gentleman and tried to move away. He was right, of course, she was hun-gry and weak and the woman was probably right too, she did have some kind of disease, not the kind you can catch, but a disease of the mind. She was mad, totally mad and now she had nothing left to fight with. Allowing herself to be coaxed along the path to a carriage that was waiting, the gentleman helped her inside. He turned and spoke to his wife before climbing in to sit opposite Emily and smiled at her as the carriage moved away along the street.

Chapter Eleven

Emily

There is no measure of time when you are mad. Days, nights, hours, minutes, a jumbled mass of horror, shutting out memories and thoughts.

Emily lay on her bed, looked about at the room and tried to put her thoughts in order.

The sign at the gate had made her shudder. She'd heard stories about the asylum. The drive was long, tall trees showed the way to the building. She'd looked up at the windows glaring down at her. There were stairs leading up to the door and she'd wondered how many feet had climbed those steps. Her body was raw, bruised on the outside and numb on the inside. She'd resisted, held back, but they'd led her on and pushed her through the revolving doors into her future. How long would it be before she'd pass this way again?

The ward was well lit by the natural light of the sun after the storm, with windows reaching to the ceiling, curtains drawn back. Emily sat at a neat table and looked around. There was a piano. This was re-assuring. It was highly polished with a tidy pile of music placed on the lid. A faint smell of over-boiled greens and bees-wax polish was in the air, masked by the overwhelming hyacinths which sat on the windowsill. It was warm and quiet, no other lunatics about at this time of day.

She'd only been left alone for a moment or two. Long enough though, to panic inside recalling the treatments she'd heard about, the stories she'd been told about the screaming and enforced baths, straitjackets and padded cells.

When the nurse returned, her uniform crisply meaning business, Emily felt herself recoiling, expecting the worst. So she wasn't ready for her smile, her warm and kindly voice as she sat and asked questions. Emily wished she could have answered them but her voice would not work, her heart had shut down and no words would reach her mouth anymore. The nurse was patient, kind, writing notes.

When asked about her family Emily tried to tell her that they were all dead. She tried to say it - her Ma, her sweetheart, and her baby was gone, but she couldn't say the words as that would make it real.

She was taken to a bathroom, high-ceilinged and white-tiled. The nurse watched whilst Emily bathed. Her muddy clothes were taken away and she was given a soft cotton grey dress and apron.

They put her in a dormitory.

'You'll be fine in here,' the nurse told her. 'And we can keep an eye on you.'

The bed was hard and narrow with barely a gap between it and the next one. Emily didn't count them but there must have been at least fifty beds in that room.

'Think yourself lucky,' she was told. 'You could be in a side room with the door locked every night. Being in the dormitory is much better. You'll soon make friends,' was added almost as an afterthought.

Emily remembered thinking 'why would I want to make friends with a lunatic?' but then she remembered that she was one, wasn't she, and anyway who would want to make friends with the likes of her?

In the dark which was never dark, Emily couldn't sleep. Too much noise, too many people breathing, so much crying and the nurses walking about, up and down the row of beds. She wished they'd put her in the locked room away from all these people too close and not being able to get out of bed. She'd watched as they'd bundled one woman back to hers when she'd got up and stumbled about, sobbing to herself.

'Sheet her in,' the nurse was saying to her fellow worker. 'Can't have our ladies wandering about at night.'

'No, please, let me just sit up, I can't breathe,' the woman pleaded. But they didn't seem to hear.

Emily watched as they pulled out the top sheet and turned it sideways on, then lifted up the mattress on one side whilst they tucked it in. The woman was laid down, passive now, the sheet pulled over her, arms pinned to her sides as she was tucked in tightly.

'There, now get back to sleep,' she was told before the nurses turned away.

Emily closed her eyes and tried to stop the tears from inching out as the nurses passed her bed with their lantern. Curling on her side Emily hugged the gap where her baby would have been and waited for the morning to drag her into another day. Where would it all end and did she care?

Sleep came harder than ever after that but she must have drifted off eventually, an uneasy sleep with noises in the background of her mind, keeping her from slipping fully into a deep restful state. Still, Emily was shocked awake some time later by her hair being pulled so viciously her head lifted from the pillow. Unable to fathom what was happening, she fought back, beating her attacker with one hand whilst with the other she tried to grasp the fist that was firmly gripped around her hair. Emily was still fighting, now on her feet, with the bedclothes tangled around her legs, trying to break free. She felt the pain before she registered that the woman had a blade in her hand and was trying to kill her. Fearing for her life, she fought and managed to wrestle the blade from the woman. It flew from her hand and slid under the bed.

At last two nurses appeared down the centre of the ward and between them they pulled off the woman, now sobbing and cursing, whilst straining to get free from the strong grip of the largest nurse.

'She's a witch,' the mad woman cried, pointing at Emily. 'She killed me and took out my entrails.'

Emily was horrified. Looking from one nurse to the other, she could think of nothing to say.

'I was asleep and she cut me up,' the woman was saying. 'Keep her away from me.'

'I don't know what she's talking about,' Emily shook her head. 'I was asleep and she attacked me. Look - I'm bleeding.'

'Liar!' The woman was struggling to get free. 'Let me go and I'll kill her. She's taking my blood from me.'

'Calm down, Hettie,' the nurse was trying to pull her away from Emily. 'Come on, let's get you back to your room.'

They led away Hettie, leaving Emily sitting on her own bed. She had never before felt so wretched. They said it was safe in the dormitory but so far it had been

hellish. She remembered the knife under the bed, knelt down and reached for it, slipping it under her pillow.

'This is my way out,' she thought. 'Only one way out now and this knife is the key.

Chapter Twelve

Emily

The cut was deep. Emily could see the blood was flowing but couldn't believe it was her blood. She felt no pain. She felt nothing. The room was quiet. She wondered why it was so quiet. The people around her were still, like in a frozen dream. The dream broke but her eyes couldn't see.

She heard a voice screaming in her head, or was it outside of her? Her eyes were tight shut - she didn't want to, couldn't see what was all around her. She couldn't see if there was anyone else there anymore. Was it a dream?

'Open your eyes Emily.' The voice was outside of her now and she could smell the strong odour of carbolic, sensing the person next to her. She shook her head and backed away. She was against the wall and could feel it against her back. It was cold and re-assuring, holding her there, safe.

'Emily,' said the voice again, gently this time. Emily shook her head.

'Please Emily, tell me how I can help.' It was Nurse Paxton. Emily said nothing. Her voice had gone away, too hard to speak, too dangerous.

Her mind drifted. She couldn't stop the memories as they flooded in. She was no longer in the room. No longer in that day, that week, that year. She was young and happy, in love with life and dancing. But Emily couldn't bear being there back in that time. That time was gone and the world was on fire now, everyone she'd trusted and loved was evil, had the devil in them. She'd seen it in their eyes. Everywhere was danger. She couldn't look at the world anymore and couldn't look at their faces. They could see into her soul through her eyes and the only way to stop them was not to look. Sometimes the people around her tried to catch her out with distraction so she just kept her eyes closed.

The only time she could see was when she was asleep and dreaming. Except the dreams were dangerous as well now. The devils were getting into the inside of her head and visited her in her sleep. She tried not to sleep.

Emily told them to stay outside but they got in, just like Nurse Paxton in the room with her now got in. The nurse moved away, keys jangling. Emily's gaoler. Attendant they called her, was she the devil attendant with the keys to hell on her belt? Emily held her breath, waiting to hear the turn of the key in the lock. Should she make a break for it, run for her life? They wouldn't catch her, she thought. But they would. She'd have no way of knowing the way out - not with her eyes shut and besides she'd have no idea as to what was beyond that door. The tears were seeping from her eyelids, making her angry that they came but they came anyway.

Emily had been determined not to talk to the nurse but when she'd reached for Emily's hand something shifted inside. The hard lump of ice around Emily's heart melted just for that moment, but long enough to let the nurse in.

'Emily,' she squeezed her hand. 'It's alright, you're safe.'

Those few words were all it took.

Chapter Thirteen

Emily

Weeks passed before they said she was well enough to work. She spent time each day with Nurse Paxton, talking sometimes, at other times, she was encouraged to walk in the garden with some of the other patients, escorted by an attendant.

There were weekly meetings when she was taken to the medical officer's room. Emily became familiar with the walk along the endless corridors to the office. The room was rather like a boardroom, or a dining room like the one she used to clean in Mrs. Cartwright's home. Grim portraits looked down at her from the panelled walls. There was that faint smell of bees-wax in the air. Soft carpet was underfoot, making Emily wonder if her boots were clean enough. She sat before his vast desk, he behind, safely out of reach.

The medical officer was probably called by some a handsome man, his whiskers may have been said to have been very fine some ten or more years ago. His stiff collar seemed to cut into his neck which was red from too much sunlight she supposed. Yet he was no more than another man who's role was to decide on Emily's future.

He smiled. 'How are you feeling Emily?'

Emily wondered whether she should tell him the truth. Of course she wasn't feeling anything, was completely numbed from the inside out.

He repeated his question. 'Emily, how are you?'

'I don't know.'

This was the right answer, of course. She didn't know, but he seemed to think it was enough for now. Words still didn't come easily.

'Good,' he said.

After a pause to write a note on his ledger, he spoke again. 'I think it's time for you to commence with the next stage of your treatment. It's what we call "moral" treatment, designed to raise your morale and make you feel you are a useful member of our society.'

Emily frowned, raising her head to look at him.

'Don't look so frightened. You will be helping in the laundry, working with other women. It will give you a purpose and make the days pass more swiftly and fruitfully.' He paused. 'The other women will become your friends.'

He didn't ask her what she thought of this. She had no choice, no opinion. Her life was no longer her own. But had it ever been?

When they got back to the ward, the nurse left her to sit by the window. The sun was warm on Emily's skin. In the past, sitting in the sunshine was something that had always soothed her but today it all seemed wrong somehow.

She wasn't ready to stop feeling she needed to be punished for all she'd done. But what had she done? Nothing really bad at all. She'd lost her love and had a baby. Then lost her baby too. Perhaps it was all about losing people she loved. That must be it. So careless with those who mattered to her. She did need to be punished. She did. So

Emily moved away from the window, turned her back on the sunlight and stared at the wall instead. She was still there later that afternoon when the women were called to the table for tea. But she wasn't hungry either so sat at the table with her tea turning cold in front of her.

Emily was tired, so tired even her fingers ached.

The laundry room was probably the place of all places she would rather not be. It reminded her of the long hours she'd spent washing and ironing the linen in her old home. Even so, it was with hope she had walked along the bland corridors to the laundry. This was perhaps a step towards her leaving this so called asylum. The sun had shone through the slitted windows high in the walls, too high to reach and too high to look out, but not too high for the sun to slip through and bounce on the opposite wall lifting her spirits just a little.

The laundry doors were wide open. Pausing a moment, she was pushed out of the way by the attendant with a shout, 'look out.' Pressing herself against the wall a load of foul washing was wheeled past her. Inside, the room was vast, filled with soap-sud steam and other acrid aromas she tried not to recognise.

A woman's face emerged from the steam, a smiling, kindly person, dressed from head to foot in a wrap-around overall, her hair scraped into a linen cap, just a tendril or two of damp hair escaping into her eyes. Wiping her hands on her overall, the woman greeted Emily with a laugh. 'Don't look so frightened,' she said. 'It seems like hell in here but it's not so bad. I'm Lillian, the laundress. Come in and I'll show you the ropes.'

She'd been put on ironing. Piles and piles of uniform dresses for the nurses were heaped on a table beside a heavy wooden ironing board.

'These are your hot irons, make sure you don't burn yourself. You've done ironing before haven't you?' Lillian asked as an afterthought.

Emily nodded. 'Of course,' she replied.

It was with determination that she began, pulling a dress from the pile, shaking it out and laying it on the board, sprinkling it with water, grabbing an iron - she almost burnt her hand on the first one, before she remembered to use the cloth - then pressing heavily onto the creased cotton, the aroma of clean steam filling her head. At first it was satisfying, once she got into the rhythm as each garment was smoothed to a crisp and ready-to-wear uniform. She took pride in carefully folding and neatly placing each one on the new pile at the other end of the table.

As the day sped on the work seemed to become heavier, harder to do. She felt a knot in her shoulder and tried to ease it by using her left hand for a while. Being right handed she was clumsy using the other hand so soon gave up that idea and went back to ironing with her right hand, leaning in with her full body-weight to get the desired result. Of course, the irons soon cooled and then would have to be put back on the range to be replaced by a fresh one. The work was hot and hard and it was only the monotony of it that kept her going, trying not to think about life and how it would be when she got out into the world again. She couldn't honestly see that ever happening.

Chapter Fourteen

Emily

That night, she slept well without dreaming, for the first time.

The attendant woke her in the morning, banging on the door. 'Get up Emily, time for breakfast. You'll be late for work.'

Emily groaned, still aching from the previous day's work. 'I should be used to this,' she thought, as she pulled herself out of the bed and dragged on her clothes. It wasn't much different from her previous life, working as a skivvy at the house, and then working even harder at home under Kate's evil eye.

As days rolled into weeks, the work in the laundry never got any easier. Callouses formed on Emily's hands from the hot irons, her back still ached each evening when she lay on her bed. The other women tried to talk to her, telling her about their lives, how they'd ended up in this place. They tried to be her friends, although Emily never trusted any of them. When she heard them laughing together, it was her they were laughing at. She would never confide in them the way they did with each other. She stopped herself from thinking about the past and the future. There was just the day, the hours in the laundry and sleeping in her tiny room at night, nothing else. She never went back to the dormitory.

Lillian was always kind, always smiled at Emily and sat with her when they stopped for tea. She seemed to understand that Emily couldn't share her feelings with anyone. Lillian was a woman that could have become a friend should they have been in different circumstances, but of course, Lillian was staff and Emily was a patient, a madwoman.

It was on a Thursday morning that it happened. Emily felt something different was bubbling up inside herself. Perhaps it was the nearness of a woman who seemed to be on her side at last. Whatever it was, Emily found herself talking.

'I had a baby,' she said. 'A little boy. He was taken from me.'

'What? Sorry, what did you say?'

'Nothing. It doesn't matter.'

'No, please, you can talk to me. Whatever you want to say won't go any further. I don't write down what is said to me in here. It is alright, really.'

'I said I had a baby. I had a little boy but they made me give him up.'

'You poor love. Life can be so hard sometimes.' Lillian reached out and touched Emily's shoulder. 'What happened?'

'His father went to Belgium and never came back. He kept asking me to marry him but I wasn't ready and then I didn't find out I was pregnant until he'd gone. I wrote to him about the baby but it was too late. He was already dead. At first, my Pa said he'd stand by me and I could keep the child and live at home. But after he was born, they took the baby away. Kate did it. She's my Pa's wife.'

'Not your Ma? What happened to your Ma?'

'She died too. Kate was Ma's friend. At least she seemed to be always in our house before Ma died, but looking back, perhaps she was after Pa even then.'

'Maybe. But this is what happens sometimes when a man loses his wife. It doesn't mean that she had her eye on him then. What about her husband? Kate's? I suppose she had been married before.'

'Her husband had died too. Sometimes when I'm thinking in my room, I wonder whether she did it.'

Lillian looked shocked. She laughed nervously. 'Surely you don't think she would have killed him?'

'I often overheard her telling my Ma about how he was with her. He was a cruel man. I once heard her say that she had been planning how to get rid of him if he carried on like he was. Then one morning she came round and told Ma that he'd died in his sleep after coming home from the pub drunk again. She said that he wouldn't be hurting her again.'

'I'm sure you're reading too much into this. You know your imagination must be over-active.'

Emily looked up through the clouds of steam before she answered.

'She was cruel to me before.' Emily turned to face Lillian. 'I never told anyone. I didn't want Pa to be upset, but she would try and burn me with the poker and she bullied me into doing the heavy work around the house, even though I was already working twelve hours at Mrs. Cartwright's house. She'd wait until Pa went to the pub before she started on me. She'd put her feet up and say that I should pull my weight. I know housework is hard and I don't mind doing my share, but she expected me to do hers as well. And then she told me she wanted the house for herself and Pa and that I wasn't welcome anymore. When Pa told her he would stand by me and support me in looking after the child, she said nothing but after that she was even worse towards me. It was she who arranged for my baby to be taken away.'

'That all sounds terrible. I'm not surprised you had a breakdown.'

'I used to call her the Devil. I did that when I was first brought in here. But to me she was and still is the Devil. She took away my Pa and my child. I can't trust her to look after Pa either but he won't listen to me.' She paused, stretching her back. 'I've got brothers. The eldest two are in Belgium but the youngest, Percy, lives at home. I worry for him, living there with her. I'd like to write to him but

I'm afraid he wouldn't get the letter. I think she'd stop him from seeing me too.'

Lillian stood. 'Look,' she said. 'We should get back to work now, but I'm so glad you've been able to talk to me. I've worked here now for a long time and I've seen plenty of women like yourself over those years and heard stories similar to yours. Many of them overcome their problems and leave here and never come back again. Although it may seem like you are alone now and perhaps you feel you'll never recover, things will change in time. Maybe I can help. I could take a message for you to Percy. How old is he?'

'Could you really? He's thirteen. He helps Pa in his butcher's shop after school. If you would be kind enough to do that, I'd be so happy.'

'Write a note and let me have it tomorrow. I'll take it to the shop if you tell me the address. Make sure it goes straight into his hand.'

'Thank you so much,' Emily sniffed away a tear.

Letter to Percy:
   Dear Percy,

I am writing this from the laundry in the asylum. I don't know what Pa and Kate have told you about me. I wanted to let you know that I am alright and that although I have been unwell, I am recovering and will be out of this place as soon as I am well enough. The nurses are kind and I have made a friend here in the laundry where I work each day. She's the laundress, not a patient, and has kindly said she would take this letter to you. Her name is Lillian.

I trust that you are well and happy. I had a baby boy but he has been sent away against my wishes. I would have loved to have brought him home. You are an uncle, Percy, and Pa is a Grandfather.

Pa has not been to see me in here yet. Please tell him I love him and that I'm sorry. I love you too, my dear brother. You can write to me if you like at the asylum although I have no intention of staying in here for long.

Your loving sister,
    Emily.

Chapter Fifteen

Emily

Emily spent the whole weekend thinking about Percy. Had he received her letter yet? What would his response be? She swung from excitement that he might be in touch with her, to regret that she had written at all. He wouldn't want to see her or even write. He wouldn't like the thought of his sister being in the "Madhouse" with all the crazy people and that she was now one of them. By the time she arrived at the laundry on the following Monday morning, she was trembling with anxiety.

Lillian was waiting for her. The smile on her face told Emily that all was well. 'Did you see him?' Emily asked.

'I did, and what a fine young man he is.'

'Was Pa there? I wouldn't want to get Percy into any trouble with Pa.'

'He was, but I waited across the street. I watched them as they worked together. When the elder man, your Pa, I supposed, went into the back of the shop, I crossed the street and went in. I was worried he would come back, so I quickly asked the lad's name. It was him, of course. I told him I knew you and had a letter from you. He was delighted but said that he couldn't talk to me in the shop. I think he didn't want his father to know. So I slipped him the note and said I would take a reply for him if he liked. Then your Pa came back in. Quickly I asked for an order of sausages. Once I'd paid for them I said that I would be back in on Saturday morning for one of their steak pies.'

'Oh, thank you. And did you go back on Saturday?'

'Of course. I looked in through the window again before going in. Your Pa was in the shop alone though. My heart sank and I wondered what had happened to Percy. So rather than going in I walked on and went into the grocery store for my other provisions. Then after a while I walked back, looking in the window again.'

'Yes? Was Percy there?'

'Luckily he was. I was feeling nervous and thought that maybe your father had found out and had stopped him from replying, but there he was and he was smiling and waving at me through the window. I went in, but just at that moment your Pa came in from the back room. He remembered me and started to serve me with the steak pie I'd ordered. That was a moment when I thought it would all go wrong. I was thinking that I would have to plan another way to see Percy away from the shop but then Percy took the pie from your Pa, saying he would wrap it for me. Then once I got outside the shop, and around the corner, I opened the package and found this inside.'

She pulled from her pocket a crumpled note from Percy.

Dearest Emily,

It was so good to hear that you are alright. It must be pretty frightening being in the asylum. I have heard so many stories about that place. But it sounds like you aren't being treated too badly. I miss you so much. Pa told me that you weren't going to be

coming home for a long time. He told me you had broken his heart but I think that he is just saying what Kate wants him to say.

I am sorry that your baby was taken away. It must be so hard for you after you have lost so much.

I wish Ma was still alive.

I don't think I will be able to visit you. It would be too difficult. Please let me know when you get better and can come home.

I love you Emily, whatever happens.

Your brother

Percy

Emily couldn't stop the tears from blurring her eyes whilst she read. She carefully folded the note and put it into her pocket. 'Thank you so much for this, Lillian,' she said. 'Knowing that Percy is thinking of me kindly means so much to me. It gives me hope that one day we can see each other again.'

'It was my pleasure,' Lillian said. 'In fact, it was quite fun, and I think you deserve some kindness. I will do the same again if you would like.'

'That would be wonderful, I may write to him again when I have better news.'

The rest of the day in the laundry went quickly and the weight on Emily's shoulders felt less. There was something to look forward to and she had a good friend in Lillian too.

Sadly, it wasn't to last. Only a few days later, Lillian told Emily that she would be leaving her job in the laundry.

'I don't want to go,' she explained. 'My sister lives in Cosham and she's just had a baby. She needs me to go and help her. I tried to get time off for a few weeks but they said I would have to give up my job. They need someone to be reliable they told me. So I won't be seeing you anymore. I'm sorry, it means that I won't be able to take letters to Percy for you. Cosham is too far away from the asylum and the shop. I'm really sorry to let you down, but I'm sure if you keep going the way you are, all will be well, and you'll be out of here soon.'

'I'm sorry too. You're the only friend I have in here. The only friend I have anywhere really.'

'Surely you must have a friend outside. Do you have female friends at all? People you grew up with? Went to school with? Work friends?'

'I had friends at school, but one moved away with her family. Her father was in the Navy and they travel around don't they? My other best friend, Mabel, works for the Post Office. We did try and meet up whenever we could but with her working hours and mine it was difficult at the best of times. She was someone I could talk to, but I haven't had any contact with her since I was put in here. I could have written I suppose but feel too embarrassed.'

'That's a shame. Is there anyone else?'

'I used to work in a house as a maid and there was only Mrs. Price, the old cook who worked there with me. I don't know if she's still there and we were never that close. I have two other brothers, no sisters unfortunately. I always wanted a sister.'

'Having a sister is a special blessing, I agree. Are you close to your brothers? Apart from Percy, I mean?'

'We were close before the War took them away. My Ma was my best friend and of course, I had Billy, but he's dead now. My brothers don't write any more. Not to me anyway.'

'I am sorry to hear this. You're a friendly kind of person, when you let people get to know you. I'm sure you will make friends soon enough. But you have to work at it. Make an effort to talk to more people.'

Emily sighed. 'I know you're right and I will do my best to try and be more friendly to the other ladies in here. I find it hard, but I know I must. It's just...'

'That they are damaged in some way? Hard to get close to?'

'I don't know. I suppose I'm afraid to get close to anyone after what's happened to me. But I will try.'

'That's the spirit. Sometimes you just have to smile at people and they'll let you in. Don't forget that everyone in here has their own troubles, their own stories and perhaps you could even help others if you share your own experiences. Are there any ladies on the ward you think you could be friends with?'

'Maybe. I'll give it some thought.' Emily looked at Lillian. 'You've been so kind to me though. I'm going to miss seeing you.'

'I'll miss you too. Who knows, we may meet up again one day in the future. This war won't last forever, even though it seems like it sometimes. And you have to believe you won't be in here forever.'

Chapter Sixteen

Emily

The following week, the new laundress, Mrs. Ledbetter arrived. Supervisor, she called herself, tall and thin, dressed in a long grey dress and grey overall which suited the grim look on her face and her dour character. She smiled grimly when the women arrived for their duties that morning with a steely look in her eye that Emily tried to avoid. Even more, there was something about the woman that made Emily shudder. She looked familiar and Emily tried to recall where she knew this woman from. It didn't take long to find out.

They had stopped for their short break at eleven in the morning, when the women were served cold tea and a slice of bread. Emily was used to keeping herself away from the other workers and took her bread and tea to a quiet part of the room where she sat on a stool to rest for a moment.

The shadow of Mrs. Ledbetter loomed over her. 'It's you,' she accused, her hands on hips. 'I know you. So this is where you've ended.'

It wasn't a question. At least Emily couldn't answer it. Of course it was her, and yes she had ended up in here, but she still couldn't place the woman.

'Well? What have you got to say for yourself, you little hussy?'

Emily looked up. 'I don't know what you mean. What do you want?'

'You blighted my dear friend's life. Kate - your stepmother. The way you brought shame to her and the family. Your poor father - ruined, completely ruined.'

'You know Pa?' Emily's heart burned. How she missed him. If only he would visit and tell her he loved her like he once did. She had lost so much these past few years and always hoped that one day she would see her Father again. But the woman was goading her.

'Poor man, of course I know him. And how you shamed him with your sluttish ways. Kate told me all about you.'

Emily said nothing. She stood and turned away, her only thought to get back to work, anything to take her mind off what she'd lost.

'Don't walk away from me,' Mrs. Ledbetter was behind her, so close, Emily could feel the woman's breath on her neck. 'I'm in charge here and you'll not ignore me,' she spat.

It was the burning inside that did it. Everything that Emily had held safely there, tight in her heart, was bubbling up, trying to find a way out. Taking a deep breath, she felt her hand pick up the hot iron. The pain searing through through her palm was fleeting as she swung the weapon hard against Mrs. Ledbetter, the smell of burning cloth and flesh overpowering the screams that came from both the woman and herself. Fleetingly she saw the look on the faces of those women who had stopped chatting and were staring, their mouths open in horror.

Chapter Seventeen

Kate

Although life is so different now I have always stayed friends with Ruby Ledbetter and we still see each other sometimes. Only the other day she told me she was started a new job at the asylum. I wondered if she would come across Emily there and I found myself telling her my side of the story, just to make sure she heard it from me first. I had heard that Emily is telling lies about me, saying I was cruel to her. Maybe I had been cruel, but it was all done for the best of reasons. Life for women is hard and always will be. You have to get used to the beatings, the sacrifices, and the sooner you learn that the better.

Ruby listened to my story with great relish. I know I shouldn't have but I'd kept my feelings in for so long and it was good to have a sympathetic listener. I might have laid it on a bit thick - the way Emily had been, her self-ishness, laziness and the way Harold had always put her first. Ruby had a glint in her eye whilst I was speaking and

I do confess that afterwards I felt a little uncomfortable, thinking about some of the things I'd said about Emily.

I walked away from our meeting wondering if I should try and let bygones be bygones and to welcome Emily home to be cared for by us once she was deemed well enough to leave the asylum. By the time I'd walked through the door of the house, I'd already almost talked myself out of it and when Harold came in from his day in the shop, I pushed all thoughts of her coming home out of my mind. Harold always had a sour look on his face these days, all the warmth he had ever shown towards me was gone. It was her fault, that was obvious to me. I hardened my heart to her and smiled at Harold. He had never hurt me, not the way that William had hurt me. Yet it was still painful not to have him smile back at me. I was in a turmoil. Perhaps if I'd opened my heart to Emily more, then Harold would open his heart to me once again? The more I thought about it, the more my head spun. Could I risk it?

'Harold, dear, I've been thinking about Emily.'

'Leave the poor girl alone!' He'd snapped at me before I could even say a word.

'I'm sorry, Harold. I just thought...'

'That's your trouble. You think too much, you scheme too much. I don't want to hear any more about Emily from you. Haven't you done enough damage to her life, to our lives?'

'Harold...'

'Enough, woman. I said, enough, and I will hear no more. Let the poor girl alone in peace. God knows how much she must be suffering in that place, and it's all down to you.'

It cut me to the core to think that he blamed me for what had happened to Emily. It wasn't me who got her pregnant, was it? It wasn't me who couldn't let the baby go and get on with life. She could have come back here and life could have gone on, she would have met someone else one day and been a respectable married woman with a proper family. His words hurt me deeply. I went into the scullery to get away from his anger, his dark looks, and sat on the stool in the chilly air, not wanting to be in the warmth of the kitchen whilst I was feeling so hated.

It was some time later that the door opened and Harold came in.

'It's cold in here,' he said. 'Are you going to sit in here all night?'

I stood and looked at him. 'I'll get your tea.'

Harry made a move to take me in his arms but I pushed past him and swept into the kitchen, leaving him standing there, looking like a fool.

Chapter Eighteen

Emily

Bundling her out of the laundry and along the corridors back to her ward, their strong and spiteful grip on her
arms, only made Emily more angry. She struggled, kicked
and screamed all the way and only quietened when the
door to the cell was locked behind her.

She lay on the mattress, now dressed in a gown made
of rough material, too strong to tear. Looking about the
room she saw that the walls were padded. Feeling sick she
turned her face away from the door and sobbed. She'd
been told that this room was only used on rare occasions.
Her heart was beating so fast in fear, wondering if she
would ever be let out again. What had made her do such
a terrible thing to another person? It was as though the
words that came from Mrs. Ledbetter's mouth had burst
open a poison that she'd been struggling to keep within
herself. But now she felt only shame for what she'd done
to the poor woman.

Later a nurse came to the door, peered at her through
the small glass window and Emily heard the key turn in

the lock. She sat up and watched as first one nurse, then another, entered the room.

'Take this,' the first nurse held a medicine glass half filled with a clear syrup. 'It will help,' she said.

Emily just stared at the glass, unwilling to drink whatever it was.

'Come along.' The second nurse was less than patient. 'We haven't got all day. Now drink it down young lady.' She nodded to her companion who pushed the glass towards Emily's lips, holding the back of the young woman's head with her free hand. 'Lucky for you Mrs. Ledbetter has only mild burns. She felt sorry for you for some reason and didn't want you to be punished. Come on, drink it down and think yourself very fortunate.'

It wasn't unpleasant, quite sweet, Emily thought to herself as she meekly swallowed it down. All fight seemed to have left her. What else could she do, locked in this room, all dignity removed from her? She'd been stripped and dressed in this canvas gown, forced into a padded cell, and now was being drugged against her will. There's no point in fighting anymore, she thought. She wondered why Mrs. Ledbetter had been so understanding although in Emily's opinion she had brought it on herself. No doubt she'd find out in time.

The nurses left and Emily let the medicine do its magic. She closed her eyes and hoped for sleep to come.

She woke in the night, cold and confused. The room was black, no light seeping in from anywhere. Emily noticed the smell of disinfectant, or carbolic, or something else which had been used to clean the place. She tried not to think about what the smells were covering and who may have been in this room before her. They'd said she wasn't being punished but this room was a prison of sorts wasn't it? There was only one way out, through the padded door which had no door handle on the inside. All of the walls were padded in the same canvas that she'd been dressed in. As she felt her way around she realised that there were no windows so natural light would get in. They'd taken away her shoes so her feet were bare and there was no blanket to cover herself with. Curling up on the floor into a tight ball, Emily tried to keep herself warm by wrapping her own arms around herself and she felt such an emptiness in her heart. 'I will never recover from this,' she whispered to herself.

Emily had finally slipped back into a deep sleep which had initially wiped out the memory of the day before. It was only once they came to take her from the room the next morning that it all came back to her. She was taken to the bathroom by the same two nurses. The sinking feeling grew heavier as she realised how hard it was going to be to get back to some kind of normality after this. It seemed to her that however hard she tried to recover, there was no going back, or going forward either. The world was dark and heavy with no hope for her ever again.

Even though she dreaded the bath, Emily passively obeyed the instructions of the nurses as they helped her to strip off and step into the tepid water. It did help. The warmth of the water washing over her and the cleansing of her skin was a relief, as though washing away some of the troubles that weighed her down. Her spirits raised a little more when she realised that the nurses had brought her own asylum uniform clothes into the bathroom and had taken away the canvas dress she'd been forced into the day before.

'You're going back to your own room now, Emily,' she was told. 'I'm sure you're going to behave yourself aren't you?'

'Thank you,' Emily managed to whisper as a tear dropped from her eye.

'Now don't start that.' The other nurse roughly rubbed at her back with the coarse towel. 'No time for sympathy. Just stop playing up and do as you're told and you'll soon be better.'

Emily found it hard to believe that she would ever be well again. There seemed nothing left to live for but doing as she was told was something she could do. She let them lead her back to her room and sat on her bed looking out of the window into the courtyard below. She shuddered as she watched women walking in circles, not talking, not even noticing each other. The thought of being in here for so long that you have no idea of the world outside any more was almost too much to bear. 'There must be a place in the world for me,' she thought. 'I just have to find it again.'

Chapter Nineteen

Emily

The next morning they let her out into the main ward again. She sat in the day room with a handful of ladies who all sat around the walls. The piano stood in the centre of the room, music ready on the stand as if waiting for someone to sit and play. Emily couldn't actually remember the last time she heard a piano and wished that she had learnt to play.

A nurse was helping another patient with some sewing. Emily noticed her glancing over from time to time and wondered where Nurse Paxton was and whether she'd be able to help Emily again like she had before, letting her talk and giving her so much encouragement. Looking up, she saw the nurse looking at her again. 'She's watching us all,' she thought. How uncomfortable it felt to be always under someone's eye.

Determined to get her dignity back, she stood and crossed the room. 'Is Nurse Paxton not here any more?'

'She's on her day off. She'll be back later this evening, don't worry.'

'She has been kind to me.'

'She's a good nurse.'

'Is there something I can do? I need to keep busy.' Emily asked.

The nurse smiled at her. 'You could do some mending,' she said and passed an apron to Emily from a small pile on the table. 'Here, this needs sewing around the hem.'

Emily felt the warmth of the sun shining through the windows as she worked. Stitching the cotton material was soothing, the rhythm almost easing some of the pain. She tried not to let her thoughts drift too much, concentrated on the stitches, now and then glancing around the room to the other women as she wondered about their stories, their lives, what could have happened to bring them in here. She was exhausted by the time she was sent back to her room after supper that evening. It was such a relief to be back in her own bed. She realised how far she'd come, feeling at home in her room in the asylum. This was frightening. Feeling at home in this place was the last thing she wanted.

And so the time moved on. Emily continued to do as she was told, took her medicine and as the days passed, chats with Nurse Paxton began again and Emily felt herself improving. After the first week they stopped giving her the medicine and gradually her old self seeped back into place. She became accustomed to the routine of the ward, rising in the morning early, helping the nurse and attendants to lay the tables, clean the wash-room and to sit and sew for hours every day with a short walk in the courtyard whenever the weather was suitable.

All of this was to change when the medical officer called her for a meeting.

'It's time you started to leave the ward and go back to work,' he said.

Emily sighed, dreading having to go back to the laundry, to be face to face with Mrs. Ledbetter again. But he had something else in mind.

'I'm going to send you to work on the farm. The fresh air and exercise will be much better for you than being in the heat of the laundry.' He looked at her. 'And besides, Mrs. Ledbetter has said that you won't be welcomed back there again. Can't say I can blame her,' he added. 'What do you think of that?'

'I would prefer not to go back to the laundry either. Being outside would be wonderful. Thank you.'

'Good. You'll start on Monday. And well done. You have made a good improvement. We'll have you well in no time at all.'

Emily's spirits lifted. 'Will I really go home again?' she asked.

'Of course. That's always our aim. This is a hospital, not a prison. As soon as you are well, we will ship you out of here as fast as you like. Just make sure we have no further upsets with you. Behave yourself, work hard and all will be well. Now off you go.'

It was with a lighter step that Emily walked back to the ward with the nurse.

Chapter Twenty

Emily

It was a new day and Emily had hope in her heart as she stood by the door of the ward ready to be led out to the fields. She wondered what kind of work she would be given and hoped she would be able to manage it. Emily had no experience of working outside before. She'd always worked inside, cleaning, washing and doing basic cooking tasks. She felt a glimmer of excitement as she waited.

And she'd made a friend. Janet had been in the ward from the day that Emily had arrived. Another woman with a turbulent past, at times she had been sullen, looking away when she spoke to anyone. Emily had often wondered about her story but was too afraid to ask. She'd seen the woman at her worst, screaming at the nurses and attendants at times. Recently though, she was calmer and today she was standing at the door with Emily waiting to go out into the fields. Her hair was wild and a dirty brown, her face was round and maybe had once been jolly-looking. Today her deep brown eyes had a sparkle in them.

'Looks like we're going to be working together,' she said. 'I can't wait to get out of this place, can you?'

Emily smiled.

'I mean, we're still imprisoned I suppose, but being outside during the day will be so good. Shall we be friends?'

'Yes, we will.' Emily wondered why she'd agreed so readily. It was probably the easiest thing to say, she thought.

The attendant opened the door with the key on her belt and ushered the women through. Passing down the dark stairwell felt like going down Alice's rabbit hole, and Emily wondered what was in store for her, but it was the moment that she stepped out into the sunshine, walked through the courtyard, out through the gate into the lane beyond when she felt the huge weight lifting from her shoulders. The first few steps towards what she hoped would be her freedom, her road home, wherever that may be. She reminded herself that she no longer had a home to go to outside. Life had changed beyond all recognition for Emily and there would be no going back. Even if her Pa ever wanted her back, she would not want to go there, not whilst Kate was his wife. And how could she ever forgive him?

They were at the five bar gate to a field of cabbages. She could smell the richness of the vegetables even before they'd entered the field. A farm boy was sitting on the gate as they approached. Jumping down, he swung open the gate, cheekily grinned at the attendant as he quipped, 'Good morning ladies.'

The little band of women were led through into the field. Each one was handed a trowel and the attendant placed a woman at the start of each row. They were shown how to weed between the vegetables, to clear the ground around each plant to enable growth.

Emily hitched up her skirts, knelt in the dirt, loving the feel of the earth between her fingers as she worked. She loved the feel of the sun on her back, the gentle breeze rustling the leaves of the plane trees, creating nature's music, the sound of the birds shrill song, and just being outside of the asylum walls which loomed a few hundred yards away, reminding her that she was still a prisoner but there may one day be an end to it.

The work was hard and she was ready for the break when the sun was high in the noon sky. It was at that moment, as the attendant called for them to stop for a rest and something to eat that she looked up and caught his eye. The farm boy from the gate had moved down the field, watching the workers. Standing a few rows away from Emily, he was staring at her and their eyes met, briefly at first, then when she looked again, he smiled. She held his gaze for a short while, wondering if she had imagined it. He was blushing, she was certain, but was it only the sun burning his face? Then she felt her own face burning too. She quickly looked away. 'I must be imagining it,' she told herself.

Emily tried not to look his way again, but focussed on her bread and cheese, going back to work as soon as she'd eaten. She kept her head down, but her mind was unable to stop thinking about him. The day was nearly over by the time she took the courage to look up again. He was at the end of her row now, only a few yards away and he was looking at her again. Surely she wasn't imagining it? There was something warming about his look. But he was so young, far too young to be serious, and besides it was ridiculous even thinking about anything happening for her now. She shook her head at him and turned away.

When they took her back up the stairs and opened the door with the clanking keys she felt different. Was it the sunshine on her back that had burned all day, making her delirious, or was it true that the farm boy had really looked at her with such a longing in his eye? She thought it must be merely a part of her madness, her lusting after a young man, her longing to be loved and held close again. She'd been asleep for so long, unable to speak even to herself, the darkness like a kernel inside of her, black and rotten, evil, like the world outside in the city. Thinking had been beyond her for so long. Now thoughts attacked her all the time and she tried to ignore them, toss them away again. No thinking! No thinking!

The noise of the ward hurt her head, the shrieks and orders, the clattering of the cutlery as the tables were laid, the scraping of chairs as they were dragged across the floor. She longed to hide in her room and dream of the day, stare up at the clouds passing the window of her tiny room but that was not to be. She had more duties to carry out before the meal was served.

The water in the washroom was icy cold, her back aching as she worked scrubbing the bath tubs and wash basins, glad that she only had to do these and not the water closets which were cleaned by the trustee patients, those that had been in here for years and would never be released.

Her mind was on the sunshine outside and the look in his eye when she'd glanced up. Her heart was waking up as if from a long sleep. She wondered if the future could be better than the past. But this had happened before and she knew she couldn't trust what she saw, or thought she'd seen. It was all a ploy to make her feel she could live again. She had to push it away, protect herself, stop the devils from trying to trick her.

The nurse was calling her. She would go into the dining room and pretend all was well. She would sit at the table and be on her best behaviour, and take the bread and cold meat that they offered, using the spoon to drink the soup that they served and clear her plate of every crumb. She would be watched and see the looks that they passed between each other and she'd know that they were noting how she was. Sometimes, one of them would smile at her or at one of the others at the table.

She didn't trust the smiling ones, they were only trying to get inside her armour, to make her lower her guard and then they could control her thoughts.

She would pretend and then be safe. And tomorrow she would go out into the field again, weed more cabbages and see the farm boy once more. Her heart was lifting until she had to tell it to stop - this was not real, it was just a dream. But there could be hope, she told herself. Hope.

Chapter Twenty-one

Joe

Life on the asylum farm was so different to what it had been like at home for Joe. His Pa's farm was in the countryside just outside Droxford. It had been his Grandpa's before and they'd always said that it would be Joe's one day but he couldn't imagine being stuck on the same farm all of his life. He didn't always see eye-to-eye with his Pa and although it had made his Ma unhappy, Joe couldn't wait to get away. When the war started, he was too young to join up but wasn't too young to move away from the village. He was excited to be moving to Portsmouth and although the asylum was in the countryside, it was nearer to the city and there would be so many more opportunities for a young lad.

The asylum walls enclosed the looming buildings where the inmates were kept, the lunatics as they were sometimes called. Joe was surprised when he first started working out in the fields. He'd not realised how ordinary-looking the inmates were. No different to any of the people who'd helped on his Pa's farm back in Droxford really. And the countryside was not that much different. The land was flat, being a small island, the fields surrounded with trees, growing vegetables and wheat, with orchards full of apples and pears too. The narrow road that passed the asylum led to the harbour where the now disused canal entrance was. House-boats sat in the mud beside the shore and you could see across the inlet to Eastney and even further to Hayling Island.

Sometimes he worked in the stables, helping with the horses, mucking out and keeping the stables clean. On other days, he had to help with the cows, taking them to the milking parlour each day. He already knew how to milk a cow and had spent many mornings in the dairy. But Joe's favourite place was in the open air, overseeing the workers in the fields.

Life moved on from day to day until the day he first saw Emily.

His first impression of this untidy woman was one that would never leave him.

He was in the field of cabbages, overseeing the patients who were stooped, weeding along the rows. He'd been shocked when they stopped for tea and she looked up at the sun, craning her neck and stretching her back. Shocked at the beauty in her face as the sun eased out the lines that he had thought were a part of her, ingrained in her being. Her clothes hung loosely on her slender frame, her hair was loosely plaited, strands escaping into the breeze.

The sunlight glinted gold around her head, like a halo, he thought.

Telling himself he couldn't be in love with a lunatic, he tried to turn his face away. He tried several times, finding himself drawn to her again and again throughout the hot summer day until, relieved, the sun was lower in the sky and the women were escorted away from the fields and back into the looming building beyond the wall. He wondered what her story could be. he'd worked on these fields for a while now and had seen many women from the asylum but never before been this curious about any of them. He checked himself. No longer called an asylum, now a mental hospital, although the place was no different, the patients still looked the same: often vacant, sometimes troubled. Usually he just got on with his work and tried not to think about why they had ended up in here.

Sometimes he longed to get away, to join up and fight on the front like the other older lads had done. He was nearly old enough now. His Pa had wanted him to help on their own farm and maybe he should have gone back to do that instead. But he'd liked the life here so much nearer to the city. He could work on the farm and it was only a walk away to the bustle of the town. Of course things had changed since the war began and it seemed like it was coming closer the nearer Joe got to adulthood.

His mind insisted on drifting back to the woman. He tried not to hope, but there was something about her that had wrapped itself around his dreams.

Walking home that night Joe wondered if his life would ever change.

Chapter Twenty-two

Emily

The next day Emily struggled to wake. She knew all was not well when the room was spinning around and everything was blurred. Her limbs were heavy and her throat sore.

'You've got a fever,' the nurse told her. 'No field work for you today.'

Fearing the worst, Emily remembered how her Ma had been when the fever had taken her such a short time ago. Surely this wasn't how it was all going to end for her too?

Over the next days and nights, Emily slipped in and out of delirium, the nurses trying to keep her cool with tepid bed baths. Sometimes she threw the bedclothes off and then later she would wake, freezing cold and crying for more blankets. At times, they tried to feed her broth, most of which she vomited back up almost as soon as it reached her stomach. Her throat felt like she'd swallowed gravel and even taking sips of water was torture.

Gradually she improved, became stronger and after a week the nurse told her she was to go back to work.

'You can do half a day at first,' she was told. 'See how it goes. The next few weeks are crucial for your complete recovery. It will be hard but the fresh air and exercise will do you good.'

Emily was helped down the stairwell by the nurse. As she carefully trod her way, she stumbled.

'I think we're hoping for too much, Emily,' the nurse held onto her arm as they finally made it to the ground floor. She called to the other escort. 'I'm going to have to keep Emily back. You go on ahead.'

'Please, could we just go into the courtyard for a while. I can't bear the thought of spending another day in that ward with no fresh air.' Emily looked longingly out of the window.

The other women had all passed through the doorway and the hall was quiet. The nurse hesitated with her keys, about to lock the door. 'Come on then,' she said. 'I don't suppose it'll do any harm to have a little walk.'

How wonderful it was to be out in the sunshine once more. The brief time that Emily had been in the field before had given her a sense of hope and being out here again, feeling the warmth of the sun, the soft summer breeze on her face, was the tonic she needed to make life almost worth living again.

'Give yourself time, Emily,' the nurse was saying. 'It won't be long before you're strong enough to work again.

She led them to a bench nearby. 'We'll sit here for a moment, shall we?'

Above them was a cherry tree, its blossoms no longer on the tree, the ground around the bench still covered in the petals, now turned brown underfoot. New leaves adorned the branches as well as the tiny beginnings of cherries hanging there, a promise of the abundance for the future.

Emily's mind drifted to her past, wondering where she would have been if her Ma hadn't left them, if her Pa hadn't remarried, and if she and Billy had married before he went off to war. She realised how pointless it was to think such thoughts, even though it was easy to allow her mind to drift in this way. But now was there any hope for the future?

Of course, there was that lad in the field. Surely she hadn't imagined the look on his face when they'd met? She immediately scolded herself. 'It was the beginnings of the fever, merely your imagination,' she told herself.

'What are you thinking about?'

'About what you said about me getting strong again. I can't seem to imagine a future for myself at the moment. Locked up in this place.'

'Well, I've seen many women come and go. It's not like the old days when you might have been locked up and forgotten about. We don't want people to stay here unnecessarily, that's the truth of it. You are young and do have a future in the world.'

'I hope so.'

'You just need to believe in yourself. Come on, let's go back to the ward. It's a lovely day but we can't stay sitting here for much longer. I need to catch up with the ladies on the farm.'

Chapter Twenty-three

Joe

It was some time before he saw her again. Days probably although it seemed like weeks. He looked for her every
day with hope in his heart. For what? He was just a boy,
too young to be of use to anyone yet and by the time he
was older she would be gone, back to her family if they
ever cured her. Yes, he'd heard that those with madness
were often cured these days and went on to live in the
world outside. She may have been sent home already and
he'd never see her again. Was he imagining that she'd be
interested in a boy like him? Maybe it was this place that
made him dream so.

Outside the asylum, across the city, the war was alive.
It was eating away at all that was good, taking away the
fathers and sweethearts, putting suspicion into the minds
of friends and neighbours. It was sucking the energy and
hope for the future out of the women who were left to
work and scrape together food for the table. No wonder so
many came through those gates to this place. No wonder.

Joe went to work each morning, toiled in the fields and every evening he walked back to his lodgings, his heart heavy as the days passed and he didn't see her. Unable to talk about his feelings to anyone, he kept his thoughts to himself like a secret love that was so far out of his reach. Sometimes he drank in the Farmhouse pub just down the road from his lodgings. His pal, Jack, had no idea that he was suffering. Joe told himself to forget her but each night in his room, he lay in bed and couldn't erase her face from his memory.

One day the two friends took the bus to the city centre. It was Jack's idea, to explore the "city lights", although the city wasn't like it used to be. The streets were filled with hungry looking people, so many more women than men, and those men that he saw were in uniform. Some were soldiers, but there were more sailors, home on leave. There was an atmosphere of determination. Despite the hungry looks, people were greeting each other with salutes and thumps on the back between friends.

Being in the city made Joe feel even more out of place. 'Shouldn't we join up?' he asked Jack.

'They wouldn't have us yet, would they? They want men, not boys.'

'I'm old enough now and I feel bad not being in uniform like all the other young men.'

'You can join up if you want. Although as farmers we aren't expected to go. Someone has to keep the country fed. That's our job. Or in our case I suppose it's to keep the asylum fed first but much of our crops goes to feed the navy too, remember.'

'I do know all that. I still can't help how I feel though. And now that the women are starting to do more men's work...' he paused. 'There are land girls working on farms now. I know they don't do the work the same as a man, but some of them are good, and they work really hard. I don't know what's right or wrong.'

'Well I agree with you. I will probably join up soon enough. If the war carries on, we might have to anyway.'

'What do you mean?'

'So many are not coming back. And a whole lot more coming back maimed.' He looked across the street at two men who were struggling along, both with crutches, one with no legs at all and the other only had one.

Joe shuddered. 'If that happened to me I'd be no use on the farm afterwards. Still, it makes me feel I should do more. Let's hope that it's over soon. Although if I don't go, I will always wonder if I should have gone.'

'It's not easy, I know. Come on, let's stop thinking about what might or might not happen. I want to enjoy my day off. Now it looks like rain, bloody typical, one day off in a month and it rains.'

It rained for another week, making work in the fields miserable as he worked alone. None of the women came out to work in this terrible weather. Joe felt life would never get any better. Then one day, he looked out of the window early in the morning and the sun was shining.

He arrived at the farm, his spirits lighter, hoping that today the women would be allowed to come out to work again.

He saw them walking down the lane towards the field. He waited, his stomach churning with anticipation. He dared not hope, but was that her, near the end of the straggling line?

Turning away he put his mind to his work with the hoe, not wanting to show how red his face had begun to glow. Throughout the next few hours, although he'd longed for this day, he kept himself aloof from the women, head down, digging and hoeing, bending and pulling weeds. When they stopped for their first tea break, he stayed as far away from the group as possible. He was afraid of what might happen, of what he was feeling. He told himself he was being stupid, imagining something that could never be. This was nothing like he'd experience before. This woman had seen so much more of life than he ever had and he just didn't know how to behave.

Joe worked through the day, his determination swinging from staying away from her to trying to speak to her before the women were taken from the field back to the asylum. He couldn't go through another night without at least trying. Of course, nothing ever works how you hope. The rain started again not long after dinner and the women were all ushered away again. When his day was done, he made his way to the stables to wash the mud from his boots before he went home. The farm manager was waiting for him.

'Joe, I'm glad I caught you. Jack's hurt his leg and can't come in. It looks like a sprain but he can't walk so you'll have to take on his work in the stable for a week or so until he's back on his feet. You'll need to come in tomorrow at dawn. There's plenty needs doing. I'll do the cows.'

Joe looked across the yard, his face dropped.

'You alright with that?'

'Sorry, Yes of course. I'll be here.'

'Good. See you tomorrow then.'

Chapter Twenty-Four

Emily

'I really should get some boots that fit.'

It was a fleeting thought, soon pushed away as ridiculous. There was nowhere she could get new boots. Not in this place. The boots she wore every day, inside and out, whatever the weather, were the same boots that Kate had brought in for her, that she'd worn before. Before the birth of her son. The pain of realising her loss pierced her again and again. Thinking about boots and the rubbing on her heels took her mind off the emptiness in her arms.

'It's no good living in a past that'll never be different,' she told herself. Her child was gone, the world a place where she had no power, no right at all to claim back that which had been taken from her. She was a mere woman, one without a husband, and even in the twentieth century, the modern world, she was still owned and ruled by her father, a father who only listened to his new wife and never his daughter, at least not any more.

Walking to the fields, glad enough that she was at least outside and not in the laundry, Emily felt the blisters on her heels. It was almost welcome, the soreness of her feet kept her grounded somehow. Each step was heavy, the earth underfoot, the mud kicking up as she moved along behind the other women making their way to the cabbage field. 'Thank heavens that the rain at last stopped,' she thought. 'This last week has been a long one, not being able to get out of the ward.'

Emily wore a kerchief around her face, covering her nose and mouth, her hat low over her head, more as a way to avoid others, rather than to protect her from the weather. She spoke only when she had to now. Mindless chatter was something she'd been accused of once, in the world before the war. Now she kept quiet, away from happy voices, away from spiteful gossip. The work was hard enough without having to be sociable.

It was nearly noon before she noticed him. She recalled the last time he'd looked at her and smiled. She'd been alarmed by that. They weren't allowed to talk to the farm workers. She had looked about to where the attendant was standing, ushering the women back to the high-walled building with sad-eyed windows gazing across the fields. She'd not been noticed looking at him that day. The attendant had said nothing anyway, but Emily made a pact with herself that she'd keep away from the boy in future. She had too much to lose. The mere thought of being back in the laundry sent a panic through her. Being in the fields was hard work but at least she felt a kind of brief freedom being outside in the sunshine or the rain, the breeze on her skin, the sound of birds singing as though there was no war, no death of all that was good, and no mental asylum incarcerating her.

Knowing all this didn't stop her wondering. What if it was true, there had been a spark that day? When he'd looked at her and smiled it was as though she'd woken from a dream. Each time she thought of that moment she felt herself drifting into another dream, a day-dream, one in which he was the centre of the story. 'It can't do any harm,' she'd told herself. It was a way of escape from the monotony of every long night in this place, to take her mind from the sounds of the ward, from the miseries of the other women, the wailing, the fighting and sometimes the hysterical laughter. But that was all it was.

Chapter Twenty-five

Joe

Every day he'd walked to the asylum from his lodging house, hoping he'd see her again if only from a distance. He was torn in two with hoping, whilst knowing at heart it must be hopeless. She could never be his, never. But still, he walked to work in hope.

It had been frustrating working in the stables, making him miss a whole week of not seeing her, knowing she was there in the cabbage fields but somehow out of reach. Still he kept his head down, fed the horses, turned them out into the meadow, mucked out the stables and somehow the rhythmic work was soothing and helped the time pass more quickly.

Joe loved the horses. He loved their quiet strength. They seemed to understand his mood and gave him comfort. He couldn't help wondering about the horses on his Pa's farm, especially the one's that had been taken by the army to France. Would they be safe, or would they suffer somehow with all the noise of the battle-field and the danger? Joe couldn't imagine what it must be like for them and didn't like thinking about it, knowing that he was safe whilst they were far away helping to fight a war.

Today at last, Jack was back at work and Joe walked from the stable to the fields with a lighter step. The women were already there when he arrived. He was greeted by one of the attendants, a large woman with a gleam in her eye.

'Back again then, young Joe?' She winked at him. 'Couldn't stay away from me, eh?'

Joe felt the blood rush to his face.

'Don't be shy, lad,' she said. 'I could tell you were keen to get back here. You were falling over yourself in haste.'

Joe coughed and moved away towards the far end of the row, glad to be as far away from this rude and forward woman as possible. He only glanced back when he'd reached the fence. Thankfully the woman had been distracted by one of the inmates who was sobbing loudly to herself in the middle of a row.

Joe sighed. He'd have to learn how to harden himself against pushy women. Some of those who worked in the asylum had no shame, were brazen and outspoken. Not the kind of woman he could be happy with. He leaned on the hoe and let his eyes wander to the other women in the field.

He was drawn to her. Her face was covered but he'd never forget the shape of her back, stooped over the deep green of the cabbages, nor would he forget the graceful way she moved her arms as she pulled the weeds from the earth.

She looked up, just briefly, but their eyes met in that moment and he knew he hadn't imagined it. All the dreaming hadn't been in vain. He needed to find a way to spend a few moments with her, not here, but in a place where they could both be free. Was he every going to succeed?

Ever since the day he'd first cast eyes on her in the fields when she'd looked up at the sun and stretched her neck, he knew he had to be with her. It was a dream at first but somehow just having her in the world at the same time as him was almost enough. It was just one day in the sunshine and then he'd not seen her again for what seemed like forever, but still it was enough for him to know he was in love.

Leaning on his hoe, he'd watched as the women walked from the walled garden in their grey dresses, overalls wrapped around them to keep them clean. They all looked the same, those women, their hair tucked into cotton scarves, or covered with straw hats against the sun. Their faces all had the same expressions, troubled with suspicious eyes. Except for hers. He sensed her nearness before she even came through the gate in the wall. When she stepped through, it sounds unbelievable, but he could have sworn at that exact moment the sun came out from behind the clouds and he felt alive again.

What a strange wooing, an unusual courtship. He kept telling himself that it could come to nothing but still he was full of hope, watching her from afar until, as she stood at the end of a row, the attendant passed her a drink of water in a tin mug. She was so close to where he was working now, he could almost hear the sound of her breathing. Or was he imagining it? He knew the blush was blooming through his face and he felt a fool. The attendant had moved away to the next row. He stepped a little closer to her now, holding his breath, wondering how to speak, what to say, should he say anything at all?

Then she spoke.

'It's good to be outside,' was all she said.

'It is,' feeling so foolish and wishing he could say something meaningful, this was all he could say.

Then she laughed. 'But you are out here whenever you want.' Her voice was low, the laugh was humourless.

He looked at her and saw she was smiling a sad smile, almost as if she pitied him and not herself.

He wanted to say so much more. His tongue was caught up like a fish caught in a net. And then it was too late. She was bustled back into line by the attendant. He watched, as she wiped a hand across her face and stooped to the ground once more, regretting that he hadn't told her how beautiful she was, but that would have been impossible, wouldn't it? Then she looked up at him and smiled, this time a real smile, no sign of sadness but only of hope.

When the rain came, there was a rainbow.

Chapter Twenty-six

Emily

There was a rainbow.

Rain splashed down on the field, creating diamonds on the cabbage leaves. Emily turned her face to the sky and revelled in the cool water washing her face clean. A bubbling in her throat unrecognisable, it had been so long since she'd heard herself laugh. When it was released, she felt her whole body relax, the tensions slipping away. She pulled off the straw hat and felt her hair grow heavier, the rain now running down her neck.

The days had passed without her seeing him. She'd convinced herself that he had left the asylum, probably gone to the front with all the other young men she'd known. Her life was so broken that she'd convinced herself she wouldn't see him again, so she wasn't expecting him to just turn up this morning. And he'd seen her, even spoken to her when she'd said those few words to him. He hadn't shunned her like she'd expected him to. Everything in the world seemed lighter now even in the rain.

The farm boy spoke. 'You should go in, now,' he said. 'You'll catch your death of a cold.'

Emily remembered her Ma saying that to her brothers when they'd been out playing in the street so long ago. The smile on her face faded as she lowered her head once more.

Trying to ignore the boy, she continued to pull out the weeds, digging with her trowel to loosen the roots. It was only when the attendant, who had been sheltering in the far wooden hut, called out for the women to get back to the ward, that she stopped.

Squelching through the muddy rows to the gate, she tried not to look at the boy, but was unable to be indifferent to his stare as she passed him. Convinced that he was laughing at her, or disgusted with her plight, she could not imagine there would ever be anything to bring them together. And yet...?

She was being ushered through the gate back to the asylum. Unable to resist it, she glanced back over her shoulder. The rainbow was an arch in the sky passing over where the farm boy stood, looking back at her. Was he smiling at her? Emily felt the warmth spreading through her heart. She smiled back as he lifted his hand to wave.

Joe

She had gone and Joe couldn't stop thinking about her and how she'd looked.

Her hair flopping against her face, rain trickling down. Her inner beauty shining in the jewels on her cheeks. He believed he loved her now even more, as he remembered that first day when she'd smiled at him in the sunshine. But it was a love he thought would never be reciprocated or ever even be spoken of. It was forbidden for them to

know each other, as they stood on different sides of the dividing line. He was too young, inexperienced, preparing for a war, or for a life on the farm. Whereas she was older, wiser perhaps, but damaged both from without and within, already tarnished by life and labelled as mad.

Even should they come together in the future perhaps after this war was over, after she had been cured, and they were both out there in what they call the "real world", his family would never accept her, nor hers him.

But he would see her, every day in the field, and know that he'd never love like this again.

Chapter Twenty-seven

Joe

It was Jack who pestered him into going to the asylum dance. He'd talked about it before he'd hurt his ankle but that had put a stop to doing anything about it.

'Come on Joe, it'll be fun, a change from going to the local. The Farmhouse pub's alright but this is just what we need.'

'I don't know. I'm not sure about being in there. I mean, it's alright to work on the asylum farm, but to go there to dance?'

'You can dance can't you?' Jack had asked. 'There are always a few nurses there, hungry to meet some men. And there's refreshments. Not beer, but tea and sometimes cake.'

'How can I resist,' Joe had said, grinning. 'I don't know though.'

'Go on, Joe,' Jack nudged him. 'Sally, the nurse on B Ward will be there, but I can't go on my own. She's going to bring her friend.'

'Alright, I'll come. Just for you, because you're a mate. But if I don't like her friend, I won't stay.'

The music coming from the hall was already playing as they walked towards the doors. Joe wondered why he felt nervous. Perhaps it was the thought of being in that room full of lunatics, or maybe the prospect of being with all those dignitaries who liked to come along to see how well the inmates of the asylum were cared for. He'd heard it said that they believed madness should be treated with fresh air, good food, and raising morale. A regular dance would be perfect for doing that, as long as you could dance, he supposed. It seemed strange to him that whilst the world outside was a place full of danger, turmoil and madness, in here it was as if nothing had ever changed. Was that why they called it an asylum?

Jack led the way, walking straight across to the refreshment tables on the far side. The room was full - ladies in rustling gowns, glittering jewels adorning their necks, men in tail suits with bow ties, nurses in uniforms and attendants in white coats. And the patients of course - men along one side of the room and women on the other all still dressed in the uniform of the asylum, men in woollen suits and the women in drab grey dresses, the same dresses they wore in the fields but without the overalls covering them.

He saw her almost at once. It was as if a light was shining from her - perhaps it was the gas light behind her but to him it looked like a halo. And he could see no-one else after that. Would he have the nerve to ask her to dance? How he wished that they were serving beer not tea. A drop of courage would have been the answer.

Jack elbowed him in the ribs. 'Over there.' He nodded towards a couple of nurses who stood together beside a table.

Joe dragged his eyes away from the light.

'Come on,' said Jack, who without waiting was making his way across the room.

Joe glanced back to where the woman had been. She was gone. His heart in his boots, he followed Jack and stood shuffling his feet.

Sally's friend was pretty. She smiled coyly at him when they were introduced.

'Joe, pleased to meet you, I'm sure,' said Sally. 'This is my friend Maisie. We work together.'

When Jack and Sally took to the dance floor, Joe stood for a moment. He coughed awkwardly when he realised what was expected of him. 'Would you like to dance?' he asked, thinking 'how pompous I sound'. This was not like the country dances he'd been used to, it was so formal and stiff.

The Waltz was not a dance he was comfortable with. The basic steps, of course, he'd learnt at school, but he enjoyed the "Polka", or "The Dashing White Sergeant" best, dances he could see the purpose of. They shuffled around the floor, Joe holding Maisie at arms length. She may have been pretty, he could see that but there was no magic there, no joy in their movement together. And yes, he was distracted. His eyes were searching the room for her, the woman from the field who as yet had no name. She was here in this room but so far out of his reach. And now he was saddled with Maisie, he would never get a chance to speak to her. All he longed for was to hold her in his arms and to spin her around the floor. Would it ever happen?

'Oi, Joe, you're hurting me.' Maisie pulled at his hand which had gripped her like a vice. He hadn't even noticed, his mind on the other woman and his longing for her.

'I'm sorry.' He let go of Maisie and stood, his arms at his side. 'I don't know what I'm doing. I'm sorry, I can't do this.'

Other dancers trying not to collide with them were tutting as they passed.

'This is so embarrassing.' Maisie glared at him. 'You will not leave me here like this,' and she grasped his hand, placing her other hand on his shoulder as she led him back into the dance, just in time for Joe to see the illusive woman with the light in her hair being escorted from the hall by a nurse.

Not wishing to cause even more of a scene, Joe resigned himself to finishing the dance with Maisie, a dance that seemed to go on forever. Finally, the music came to a close and they made their way through the crowd to the table where Jack and Sally waited.

'Get the ladies a drink, won't you Joe?' Jack was nodding towards the bar area. 'You'd like a lemonade, wouldn't you?' he asked Sally.

'Yes, please. That would be lovely,' Sally nudged Maisie. 'Wouldn't it, Maisie?'

Maisie, still looking annoyed, said nothing.

'Of course,' agreed Joe, as he moved towards the refreshments, a feeling of relief that he'd escaped, if only for a few minutes, washing over him. He didn't look back. If he had he'd have seen Maisie and Sally, heads down, furiously arguing over something. Jack stood looking awkward beside them.

There was a queue. He glanced with envy at the waitresses serving those in fancy evening dress. He'd heard about the wealthy do-gooders who supported the asylum financially and came to the functions such as this one held in the ballroom. Only inmates who had earned a place here by their good behaviour and willingness to work within the asylum were privileged enough to be able to attend. As well, of course, the attendants who lived within the asylum, and the other workers, such as himself. Looking about the room, he saw a couple of the carpenters with their wives, sitting looking bored, and he recognised other nurses that he'd seen walking in the grounds.

He was almost at the front of the queue when she returned through the doorway, still escorted by the nurse she had left with. All thoughts of Jack, Sally and Maisie left his head. He was lost to everything else but the woman with the light in her hair. He could have sworn at that moment that she looked across at him and smiled. He may have imagined it, but would always look back on that moment and know that there was no one else in the room that was important.

Joe left the queue and made his way to the door. He stood in front of the woman. 'Hello again,' he said. 'I've seen you working in the field.'

The nurse looked at him suspiciously. 'And you are?' she asked as she pulled herself up to her full height.

'My apologies,' Joe, feeling clumsy and crass, knew his face had turned a bright beetroot red. He looked again at the woman beside the nurse. 'My name is Joe. I work on the farm. I spoke to you in the field last week. I don't know your name though.' The words seemed to choke in his throat.

Her voice was low, sweet like violins in a midnight Christmas song that he'd heard once in passing the Cathedral. One word she spoke, one beautiful word, her name. 'Emily.'

He smiled but his heart sang in tune with the violins. 'Hello Emily, pleased to meet you,' he said.

He turned to the nurse. 'Are we allowed to dance?' he asked, then to Emily. 'If you want to of course?' He held his breath, the seconds passed whilst he waited for her reply, seeming like minutes or even hours.

Her smiling reply was the sweetest thing. 'I would,' was all she said.

'You may dance,' the nurse put in. 'But I will be watching. You must stay in the ballroom and not go out of my sight.'

The music had begun. Joe took Emily's hand and led her into the throng of dancers. It was his favourite, the Polka, a dance which sang with the joy he was feeling. The room was crowded but there was only Emily and himself, spinning and dancing as though they'd always been dancing even though this was their first time. He looked into her eyes and knew this was the woman he had to spend the rest of his life with.

The dance was over far too soon, leaving Joe wondering what he could do to make this evening last for ever. The nurse was at their side again before he could think.

'It's time to get you back to the ward,' she was saying.

Joe glanced at her then back to Emily. 'I'm sorry you have to go so soon,' he said. 'Perhaps we can dance again at the next one?'

'I would like that,' Emily replied.

'And I will see you in the fields?'

She nodded.

'Come along. It's time to leave, Emily. You've already had more than the hour you were allowed.' And the nurse gripped Emily by the elbow, steering her towards the doorway which was already full of people being herded out to their mundane lives in their prison-like rooms in the airy Victorian wards.

The last he saw of her that night was when she reached the door and glanced back at him. Their eyes met and the light was shining across the room to him. He sighed to himself, then remembered Jack and the ladies waiting for their lemonade. 'Damn it, I'm not doing this,' he said to himself as he turned and made his own way out of the ballroom and was soon walking along Asylum Road back to his lodgings. 'I'll face Jack tomorrow,' he thought.

Chapter Twenty-eight

Emily

When she closed her eyes she could see him. When she lay down on her bed, she heard the music they'd danced to, a wonderful Polka, not a romantic dance, but full of the kind of joy she thought she would never feel again. They'd whirled around the floor, all the other dancers had dissolved into the ether, never to be acknowledged. She didn't care that they were dressed in finery whilst she and Joe were in their everyday garb. She only saw him, only felt the touch of his hand on hers, his other one on her waist, its heat through her cotton dress. She placed her own hand now on the place where he'd touched and still could feel the warmth, the blood coursing through her veins, longing for more of him. Yet it was just one dance and then it was over.

She remembered that last look as she'd left the ballroom, could feel his eyes on her even as she lay alone in her room, awake and dreaming of the night, looking forward to the morning when she'd be back in the fields, working with the other patients. She'd look up and their eyes would meet again. She'd speak to him in her dream, they'd walk along the lane together, would sit on the grassy bank and talk of their future together, after the war, after this nightmare was over.

She'd been marched back to the ward by Maud, the nurse. She was nice enough, had allowed her longer at the dance than was usually allowed. And she was always nice to Emily, even in sharing her christian name. All the other nurses only used their surnames. She was Nurse Paxton to other patients. Emily didn't know why she was so kind to her; perhaps she'd reminded her of her sister. She'd told Emily about her sister once. That was before she remembered that they were not supposed to tell the patients about themselves.

'You are a silly girl,' nurse Paxton had said to Emily this night as they made their way along the corridors. 'Enjoy the moment, it will only be fleeting. He is too young for you and he'll soon be going to war with the rest of them. You,' she paused. 'I'm sorry, but you will always be damaged goods, people will call you a lunatic now and you will be labelled as such for ever. You may as well get used to it. With so few young men left, it'll be hard enough to find a husband for any woman.'

Perhaps she had meant to be kind but it cut to Emily's heart. She pushed it away, preferring to hold onto the dream, to believe in the warmth that was still wrapped around her, the glow from that one short dance. It would have to be real, Emily thought, or she'd would never get through those days and maybe even the years ahead.

Chapter Twenty-nine

Joe

Joe didn't need to wait long to face Jack. He was waiting at the end of the street the next morning and he was not happy.

'Bloody hell mate, what happened to you last night? You left me right in the shit with the ladies. What were you playing at?'

Joe cursed himself for blushing. 'I'm sorry. I couldn't do it. Maisie is nice but she's not the girl for me.' He began to walk away towards the asylum.

'Sorry Joe but that's not playing the game. You knew I was sweet on Sally. You've messed it up for me good and proper now. I could swing for you.'

'I said I was sorry. I'll make it up to you. Buy you a pint later. Sally'll forgive you, you didn't do anything wrong anyway, It was me.'

'I saw you.'

'What?' Joe clenched his fists.

'I saw you dancing with that lunatic woman.'

'Don't call her that.' Joe stopped walking and turned to face his friend, hating the smirk on Jack's face. 'She's not a lunatic.'

'What is she then? She wouldn't be in there if she was normal. Obviously mad in some way.'

'You know nothing about her,' Joe said, thinking to himself, and neither do I.

'Neither do you,' echoed Jack. 'I don't know why you're so bothered anyway. You'll probably never have a chance with her. She's damaged goods, an inmate whether she's a lunatic or not, and she'll always be someone who's been in the asylum whatever happens. Not only that but she's old. Must be at least twenty eight and you're only a lad.'

'Shut up, Jack!' Joe glared at him.

'It's true. Anyone can see it would never work. She's just an old, mad woman and you're a fool.'

Joe's temper flared over as he lost control. His arm swung back and forward as he punched Jack in the face. He felt sickened as the sound of Jack's nose cracked under his fist. But he had no time to think as the other man leapt forward and punched him back. Soon they were both on the ground, wrestling in the dirt of the road, each trying to hurt the other in any way they could. All the frustrations in Joe were flying out in his anger towards his friend. Later he would only feel shame in his behaviour but now he could see nothing but fury and a need to fight.

How long it would have gone on, he couldn't say. It was only when they were pulled apart by the passing ploughman who grabbed Jack and dragged him across the street whilst at the same time shouting at Joe to stay back.

'What are you two playing at?' he yelled. 'Two friends trying to kill each other?'

Joe staggered to his feet. 'Keep him away from me,' he pointed at Jack.

'Don't worry, I won't be seeking you out,' Jack shouted then turned to the ploughman. 'He's no friend of mine.'

Joe leaned on the wall and watched Jack walk away with the ploughman. He shook his head, wondering what the hell had just happened. His best mate and all that anger. It had touched a nerve in him when Jack had said all that about Emily. How could it ever be resolved now? How could Emily and he ever be together with so much against them? And how could he ever find out whether she felt the same about him?

The day got worse. Joe had already started to walk towards the fields when he was called back by the ploughman. 'The farm manager wants to see you, boy.'

Joe stopped and looked back. 'What now?' he asked.

'Only one way to find out.' The older man shrugged and then walked away. 'You'd best not keep him waiting,' he called over his shoulder.

It wasn't good news. Joe was given a warning over his behaviour.

'Sorry lad but can't let it go without seeming to do summat about it.'

'I know. I don't know what came over me,' Joe said. He felt ashamed of himself. There was enough trouble in the world without falling out with your mates.

'Well, whatever it was, I've decided to take you off the fields for a bit. I seem to think it has something to do with a woman, perhaps one of the women who comes down from the asylum to work. It won't do lad, you must know there could be no future for you there. Unless you see yourself as an inmate,' he added.

Joe was aware of his face reddening but he shook his head in denial. 'It's not anything to do with those women,' he said. 'We just had a barney, that's all. I'll buy Jack a drink later and we'll be back to normal.'

'Sorry lad. I've made up my mind. Anyway I was going to put you on this job before all this happened. I need you to get mending the fences on the bottom fields. Stop the sheep getting out into the lane.'

Joe stood, wondering if there was any point in trying to get the man to change his mind.

'Off you go, then,' was his answer.

Joe turned and left the office, his shoulders slumped in despair.

Chapter Thirty

Emily

When the sun finally came up she was still filled with hope, excited to be seeing him again in the field. The work was hard but she wouldn't notice the aches in her back because her heart would be full. Rushing through breakfast and the clearing up of the tables afterwards, not even noticing the other women shuffling around the place, Emily donned her overall and waited by the door to be led down those narrow stairs and into the sunshine.

The walk to the fields was short. They passed through the stable yard. The smell of the horses hit her senses as they approached. In the air were particles of dust from the hay bales that the horses feasted on. It promised to be a hot day and she was glad of her sun hat. She noticed the other young man that she'd seen Joe with last night across the crowded ballroom, his hob-nailed boots now sounding like flint against the cobbles. Making a passing glance at him she noticed his right eye was blackened, his face was bruised as though he'd been in a fight. Emily could have sworn he'd glared at her as she walked quickly by with the other women and she had a faint uneasy feeling in her belly but shook it away, turning back to the sunshine and the field ahead.

Janet, who was walking alongside, sniggered.

'Who was that?' She prodded Emily in the ribs as she spoke. 'Did you see the way he looked at us?'

'I didn't notice. He's just another stable lad,' Emily managed to reply, her stomach churning. 'I'm not interested in any man.'

Janet laughed. 'Pull the other one. I've seen the way you look when that other lad is around. I wonder where he is today.'

Emily felt herself blushing as she rammed her hat onto her head, hiding her face from the world as they walked on.

Working in the second field further away from the asylum walls, it felt good to have so much distance between herself and that gloomy building. Tall trees surrounding the fields shimmered in the breeze, whispering their scorn at the weary workers. But where was Joe? Emily searched across the cabbages, hoping that she was mistaken, but he was not there. She tried to work, to take her mind off him. How could she, distracted with searching, head down, pulling weeds, then looking up and gazing desperately into the distance, wondering what could have happened to him.

Janet noticed, of course. 'Still looking for your sweetheart?' she teased.

'Leave me alone,' Emily turned away from her bending to her work.

'Don't be like that. I'm only teasing. Why shouldn't we have our dreams, eh? We still have feelings even though we're written off in here. He's a nice looking lad, even if he is still a boy.'

Emily couldn't answer that. Keeping her head down, she worked harder than ever to make the day go quickly and couldn't wait to get back to the safety of the ward, away from any hope she may have mistakenly had.

Chapter Thirty-one

Maud

It was difficult to carry on at times. She was nurse Paxton and working was her life now, from before dawn until she lay her head on the pillow at night. Normally it was automatic. The night attendant woke her with a knock on the door, she'd splash cold water on her face and arms, pull on her uniform dress, tie the ribbons of her starched apron. Then she would scrape her hair into a bun, don the cap, check the apron for stains, tidy her bed before leaving the room to enter the early morning snoring odours of a ward full of troubled women.

Today felt different. The world had changed beyond recognition because her own sweet Oswald was never coming home. They should have married before. Maud was ready - oh yes, they'd dreamed of a future together, walked along Eastney promenade, arm in arm, planning. When the war came, he came to see her that last time, told her he was going off with his pals to fight for his country. 'It'll be a grand adventure,' he'd said. 'I can't watch my pals go without me. We'll marry when I come home.'

From the front, he'd written letters, mud spattered and filled with love. Again and again he talked about the wedding and how wonderful if would be when he came home. They said it would be over soon. They said it would be Christmas but Christmases came and went with no sign of his return, not even for a few days leave. Working in the asylum kept Maud occupied enough, with little time left over at the end of the day to think too much. She tried not to imagine where he was or what he was doing, setting her mind on the next time she'd see him - how she'd smile and he'd kiss her. And they would marry.

But no. Because yesterday she walked through Kingston cemetery to see his Ma and she broke the news. A telegram had come just that very morning. He was lost forever, would never be back and so now the world would never be the same.

Maud walked down the ward, past the dormitories and the locked rooms, her mind numb and her body automatically going through the usual things that had to be done each day. The other nurse, Ellie, was already in the dining room, the tables all laid. They made the porridge and cut the bread. The trustees were already up and about their work, waking the other patients, ushering them to the bathrooms, making the beds, changing sheets that were soiled and bundling them into the laundry bags.

One by one the ladies straggled to the tables, each one knowing their place, scraping the chairs as they sat and waited for their meal. Maud looked around and wondered what it was all for. This madness in the world. Why were all these people here, not able to carry on with their lives? Life was good before - the birds still sang and the cattle still low in the fields outside of the asylum walls even though everyone knew that the world would not be the same afterwards. How could it be when so many young men were dead? How could it be when so many young men had lost their minds? How could it be when so many of young women were widows?

Maud thought about her sister. She'd said she loved the war. It had given her a chance, she'd said. A chance to get out of working in service, a chance to work in the factory with her friends, to earn good wages and have the freedom to walk out each evening if she chose. She didn't see the colour of her skin as it yellowed from the cordite, spending all her time with women the same as herself. Maud said nothing about this when she saw her. Her sister would never work in a place such as the asylum and would never want the war to end as that would mean she would lose her job to a man and anyway there would be no call for such weapons then.

Maud stood, stirring the porridge and wondered how long she could go on like this, in this uniform. How soon would it be before she too, lost her mind and changed her uniform for the grey dress of the inmate.

She'd known it was against all the rules, but when she'd seen the spark between Emily and the young lad at the dance, she'd realised that in these times you had to grasp onto any opportunity for love, however futile it may be. If she'd had her time again, she wouldn't have wasted it. And now she couldn't stop thinking about Emily and the chances that she could have if someone took the trouble to help her. Perhaps that person was her?

Maud decided that she would speak to Emily as soon as she could. The women were out in the fields now so she'd have all day to come up with a plan on how she could help. Meanwhile, there were other people to worry about.

A new patient, May Pullman, wife of a naval officer and very disturbed in her behaviour was one of those who were kept locked in the ward apart from short periods of exercise in the courtyard. Maud was writing notes at the table at the end of the gallery and watched May from a distance. The woman sat by the window, picking at some embroidery that she had been given to do to try and stop the restlessness in her fingers. She didn't seem to notice the sounds of the other women. Not even when their wandering paths crossed close to her. It was as if she were alone in the room.

Chapter Thirty-two

May

Deep in thought, May didn't see what was happening around her any more. Her life, their lives, had been perfect. The wonderful wedding, walking down the aisle on the arm of her proud father, her mother watching from the first pew with tears in her eyes, their family and friends all craning their necks to see her in that beautiful gown. The music had played with fierce abandon from the organ as she glided towards James waiting at the altar. His face was alive with love for her then. What had changed?

Just one year on and everything was broken. Mother had became ill and had stopped leaving her house. She missed her mother so much but married life was all consuming and there never seemed to be time to go visiting with always some occasion to prepare for. Hardly coping, she'd been terrified when the doctor had told her there was to be a child, a premonition that life would never be the same again. Her dreams of travelling the world with James, following his career in the Royal Navy, were swept away in the morning sickness which lasted all day. Why did they call it morning sickness?

'We'll name the baby George,' James told her. 'After my father.'

The birth she would not think about. It was something to be forgotten, never spoken of. Now she knew why no one had warned her. She understood but never could believe that any woman would have more than one child.

After the birth it should have got better but it hadn't. May couldn't look at the creature. She was angry that having given so much of herself, when friends came to visit she was ignored. All attention was turned to the mewling imposter which always seemed to be there, unceasingly needing something. Her own mother never even came. If she had, perhaps that would have helped.

Finally, James brought his own mother to stay. 'To help you cope,' he'd said. So then May had to put up with the looks of disapproval as well as the screams from the crib. She was relieved in a way as she no longer had to care for the child. His mother did everything for it, except it still had to be fed. The pain was excruciating. Her breasts were no longer her own and still the creature was hungry for more.

The fever came and she began to lose her mind.

May's mother-in-law meant well. 'I only want the best for my grandchild and James, and, you of course,' she'd added.

'I'm dangerous,' May said to her one day. 'My milk is poisoning George. I have to stop feeding him.'

So they'd taken the child from May's arms and left her to let the milk curdle inside her. Now, instead of poisoning George, it was poisoning her. After three more days, James brought the doctor home. He gave May a draught and she slept. The fever raged within her, giving her visions of devils in the room whenever she was awake. She saw the fear in James' eyes as he told her she would have to be cared for in a safe place.

Safe for who? May wondered. But of course, she was a danger to the child, this brat that had grown inside her, sucking all the good from her, all of the life force, leaving this shell of evil. All she had left was the poison in her breasts, still full of sour milk that was trying to kill her and her baby.

James did have tears in his eyes when he turned away and left her in the room at the asylum. He had held her hand and said 'I love you,' but she couldn't believe him. She had poisoned everything and nothing would ever be the same again.

The nurse was speaking to her now. The same nurse who was there when she'd been brought to this place.

'How are you feeling today, May?'

May looked up from her work. The nurse was smiling as she spoke. Was this a good sign? Should she reply or just ignore the woman. She supposed she meant well but you could never be sure. Not in here. How long had she been here? A few days? A few weeks? It was hard to tell. There was nothing to count the days for, no getting up for the baby, no walking to the sea with the perambulator in the afternoons. Everything had been taken away from her. She looked out of the window. It was still morning, she knew that much. Lunch would not be ready for some time yet. She looked at the nurse.

'I'm better, thank you.' She wasn't sure whether that was the truth. How could she know what she was feeling when everything had been taken away from her. 'When is James coming to visit?' she asked.

'I think he'll come again on Sunday. That's in two days time,' she was told.

There was a silence. May could think of nothing to say.

'If you're feeling better, you could perhaps go outside together for a walk.'

'On Sunday?'

'Would you like that?'

'I don't know. I would, I think. If he comes.'

'He's been every week so far.'

'How long have I been in here?'

'Five weeks now. You seem a lot better than when you came in. Hopefully you'll be well enough to go home soon.'

'He won't want me home. I'm not capable of being a good wife any more. And the baby, I couldn't care for my own child.'

'You have been ill, but it's not forever. This happens sometimes after childbirth. It doesn't last. I've seen many women like you who have recovered and gone home to live a good life as a mother and a wife. You can too, I'm sure.'

Another silence. Then May looked out of the window again, noticing the clouds now forming over the distant plane trees. 'I hope you're right,' she said.

'It would help if you maybe spent a bit of time with one or another of the ladies in here. You may find you have some things in common with others. Perhaps chatting to another woman would be good for you, take your mind off your own problems.' She stood and started to walk away. Turning back to May, she added, 'you could come and help me lay the tables for lunch if you like.'

May sat for a while after Maud had walked away, then putting aside the embroidery she'd been destroying, she stood and followed the nurse into the dining room.

Chapter Thirty-three

Maud

'How am I going to help Emily?' Maud was constantly thinking of some way to help the young woman. After losing hope for a future with Oswald, she was determined to help as much as she could, to ensure that Emily's future would be happier than her own.

The official hospital visitors would be coming in a few days time. She wondered if that would be the opportunity to do something. She was still mulling over the situation when she was on her afternoon off in Southsea. The sea was choppy, the waves topped with white foam. In the distance she could see a steamer making it's way across to the Isle-of-Wight. Gulls screamed in the wind, the world loud and alive. One could almost imagine there was no war.

The tea room by the pier was busy. It was always awkward for a young woman to sit alone in such a place which was normally filled with couples or women with their families. Still, times were such that many women were on their own now. Maud sat with her back straight, trying to look confident in her own space. She ordered tea and a plain scone, a treat at such a time when fancy foods were difficult to find. As she looked about the room at the other customers her mind drifted to thinking about her situation, her job and the women she looked after in the asylum. She was wondering where it would all end, this war, this madness in the world. She didn't notice the woman entering the room until she had reached Maud's table.

'It's nurse Paxton, isn't it?'

Maud stood. 'Yes. And you're Mrs. Simpson, one of the visitors.' She looked about her, wondering if it was appropriate to let on how they knew each other. She was aware of the stigma connected with those working in the asylum, as though it was contagious in some way.

'Please call me Marjorie. May I join you? It's always nicer to share a pot of tea, don't you think? Or would you rather not? Are you meeting someone?'

'No, of course that would be nice. I'm not meeting anyone. I'm Maud.' She indicated the empty chair across the table. 'I was wondering how I could make contact with you actually.'

'Really? Well this is fortunate then.'

Soon they were sipping tea and chatting like a pair of old friends. Maud cut the scone in half. 'Would you like to share this?'

'Thank you, that's very kind.'

Maud pushed the plate to the middle of the table and Marjorie took a bite before placing the rest down on her saucer. 'What did you want to speak to me about?' she asked.

Maud looked around the room. It was busy enough to be able to talk without being overheard, as long as you didn't raise your voice.

'I've been thinking about one of the ladies in my care. Emily is her name. She is so much more settled than she was when she first arrived at the asylum. Her story, like many of the women's, is a sad one and she won't be able to leave the ward to go back to her family home. Her father has remarried and she's no longer welcome there. Her mother died a few years ago, sadly. Previously she worked as a house-maid and she could perhaps go back to that again although her present situation might make that difficult for her. I was hoping that you might help her somehow, knowing that you're one of the regular hospital visitors and have an interest in the welfare of the women we care for. I hope you don't mind me asking you, but you must have many contacts, friends who might be happy to employ her?'

'Emily? I am not sure who you mean, but I am coming to the asylum to visit soon and I will make sure that I take time to speak to her. Of course I would like to help her if I can. It's very kind of you to think of her. Your job must be very difficult and I know you work long hours. To be worrying about your patients on your day off - it's very kind of you.'

'Her situation could happen to anyone. I know what it's like to lose loved ones, as most of us have during this dark time. Also, I've seen too many women left in that place with no future. It's so frustrating sometimes, not knowing how one can help, other than just the day to day care. If you could speak to her, that would be a great help, I'm sure. Thank you.'

'It would be a pleasure. Now, shall we have some more tea? Or perhaps another scone?'

Chapter Thirty-four

Emily

It had been days now and still no sign of him. The nurse was right it seemed, he had only been playing with her heart and now he'd gone out of her life without so much as a thought for her feelings. One minute she was blaming him for taking advantage of her and the next she berated herself for even thinking this. He owed her nothing, she was nothing to him and never would be. Each day in the fields she looked for him and each day her heart hardened a little more. There was no way that she would let a man hurt her again.

As the days passed, Emily began to think about her future. She would never be the same again, she knew that, and even if she wanted to find another, no man would ever want her. She day-dreamed about leaving the asylum one day, about leaving the town that was familiar to her. She would find a cottage somewhere in the country, work and pay her own way somehow. If she ever stopped and thought about what she would do or how, she would just push it away and turn her mind to her daily work.

Plodding back to the ward late one afternoon, her head lowered, Emily only saw the heels of the woman in front of her. She didn't want to look up. However much she hardened her heart, it was still too painful for her to see that he wasn't there yet again.

Once in the ward, Emily peeled off her overall and donned the apron ready to start her duties cleaning the washroom. Only the heaviness of her limbs kept her mind off other things. The loss of her child already seemed like a distant event, only surfacing in stabs of agony every now and again when she let it in.

Once she'd finished cleaning the washrooms, Emily made her way along the gallery to the day room and sat beside one of the windows. She glanced around at the other women. 'I'm not like these,' she thought. 'I'm not going to end up staying here for the rest of my life.' She remembered how frightened she'd been when they'd first brought her in here. Watching these women then had been something she'd thought she'd never get used to. But they were all like her in a way, in their different hellish worlds, each struggling to live through each day in any way they could. To Emily, they were all nameless faces; her so-called friendship with Janet had come to nothing other than the occasional chat in the fields. Janet didn't seem interested in talking to her back in the ward and had other friends that Emily never really got to know. She felt so alone, her heart was hardened - she had not attempted to make friends or even speak to anyone else.

So it was a surprise when the woman approached her. She was tall and graceful, poised in a way that Emily felt she never would be. Her hair was neatly braided and wound around her head. She wore a tailored dress in a lovely shade of lavender which marked her as a private paying patient, and she was smiling shyly at Emily.

'May I sit here?' she asked.

Emily looked at her, wondering what she wanted, then nodded briefly.

The woman took the chair opposite Emily and offered her hand. 'I'm Mrs. Pullman,' she said. Her voice was quiet and well educated. Emily took her hand, feeling the smooth coolness of the young woman's skin, which told her this was a woman who hadn't known hard work. Still she seemed pleasant enough and Emily was starved of company so shook the proffered hand and smiled.

'I'm Miss Harris but please call me Emily. It seems ridiculous not to be on first names here. I'm pleased to meet you.'

'Thank you, and you must call me May.'

'You've been in here a while now, I think?' Emily felt a bit awkward about asking May how she had come to this place. It was obvious there must have been a reason, a moment when her sanity had fled but it seemed impolite to ask outright. Emily had noticed her when she'd arrived but she'd been so reserved and never spoke to anyone else.

May sighed. 'It seems like an age although it's only a few weeks. I have a child at home who no doubt I need to be back with soon.' She paused. 'The doctor told me I had suffered from a fever after the birth and that turned my mind. Once the fever was gone, so had the symptoms, although it's left me with a feeling of doom, of not being able to cope as a mother. Does that sound silly?'

'Not at all.'

'I'm sorry, you don't want to hear all about my sordid life. I'm telling you too much. I do apologise.'

'Please, it's not too much. It's more of a relief to be honest, to hear of another's troubles. I've been focussed on my own for so long. You see all these other women in here and you never think of what they might have been through, what may have brought them to this state of mind. Thank you for sharing your troubles with me. Tell me about your child.'

'Little George is a wonder. At least that's what people have been telling me. My mother-in-law came to stay so that I could cope with him, and we did have a day nurse to take care of him too. It should have been easy, I know, with all that help around me. But somehow it made it worse. It made me feel that I was useless. I confess that when my mind was broken I believed that I was poisoning him with my milk.'

'I'm so sorry to hear this. It must have been difficult.'

'I thought he would be better off without me. I said as much to James, and to his mother. That was when they brought the doctor to the house to see me. They didn't need to certify me as mad, I already knew I was. Does that sound terrible?'

'Not at all,' Emily said. 'Were you afraid at the thought of being sent here? I know I was afraid, when I realised where I was, although it's not so bad. I know that there are times when life in here seems so far removed from outside the walls, but in the main the nurses are kind and the other patients are not much different from us, are they?'

'I thought you were dangerous when I first met you.' May looked embarrassed.

'Well, maybe I was then. I was certainly very disturbed, and angry and afraid too, I suppose,'

'Tell me about yourself if you like.'

'I'm ashamed to tell you. I am not a respectable woman like yourself. You won't want to know me.'

'Nonsense. You seem a hardworking person. I've noticed that you have very few visitors. Do you have a sweetheart? Is he away the front?'

Emily blushed and turned away. 'No sweetheart,' she said. 'Not anymore. There was a young man. We were planning to marry but he didn't come back from the war. We didn't even get to say goodbye.' She lowered her voice. 'I didn't tell him before he went. He never knew I was with child. There, now you'll hate me.' She wiped away a tear that had somehow slipped from her eye. 'I'm sorry,' she added.

'My dear, please don't apologise to me. No, I am sorry and I certainly do not hate you. You're not all that different to me. We both have had a child and I know how hard that can be. Where is the child now?'

'My little Billy. I named him after his father, they took him away from me as soon as they could after his birth. I never got the chance to say goodbye to him either. My Pa said that I could keep him and bring him up with his support, but my stepmother made him change his mind and I had no say. I don't know where little Billy is any more. Everything after that day is a muddled nightmare. I was brought here by strangers after I collapsed in the street. It was so shameful.'

'It is a tragedy and that is the way of life for women, sadly. You can only hope that in the future you may meet him again. And you must pray, of course, that he will be well cared for, wherever he is.'

'You are right, of course. It's so painful to think of him, and of his father, lost to the war.' Emily paused, gazing around the ward. 'And of course, I know that I am starting to heal and hope to get out of here one day, in the not too distant future. This can't be the end of my life.'

'Quite right. And I will be going home soon also. Let's hope that our lives will get better sooner than later. Maybe we could remain friends even after we leave here?'

'I would like that, but perhaps once you are home, you won't have much time for the likes of me. You must be used to much more genteel company.'

'Pah! I've done with genteel company. When I get out of here I will chose my own friends. I know it may cause you a little pain, but it would be wonderful if we could walk on the common together from time to time, with my George. If you would like it, I mean.'

'I would indeed.' Emily smiled. 'Come, I think we are being called to supper. Shall we sit together?'

Lying in her bed that night, Emily's thoughts went over the conversation with May. Had she shared too much of herself? Would May have walked away and realised that Emily was not the kind of woman she should have as a friend? How could they continue such a friendship once they were discharged from the asylum, coming from such different worlds? Emily knew that May was a private patient, wearing her own clothes rather than the asylum uniform, was given better cuts of meat with her meal and that she had been well-educated. They had nothing in common apart from their madness.

Emily tried not to think too much about what could happen once they were back in their own homes, wherever that may be, and focussed on life as it was in the moment. After all, she had no home to go to herself. She would never go back to Pa's house now, whatever happened. The only thing to do was to make the most of things from now on and to grasp at anything that came her way.

Chapter Thirty-five

Emily

Opportunity was not far away. The next afternoon brought official visitors to the ward. Nurse Paxton, in her smartest dress and apron, was standing talking to a man in a dark suit, a crisp wing-collared shirt and highly polished boots. Beside him was a woman in a blue costume of the highest fashion. The overdress had a wide white collar and the skirt was narrow and shockingly short, ending just above the ankles. Emily glanced at them as she returned from the field and was making her way to the washroom when she was called over by the nurse.

'Emily, this is Mr. Johnson and Mrs. Simpson. They're here to ensure that all is well in the ward. I was hoping you'd be happy to answer some of their questions?'

Emily looked down at her grubby overall and the dirt under her nails.

'I'm covered in filth from the fields.'

'Perhaps you could quickly go and tidy up first?' Mrs. Simpson said.

Emily hesitated. 'I don't know. What sort of questions?' she asked.

'Just some general questions about how you are finding the treatment, the food and the conditions, nothing more than that.' Mrs. Simpson had a soft lilting voice.

'I suppose it can't do any harm.'

'I'll wait here, then,' said the woman as she watched Emily walk away.

When Emily had returned Mrs. Simpson stood and offered her hand. 'Thank you so much for helping me with this.'

Turning to the gentleman, she went on, 'Perhaps I could catch you up?' It was more of a suggestion than a question.

'Of course. Nurse, perhaps you could show me the bathrooms?'

Nurse Paxton glanced at Emily. 'Will you be alright?' she asked.

Emily nodded and watched as they walked away then turned to Mrs. Simpson.

'Shall we sit here and talk?' Mrs. Simpson indicated the low chairs beside the window. It was warm and comforting to be in the late afternoon sunshine and was one of Emily's favourite spots on the gallery.

'What do you want to ask me?'

'I have just a few general questions about what life is like in here. May I start with you telling me how you're finding it here?'

Emily looked across the wide gallery. 'I don't know. I try not to think about it. I just live from day to day.'

'How is the food? Do you have enough to eat?' She was making notes in a small book.

Emily smiled inwardly, she didn't want to say but the food was terrible. 'It's basic,' she replied. 'It serves a purpose in that it fills the belly, but the diet is very mundane to be honest.'

'How long have you been in here?'

'Probably about three months but the days flow into one and I don't have a calendar.' She paused to think. 'I think it was early summer when I was brought here but I could be mistaken.'

'And the treatment? How has it been for you?'

Emily laughed. 'The nurses have been mostly very kind. They treat me very well I suppose. When I was - difficult, they treated me with medicine which calmed me. I slept a lot in the early days and I can't really remember much about it. What I do remember I don't want to think about. Now I work out on the farm during the day which helps a lot. I almost feel that I'm free sometimes.'

The woman nodded.

'I worked in the laundry for a short while but it didn't suit me. I felt confined and never seemed to see the light of day. They were dark times.'

'Do your family visit you often? I'm assuming you have family out in the town, waiting to welcome you home?'

Emily frowned, glancing out of the window behind Mrs. Simpson. 'My family don't want me to come home.

I wouldn't want to go back there anyway. I have to make a new life for myself. I just don't know how or where yet.'

'Really? That's very sad. I don't want to pry, but perhaps I may be able to help if you tell me a little about your situation.'

Emily shook her head.

'No.'

'I'm sorry?'

'I'm too ashamed to tell you.'

'I'm sure it can't be as bad as you think. Please, I'm a woman of the world. You would be surprised at what I've experienced myself and I would never judge you, my dear. Was it a young man? In these times of war there are many women in difficult situations who have been left behind.'

Emily felt herself blushing. She lowered her eyes to the floor, then gaining some kind of courage from the woman's smile, she looked up at her. 'It's true, there was a young man. He won't be coming back from Belgium. We were to marry. I had a child and he was taken away from me.'

'It must be so very hard to bear. But where is your child now? You must be looking forward to seeing him again. Is he being cared for well whilst you are here?'

The tears were easing from Emily's eyes now. 'He was taken on the day of his birth and I never said goodbye. I never said goodbye to my Billy, nor to his babe.'

'What about your family? Is there no way that you could go back there with your child?'

'Let me explain. My Ma died a few years ago. Pa remarried and my stepmother hates me. I can't go back there, even though Pa said he'd stand by me and help me raise the child, she took over and now the child is gone. She took him away and now he's been taken in by another family.' She looked up. 'I called her the devil when I was in my first madness. Pa never visits me and I've not heard from my two elder brothers who are both at the front. If I ever leave here I'm on my own in the world. The only one of my family I have contact with is young Percy. He's just a boy still. He goes to school and helps Pa in his butcher shop. We have written to each other, but he can't help me. He's too young. That's a blessing though. At least he's too young to go to war. But you see there is no-one at all who could be there for me.'

Mrs. Simpson reached out and took her hand. 'Such a sad story,' she said. 'You are very brave. Please don't despair. Perhaps I might be able to help you.'

'How can you help me?'

'I'm not sure yet. Perhaps I can find somewhere for you to live, maybe a live-in position? Have you worked in service before?'

'I did work for Mrs. Cartwright in her house in Southsea, before I was pregnant. She was very kind to me but I don't expect she would want me back now that I've been ill. Anyway I never lived in the house, but just went in daily.' She looked at her hands, now rough and still ingrained with dirt from the fields. 'I'm not sure that I could work inside again. Working in the fields is hard physically, but I love it. Still, I would be grateful for any employment if I'm ever well enough to leave this place.' She looked around the vast room, glancing at the other women who were wandering about in their own inner turmoil.

'Now, let's be strong and keep a positive outlook. I will speak to the doctor and see what he thinks, but if you wish, I will do my best to try and help you find the right place to go to when you leave.'

Emily smiled as the woman stood. 'Thank you,' she said with a glimmer of hope in her voice.

Chapter Thirty-six

Joe

Days dragged for Joe working in the fields on the far side of the farm. He was to mend the fences, repairing every gap he could find. The sheep were secure in their meadow and still Joe could not stop thinking of her. Every day he walked to the lanes across the fields and hoped that she would be there. But the timing was just wrong. He started his new working day early, long before the women left the wards and he worked late, staying long after the normal working day was over. He was sure he'd seen her once in the distance and he felt himself being drawn to her but as he got closer he saw that he was mistaken. Once the fences were repaired he had hoped to go back to the cabbage fields but the farm manager had other work for him.

'The cowman's joined up, Joe. You've got to pull your weight, lad,' he was told, then as an afterthought, 'And you can forget about any young woman who works in the field.'

'What young woman?' Joe glared at him.

'I know more than you imagine. I see it all here, so don't think I don't know what's going on in your young head.'

'There's nothing going on. I don't know what you're on about.'

'Well, you're here to work the land so you'd best get on with it. You know how to handle cows so that's where you need to be.'

Another week passed before Jack spoke to him again. He'd passed his old mate in the farm yard several times and each time had tried to make it up to him. But Jack had always turned his back and gone off to do something important which was as far away from Joe as possible.

Determined at last to heal the rift, Joe tried again. He was walking through the yard when he saw Jack standing in his socks, rinsing his boots under the tap, water splashing in the sunlight.

Joe stood for a while before speaking. 'You alright, mate?' Feeling awkward, he could think of nothing else to say.

'Joe.' Jack nodded across at him.

'Fancy a pint?'

'With you? Maybe.'

'Can we talk?' Joe stepped a bit closer. 'I mean, I think I should say sorry or something.'

'Or something? What does that mean? You were an arsehole. Call yourself a mate?'

'I know. I've been a bastard. I'm sorry. I don't want us to be like this. What can I do to make it alright?'

'Yeah, well, maybe a pint would do it.' Jack shook the water from his boots, pulled them back onto his feet and turned to Joe. 'The Farmhouse pub in an hour then.'

A few hours and two pints later the two lads stood in the bar, the awkward feeling between them dispersing with each swig of beer.

'I was an idiot, I know,' Joe said. 'I don't know what came over me. I know now I was being stupid thinking that I stood a chance with that woman.'

'She's pretty. I can see the attraction, but you must have known it wouldn't work.'

'I didn't want to believe that. I'd never felt like that before.'

'It's not real though. It's like something you can never have. That's what makes you want it more. She'll always be out of reach, you know that don't you? Even if she weren't in that place and you were a few years older, and we weren't in this bloody war.'

'I don't want to believe that. I can't believe that she'll always be in that place. One day she'll be free and then things could be different.'

'You know nothing about her. She may be married, or promised to someone else.'

'She may be, but I don't think so.' Joe took a long swallow of beer, draining his glass. 'Another pint?'

Jack nodded and passed his empty glass across the bar. 'How will you find out? You'll be lucky to have the chance of even speaking to her again.'

'I don't know. I'd hoped to see her in the fields again but it seems like I'm being kept away from her. Maybe it's pointless. Maybe I should just give up. But I can't.'

'You're a bloody fool, Joe.' Jack passed some coins across the bar and the two friends drank their beer in silence for a while.

Finally Jack spoke again. 'There's another dance on Friday,' he said. 'We could go.'

Joe looked at him. 'I don't know. I'm not sure I should. I expect Sally and Maisie will be there again. I don't know if I want to face that Maisie again, or Sally come to that. I made a fool of myself, didn't I? Are you sure you want me to be there with you again?'

'Oh, Sally will be there alright and she is going to meet me again. Only Maisie won't be there. She's walking out with a young soldier and he's home on leave so you won't have to worry about her.'

'Have you seen Sally since the dance, then?'

'I have and she's forgiven me. Not sure how she feels about you though.' He laughed. 'She has a fine temper on her, that girl has. All the same, you should come with me. You might see your dream lover again.'

'Don't call her that.'

'Well she is only in your dream world, isn't she?'

'Her name is Emily.'

'Emily, then. So, are you going to come?'

'I suppose I could.' Joe looked around the room. 'Anything would be better than this, this not knowing.'

'So you are still holding out and hoping then?'

'Maybe.'

'Bloody fool aren't you? She might not even be there.'

'True, but I'll come along anyway.'

'Good, that's settled then.' He grinned. 'It's good to be mates again. We should never let a woman come between us, eh, mate? Game of darts?'

Chapter Thirty-seven

Emily

'It's the night of the dance Emily. We should go.' They had been laying the tables together and May had stopped to gaze out of the window. It had been raining hard all day and the women had been kept in so Emily had been helping in the ward, polishing the floors on her hands and knees. Now she placed the last fork on the table in front of her and stretched her back as she looked across at May.

'I don't know,' she hesitated. 'I hardly see the point. It just makes you feel more trapped somehow, knowing that life is going on outside while we're shut up in here.' She was thinking of Joe and the last time they'd met. Her heart was banging in her chest so loud she was afraid May would hear it. She knew it was too dangerous to allow herself to raise her hopes again.

'I think that's true, but I do love to dance, don't you? It would be a nice interlude.' May smiled. 'James used to take me to dances in the Mess before I was pregnant. Such happy times. Please Emily, we need only stay for a short while, we could dance together. It's not frowned upon these days, women dancing together. There are so few men to partner one any more.'

'I suppose it wouldn't do any harm. But, the thing is, I feel ashamed wearing this dress when all those ladies are in their finery. It's different for you - you have your own clothes to wear. I stand out as a pauper patient, I know I do.'

'Nonsense! You are not responsible for your situation. I would lend you something nice to wear but I know they wouldn't let me do that. Look, I know what we can do. I will wear my plainest dress so that we won't be so different. Please come, it wouldn't be the same without you there. In fact, I won't go without you, so you must come.'

'We'll have to get permission first. We should ask Nurse Paxton. They may not let us go.'

Of course Nurse Paxton said yes. She was delighted that the two women had become friends. She could see plainly that they were good for each other and immediately spoke to the doctor who gave his permission gladly.

Walking together with nurse Paxton behind them along the corridor to the ballroom, Emily felt as light-headed as a giddy girl off to her first dance. She was trying not to think of Joe and was sure he wouldn't be there, that she'd seen the last of him, but something kept a glimmer of hope in her heart. They reached the door and May linked her arm in Emily's as they stepped into the light. Even though this wasn't the first time she'd been here, Emily hadn't noticed before the beauty of the architecture in this room. Vast like a cathedral, with coloured glass windows set high in the walls which were beautifully formed with brickwork, patterned in cream and brown. It was exquisite. At one end of the room was a stage with a proscenium arch, hung with red velvet curtains. On the stage gathered the asylum orchestra who were playing with enthusiasm.

'There's a table over there,' Nurse Paxton steered them across the room. Once they were sat, she moved away to the refreshment table, telling them to wait for her to return with their drinks.

May looked around the room. 'It's very gay,' she said. 'Who would have imagined this?'

'The gowns and the jewels on the ladies are wonderful, aren't they?' May agreed. 'But you most likely have gowns like these and jewels too.'

'I have, but I never really appreciated what I had before. This is wonderful.' She shuddered. 'I do hope there's nobody here who knows me. Perhaps I shouldn't have come after all.'

Emily was looking around the room, scanning the faces in the hope that she might see him. She wondered how she'd behave if he was here, if he spoke to her again, hoped that perhaps he would even dance with her again. But there was no sign of him.

'You have nothing to be ashamed of May. I know those people mean well, but I feel like you do, that they're just here to gawk at us poor lunatics and to show off how rich and how much better off than us they are. But they are not better off than us, not really. I won't let them make me feel bad about myself and neither should you. You will leave here soon and go back to your home with your husband who loves you. And I'm not going to let myself stay in this place for ever in despair. I just won't. There, I've said too much. Let's dance and enjoy ourselves while we can. The world outside is full of much more madness than we see in here, after all.'

Dancing with May was fun if a bit awkward at first. Emily wasn't familiar with taking the gentleman's role in dancing. Even before, when she'd danced with her female friends she'd always taken the ladies position. They tripped around the floor to a waltz and May, being a strong leader, save her from stumbling. Soon Emily became used to it and the two women enjoyed moving in time to the music, laughing together whenever they went wrong.

Back in their seats, sipping lemonade, May and Emily caught their breath but still Emily couldn't stop herself from constantly looking about the room.

'Who are you searching for?' May leant towards Emily, teasing her. 'Is there a young man here somewhere?'

Emily felt herself blush. 'No. It's no-one.' She said hastily.

'Are you sure? I don't think you've told me everything about yourself, have you? You look like a woman who was hoping to meet someone special tonight.'

'Really, do I?' Emily laughed. 'Alright, I will confess. At the last dance, there was a young man. He works in the fields and we did dance together, only once. His name is Joe and that was the last time I saw him. The next day he wasn't in the field and hasn't been there since. So he's either been avoiding me, or he has gone away. I don't know. It would have been nice to see him even if it's only to know that there was nothing between us. I may have imagined it.'

'Poor Emily.' May took her hand. 'Let's hope he is here somewhere then.' She looked around the room. 'What does he look like?'

'Like a young man, I suppose. Fairly tall, his hair is dark and he has deep eyes and a lovely smile. He is very young. Probably too young for me anyway.' May smiled. 'I don't know what I was thinking. He can't possibly be someone I could ever be with. But it's nice to have a dream, isn't it?'

'Of course, and in these times, ages and other obstacles can be easily removed.'

'Do you think so? I would have thought that the obstacles I face would be insurmountable. My age, the fact that I've had a child, my madness. I am what they call damaged goods, aren't I? It's been pointed out to me more than once that there are too many younger women looking for husbands, so how does that make me a good match for anyone.'

'You mustn't think like that.'

'That's what I've been told - by my step-mother and I know my Pa believes it too.'

'Well, I don't.' May was definite in her answer. 'And neither should you.'

Chapter Thirty-eight

Joe

The room looked the same. The asylum orchestra was playing a waltz as they walked into the room, bringing memories of the other time he was here. He cringed at the thought of how ignorant he'd been, treating Maisie in such a way, embarrassing her in front of everyone. The room was filled with the same people in all kinds of finery, milling about amongst the attendants and their patients. Joe scanned the room, looking in vain for the one person he was there to see.

'Come on Joe, let's get a drink of that delicious lemonade,' Jack led the way to the refreshment table. 'It's not quite the same as a good pint of beer, but better than nothing and it's free. Then we can look around and see who's here.'

They queued for their drinks and soon were walking to the far side of the room through the crowd where Sally was standing by the wall with another nurse. Joe was relieved to see that it wasn't Maisie as they wandered across, although he hoped that Jack didn't expect him to dance with Sally's friend. He couldn't bear the thought of a repeat performance, this time with another nurse. He'd be getting a reputation if he wasn't careful. Luckily for him though, the nurse moved away with another young man before they reached Sally's side. She greeted Jack with a smile and then nodded to Joe.

'Good evening Sally,' Jack was grinning at her.

'Hello Jack, nice to see you I'm sure.' She looked at Joe. 'I hope you weren't expecting to see Maisie again. She's got herself a nice young man now, thank you very much. She's a nice girl is Maisie, much too good for some people.'

'I'm sorry for how I treated her. It was unforgivable. And I'm sorry if I spoilt your evening before at the dance.' Joe said. 'I'm glad she's got a nice young man.'

'Yes, well, let's just forget it now, shall we.' She turned to Jack. 'Aren't you going to ask me to dance?'

Watching them as they moved across the floor for a while, Joe wondered again if Emily would actually be at the dance tonight or was he wasting his time? It was already half way through the evening. They may have missed her. He thought about the last time when she'd only been allowed to stay for an hour before she was escorted back to the ward. Surely she'd be here by now. Perhaps she'd been discharged back home and he would never see her again. He leant against the wall and sipped at his lemonade, wishing that there was something stronger in it.

Then he saw her. She was sitting at a table only a few feet away from where he was with another woman and the same nurse as before. How could he have missed her? The woman sitting with her looked across at him. Their eyes met, the woman looked away, whispered something to Emily who turned around to look in his direction. Her eyes lit up and she smiled. Suddenly he felt himself come alive once more, like he'd been asleep for a long time and as if the snow had melted after a long winter. She was here and she was smiling at him. She hadn't gone home. He hadn't missed her. She was here and she remembered him.

Making his way across to the table, Joe could think of nothing to say, no way to make it easy to overcome the awkwardness of their situation. He only knew that he had to be near her, to look into her face and be sure that what he'd felt was real. Nothing else mattered. As he reached the table, the nurse who was sitting there stood up and greeted him with a smile.

'I'm going to dance with Mrs. Pullman. You may sit here with Miss Harris whilst we are on the floor. If you wish to dance, you may but please stay in the ballroom. Can I trust you?' she asked.

Joe could see that she had a twinkle in her eye. 'I think you can trust me.' He said and he watched as the two ladies danced away together.

Emily was laughing at him. 'It's good to see you again,' she said. 'I thought you'd left the farm. I thought you'd gone away - to the front or, I don't know what I thought.'

'I was stupid,' he said. 'I got into a fight with my mate and was in trouble with the farm manager. He moved me off the fields where you were working and he's kept me away from there ever since. I think he got wind of the fact that I was interested in seeing you and this was my punishment. It's not looked upon as the right thing to do, fraternising with the patients. Your nurse doesn't seem to mind though, does she?'

'Nurse Paxton has been very kind to me. She understands, I think, how difficult life can be.'

'That's unusual in these times although I suppose the world is changing everywhere outside. It's been a hard few weeks but better now that Jack and me have made up our differences. I don't suppose I'll see you out in the fields again though as I've been put on the dairy herd so have to start earlier to get the milking done.'

'I'm pleased that you're still here. I wondered if I'd ever see you again. There are so many obstacles aren't there?'

'Nothing that can't be overcome. I thought that you would have been sent home and I'd never see you again.'

'I don't have a home to go to.' Emily looked at him. 'The doctor has said that I will go home but I won't go back to live at my Pa's. My Step-Mother and I don't get on and I couldn't go back there. She wouldn't want me that's for sure.'

'Then what will you do? Where will you go?'

'I may find a position where I can live-in. There's a visitor woman who comes here, Mrs. Simpson, who said she'd try and help me. I'm not sure yet. To be honest I'm not sure I want to go back into service again. I like working outside. I know it's hard and sometimes dirty work but being outside in the fresh air is so much better than working in a kitchen or cleaning floors. I feel alive outside.'

'I understand that,' he said. 'I couldn't work inside. Life on the farm is the best of lives, hard though it can be.'

'Have you always worked on the farm?'

'I have. I was brought up on my Father's farm, not here in Milton, but out in Hampshire. A small village called Droxford is where I lived.'

'What brought you to this place? Surely you'd be better living away from here? Away from the asylum, which is not that far from the docks and closer to the war? There was a Zeppelin a while back, wasn't there? And a bomb dropped near the docks.'

'They say that was just a mistake and that's only happened the once. I certainly wouldn't feel in any danger here.'

'But why did you leave Droxford and the farm?'

'I fell out with my Father and couldn't stay there a moment longer. He has a temper. A bit like me I suppose although I hope I'm not as bad as he is. I decided to get away and try something else. I came to Portsmouth thinking that I would work at the dockyard and then when old enough I was going to enlist. But before I even found a job I was told about the farm at the asylum - here in this place. My old school mate Jack had already taken a job here and so I followed him. I realised that it wasn't the farm work that I'd hated but working with Pa. I do miss my Ma though and would go back if I could. Only now I've met you, my thinking is changing.'

'Family life can be so hard.' Emily sighed. 'Why does it have to be like that?'

'Life is never simple, is it? I don't like to pry but I would love to know you better.'

'What do you want to know?'

'I only know your name is Emily. What happened to you to bring you to this place? I don't even know your surname.'

'Well, I am Emily Harris. I'll tell you how I came to be here but you will think badly of me no doubt.'

'I don't think I could ever do that.'

Emily looked across the room at the glittering dresses of the wealthy women, dancing with their partners. She shook her head. 'We shall see. I will tell you my story. You'll have to know one day if we're to be friends. I had a sweetheart. He was killed at the front and I hadn't even told him that I was with child.'

'I'm sorry.'

'You're not shocked?'

'Not really.' He reached out and touched her hand.

'That's not all. Things like that happen to many other people and they don't end up having a breakdown. I feel ashamed that it happened but I would have coped if my child hadn't been taken away from me. I was angry too, with my Stepmother. Kate took away my Pa and my baby. I think she hates me. Ma only died last year and I miss her so much. I wish Pa hadn't remarried.'

'I'm sorry. So now you have to make a new start in life somehow. It's never easy but you will succeed, I'm sure. You have to be strong.'

'You are too wise for your years, Joe,' she replied. 'I just hope that it can be easier for us if we're lucky enough to get beyond this. I miss my own Pa, who was always so close to me before he remarried. I'd do anything to have him come and see me, to smile at me like he used to before Ma died. Please don't make the mistake of not making it up with your Pa. Life may not be simple but it's definitely too short to bear a grudge for long. This war has made me realise that you have to work hard to make life good again. Let's pray that we will overcome the things that seem against us.'

'We will,' he promised. 'I have to believe that. Now, enough of this. Shall we dance?'

Emily looked around to see whether she could see Nurse Paxton and May. They were dancing nearby, both smiling at her. She stood and took his hand. 'I would be honoured,' she said.

Holding her in his arms again, floating to the music, Joe never wanted the evening to end. It was of course, over all too soon but he left with Jack and with a lightness to his step that wasn't there before. Now he had something to live for, something to look forward to, a hope for some kind of future. If only this war was over, if only he could make things good again with Pa. He decided to write to his Ma as soon as he had time the next day.

Chapter Thirty-nine

Joe

It was a warm day that welcomed Joe as he made his way to work the next morning. He felt that every day would be filled with sunshine from now on. The cows were even gentler than usual, the warmth of their flanks as he milked them echoing the warmth in the sky and in his heart. Life was good. The hours passed quickly and he walked home late that evening after cleaning the milking sheds, mentally composing the letter he would write to Ma.

He wasn't expecting the telegram which was waiting on the hall table when he entered the house. His landlady, Mrs. Johnson took off her apron as he shed his boots in the hall. She was a kind soul and she stood in the doorway to the parlour with a worried look on her face. He picked it up the envelope, passed it from hand to hand, wondering whether he had the courage to open it. He'd seen telegrams before, many had been delivered to his neighbours in the village since the beginning of the war. He'd seen the faces of the mothers and wives as they'd hesitated to open them and then their faces crumple as they read the words. Telegrams were never good news. Not in these times. They only ever told of lost men, either dead or missing in action. Confusion swam in his head - he had no loved-ones at the front. Surely this was a mistake.

There was no point in hesitating any longer. He tore open the envelope. It was short and to the point: "Pa ill. stop. Come home. stop. Ma. stop".

Pa ill? He must be critically ill for Ma to have sent a telegram. She never would have wasted money unless it was important. Joe felt his world slipping away beneath his feet. He sat down heavily on the wooden chair in the hall.

'Come and sit in the kitchen. I'll make some tea,' Mrs. Johnson took his elbow and led him through into the back room. 'Now what's all this about?'

Joe handed her the telegram, not trusting himself to speak. He hadn't realised how much he cared about his Pa until that moment. The thought of losing him was too much to take in. 'I have to go home,' he said.

'Of course,' she handed him the tea. 'It's quite a way, Droxford. How will you get there? I suppose you'd have to catch a train?'

'No need. There's a fishmonger in Southwick who comes to the docks and then does the rounds of several of the villages, including Droxford. He'll give me a lift. But I'll have to be at the fish dock early tomorrow morning. If I miss him I might be able to get a lift on one of the carts going back to the farms from Charlotte Street. They bring in fresh produce from all over the county. It'll mean waiting until later in the day if I do that. What if I'm too late? Even if I get the train it'll take most of the morning to get there.'

'Calm down, you will get there on time. I can take a message to the farm at the asylum to let them know what's happened, and I'll make you up a parcel to take for the journey. Now, go and wash off the farm grime and then come in and have your supper. The copper in the wash house is lit and the water is hot. There's a clean shirt airing as well.'

Joe stood and went out into the back yard, crossing to the wash house. He was moving as if in a daze, still unable to take in what was happening. He thought about Emily. How could he let her know? Should he write her a note? How would he know where to send it? His mind was a turmoil wondering what he could do. Would he now lose all that he'd hoped for after all? But how could he be thinking of himself when his Pa was ill? How he wished he'd made his peace with his Pa before now. What if it really was too late?

After he'd eaten his supper, Joe packed his small suitcase then sat again at the kitchen table. Mrs. Johnson was in her chair by the range, knitting. 'I will miss you, lad,' she said. 'You know I will keep your room for you and I hope that your Father recovers quickly so you can return here soon.'

Joe sighed. 'I hope so too, although I've a bad feeling about this.' He paused. 'There's something else. A woman I care about. We have only just met but we have feelings for each other. The problem is that she is a patient at the asylum. I danced with her last night, and once before a few weeks ago at the asylum dance. I know it seems unrealistic and impossible that a woman who is in the asylum could be someone for me to have a future with, but she is wonderful. She may have had a breakdown, I know that, but she is recovering and I am sure she'll be discharged before long. And now I have no way to let her know where I'll be.'

'There's no fool like a young fool,' Mrs. Johnson shook her head. 'Does she have a name, this woman?'

'It's Emily. Emily Harris. She works on the farm. That's where we first saw each other. I know I'm a fool, but it means a lot to me that we have a chance to get to know each other once she gets out of the place. The trouble is, I don't know where she'll go once she's discharged. Her family don't want her back.'

'Her family don't want her? She must have done something awful for her own family to shun her. Her own Ma and Pa? How could they?'

'It's complicated but her Ma died and Pa remarried. She didn't do anything bad, no worse than many others have done anyway. She had a sweetheart and got pregnant but he died before they could marry. The child was taken away. That's what started her breakdown. I hope you won't think the worst of her. She is all but recovered now, she says. I only want to take care of her and to make her happy.'

Mrs. Johnson shook her head.

'I'm not going to judge her, of course I'm not. In times like these we don't need to make life more difficult than it already is. If I had a daughter, I would hope that I'd understand if she got herself into such a predicament. I know I might regret it, but this is what I'll do. You must write her a note, and I'll make sure that she gets it. I don't know how, but I will. I know one of the nurses at the asylum. She can pass it on perhaps.'

It was still dark the next morning as Joe left the house and began his long walk to the old Camber Dock where the fishermen were unloading their catch. The rain was sheeting down, adding to his misery as he walked. He felt as though life would never be the same again.

Chapter Forty

Emily

It was Sunday and Emily had been to church that morning. This was the first time she'd had the heart to go to the little church in the grounds of the asylum, having lost faith in God for so long. The weather had turned cooler again, the rain relentless that morning. It was only May's persistence that had made her go and she was glad to be there in the end. The church was a peaceful place, even when filled with nurses, attendants and patients from the asylum.

After the usual Sunday lunch of meat and potatoes, and having helped to clear the tables, it was her time for rest. There was no other work on a Sunday apart from a little sewing if she wanted to keep her hands busy. She wasn't expecting any visitors. There were never visitors for her on a Sunday as it was the usual day for family members and none of her's ever came. The regular hospital visitor, Marjorie, never came on a Sunday. She only did her 'good works' during the week.

May's husband came regularly and he was already sitting with her on the far side of the day room. Emily had glanced across at them a few times, feeling envious of the love she could see that there was between them.

So Emily was surprised when the ward maid came across and spoke to her. 'You've got a visitor,' she said.

Emily sat up and looked along the gallery to where the entrance of the ward led into the corridor beyond. She wondered who on earth would be visiting her. Fleetingly she hoped it might be Joe and as quickly pushed the thought away as being ridiculous. How could he visit her? It wouldn't be allowed, she knew that. Still, she had a visitor. The door of the ward was opened and in walked her own dear Pa, his hair wet from the rain.

Emily stood, smiling broadly at him as he approached. 'Thank heaven,' she thought. 'This can only be good news. I pray that he can forgive me and we can be like we were before.' Something about the way he was looking back at her made the smile slip a little. Had she imagined it? More than anything she wanted to throw herself into his arms for the fatherly hug that she missed so much. She wanted to tell him how much she'd missed him and how she longed to come home, but something about the way he looked held her back.

He indicated for her to sit and took the chair opposite.

'What is it, Pa? You have news?'

Ignoring her question, he looked out of the window then back at her. 'How are you Emily? The doctor tells me that you're on the road to recovery.'

'I am indeed,' Emily replied. 'It's good to see you, Pa. I am glad you've come. It's been a long time and I've missed you. I wanted to say how sorry I am about everything.'

'I've missed you too.'

'Pa, I know things have been bad between me and Kate in the past, and I know it was mainly my fault but I'm stronger now. I wish I could come home and be a good daughter to you, and to her too if that's what you want.'

'I'm glad to hear you're sorry and ready to be a good daughter. But I must put Kate first. She is my wife and you are a grown woman now, you've proved that much. The doctor has asked me about where you will go when they discharge you. I've had to tell him that I don't think it would be right for you to come back home. I don't think it would be the right thing to do at all. I am sorry about that and I wanted to speak to you first, to see how you are for myself.'

Emily tried her best not to cry in front of him, feeling desperately sad that she'd really lost her Pa after all. She swallowed her sorrow down before speaking. Her voice was clipped.

'As I said, I am well. Well enough to start a new life even though I will never forget losing my child. I still can't understand why you let her take him from me after you'd said you'd stand by me and let me bring the child up myself. You said you'd support me. You lied.'

She saw the look of pain in Pa's eye as she glanced at him. 'You are not the centre of the universe,' he said.

'Not any more,' she snapped. 'You've made that quite clear.'

'I'm sorry,' Pa's voice was quiet now.

'So you've come to tell me I'm no longer welcome in your house, my home?'

'I'm not saying that. You are alway welcome. It's just I think it would be best if you find your own way when you're ready to leave here. There must be work you can find where you can live-in. We could ask Mrs Cartwright to take you back?'

Feeling suddenly cold, Emily shook her head. 'This has come from her, hasn't it? From Kate.'

'I don't know why you can never call her Mother. She always asked that you think of her as Mother. Percy calls her Mother. Why can't you?'

'She is not my mother and she never has behaved motherly towards me. You are blind to her ways, Pa. She has been wicked to me when you've not been looking. I will never call her Mother. My Ma was a good woman. Your Kate is not and never will be. And as for working in service, I made some decisions whilst in here and one of them is that I won't be working shut up in a house any-where, not even in Mrs. Cartwright's who, to be fair, was always kind to me.'

'So what do you propose to do then?'

'I don't know yet. I've been working on the farm here and I love it. I may look for outside work.'

'Outside work? And where would you live?'

'I've heard about the Women's Land Army. I can become a Land Girl, and live on a farm. They are desperate for women I believe.'

'You're a dreamer. Working on a farm will ruin your chances of finding a husband with a good wage. You're just running away from the real world.'

'The real world as you call it has done nothing for me. The real world has thousands of men who have gone to war, many of whom won't ever come back. The ones who do come back are damaged either physically or are suffering from what they're calling shell shock. I've seen them walking in the courtyards on the other side of the asylum. I've seen them in the ballroom here at the dances with their limbs missing. This is the real world and it will never be the same again. You've made your choice, Pa and I have made mine. It's clear that I have no place in your home nor in your heart any more. I am resigned to making my own way in the world. And as you have pointed out to me in the past, I am already a ruined woman with no chance of finding a husband, good waged or poor.'

He shook his head and looked away.

She went on. 'I will never forgive you for letting her take away my son. I will always love you, Pa, but you have broken me. As I heal, I will push away all memories of you and our life as it was. My world changed when Ma died and ended when my child was taken. Now I will work at making a new life for myself and try not to look back.'

'I am sorry you feel like this. One day you will understand.'

She stood. 'Perhaps I may. Perhaps I already understand more than you think. You will never know.' And she turned and walked away without looking back. Holding her head high, she walked across the open space and entered her room before she fell on her bed, sobbing.

Chapter Forty-one

Emily

A weight seemed to be holding Emily down as she forced herself to rise from her bed the next day. She berated herself for even hoping that her Pa would have put her first in his life. Of course he wouldn't, he couldn't do that. He was married to Kate and that was the end of it. She wished that he'd never bothered to come to visit. His words made the rift between them so final. She could no longer ever hope that there'd be a chance of making amends, of being welcome into the family again.

There was nothing for it but to go forward and try not to look back. Plodding to the fields, she tried to shake off the gloom, telling herself that she had to make her own future now and her future perhaps would be better. She smiled sadly to herself as she thought about Joe and how he made her feel. Life could only get better now, surely? She remembered how ill she'd been and realised that she must be truly recovering. In the not so distant past she would have slipped into a black mood that she'd have struggled to get out of again for weeks or months. But now she had hope. She had Joe.

The hours passed slowly. Emily worked and occasionally looked across the horizon, wondering if Joe was out there somewhere. She had thought that perhaps he might be able to walk near to the fields to take a glance across at her. But there was no sign of him. Finally the working day was over and she was being ushered through the door back into the ward.

Nurse Paxton was waiting for her.

'Emily, I have something for you,' she said as she handed Emily a note. 'It was given to one of the nurses by her friend, Mrs. Johnson. She's a landlady. I think you know the young man who wrote this.'

Feeling her face burning, Emily took the note and made her way to the privacy of her room. Her hopes were high as she sat on her bed and tore open the envelope but in less than a minute they were dashed as she read.

'Dear Emily,

I have been called away. My Pa is ill and I have to go home for a while. I don't know when I will see you again but I will never forget you and will write if I can.

Your friend (I hope),

Joe.'

Such a short note, filled with so much but with so little promise. Would he ever come back? Droxford was a long way from Milton. Never had the walls of the asylum seemed so high and insurmountable to Emily. Then she thought about Joe. Poor Joe's pa was ill. After all they'd told each other about their families only a few days ago, she truly hoped that Joe could make amends with his pa. She knew what it felt like to be at odds with someone you loved so much. And of course Emily realised that he may not ever come back if he was needed at home.

It seemed like an age before she heard the knock on her door. It was nurse Paxton again. 'Are you alright?' she asked.

Emily shook her head. 'He's gone. I may never seen him again now.' She handed the note to the nurse.

'It says he'll be away for a while. That could mean only a few weeks. You don't know.'

'Or a few years. If his father is ill enough for him to be called home, who knows how long it will be. I can't imagine he'll be back now. If my Pa needed me, I'd go whatever had happened between us.'

'You mustn't despair, Emily. These are unsettled times. We never know what will happen tomorrow. Please, don't let this set you back. You must keep strong and get yourself well enough to leave here. You are almost there, you know that.'

'I thought I was, but where will I go?'

'It will all work out for you, I am sure of that. Just keep your spirits up. Now, you have work to do on the ward, and then it will be time for supper. The best thing to do is to keep busy.'

After she'd gone, Emily sat and thought about her situation again. What a rush of different emotions she'd experienced in just a few days. Last week she had been so happy and hopeful of the future, that perhaps she could have a good life one day with this young man who clearly had feelings for her, as she did for him. Then feeling so much better and being told that she would be leaving the asylum in the near future should her progress continue. She felt good working in the fresh air and had hope that one day she might work outside somewhere, maybe on a farm somewhere away from the city. Seeing her own Pa on Sunday had been a low moment, dragging her spirits down so much that she nearly lost all of the progress she'd made, with only the thought of Joe keeping her on an even keel, only to have those hopes dashed by him being called away so suddenly.

Why did life have to be so troubling, so complicated? Whatever would happen next, she wondered.

Chapter Forty-two

Emily

She thought it couldn't get any worse, but the very next day the whole ward was buzzing with an excitement that she couldn't feel. The American Army was to take over part of the asylum. It started as a whisper amongst the nurses on the ward and soon even the women at the breakfast tables were talking about it. Everyone wanted to know what was going to happen. They'd heard about the Americans who'd joined the war in April but not many had seen an American themselves. And now they were going to change some of the wards into general wards and the nurses said that they'd be admitting men straight from the front line so needed to refurbish wards into surgical areas and even operating rooms. Everyone wanted to know when these men were going to be arriving and who would be looking after them and what would happen to the patients already there.

It wasn't long until they were told. The rumour was that all of the patients were being moved. Those who could go home were to be discharged.

'What will happen to me?' Emily asked. 'Will they discharge me? Where will I go?' Any hopes that she still held sank to the pit of her stomach when she was told that she would be moving to another asylum and she felt even worse when she realised that it would be all the way to the Brighton asylum.

Her interview with the doctor was short. 'As part of the war effort, now that our American friends have joined us in our fight, we are handing over the main hospital building to them. They will adapt the wards so that they may treat their troops as the wounded are brought back from France and Belgium. This means that all of the pauper patients here will have to be moved. It will only be temporary, until the war is over, of course, and then you will be brought back here, although in your case, you are more likely to be discharged before that happens. We are keeping the villas for those paying patients. Unfortunately, you are not a private patient so you must go. You will be well cared for. Are there any questions?'

Emily felt that there were too many questions for her to think of.

'How will I get there?'

'You will travel to Brighton in an ambulance with some of the other women in her ward.'

'What about my work on the farm? Is there a farm in Brighton? What will I do?'

'There will be work for you but it's out of my hands as to what you'll be doing. You must understand that there are going to be more patients there already, from other asylums. It may be a little overcrowded but in these times we all have to make adjustments, to make some sacrifices. I am sorry.'

'How long do you think it'll be before I'm well enough to leave?'

'You are doing very well. If you had somewhere to go now, maybe it would have been sooner, but you're not quite ready yet. Try and do all you can to keep your spirits up, do your best to do everything the nurses ask of you and I'm sure it won't be too long.'

Emily felt worse as soon as she heard that May would be discharged. May was excited.

'I am to go home, Emily. Only a few more days and I will be back in my own home. I'd thought I'd never feel like this again.' She stopped. 'It will be your turn soon. Then we can meet up for chats perhaps.'

'That is good news, May. I'm happy for you but I won't be going home for a while yet and when I do, I have no idea as to where I'll be living.'

'Oh, my dear, I am sorry to be leaving you behind. You've been a good friend to me. If there is anything I can do to help, then please let me know.' She handed a piece of paper to Emily. 'This is my address. You must write to me when you get to Brighton, keep me informed of what it's like there. Hopefully you will have a sea view.'

Emily smiled at May. 'I will write to you, of course I will, and thank you for wanting to keep in touch with me. I'd thought that once leaving here, we'd not see each other again. You wouldn't want to be reminded of the dark times you've been through.'

'You helped me through those dark times so yes, I do want to see you again and I do really hope that you will have a happier time ahead.'

'I hope so too.'

Although she was pleased for May it meant she would lose her only friend here. Not only May, but far away from Percy and anyone else she might hope would visit. She would be so far away from everyone. The only saving grace was that Nurse Paxton would be going too, as were most of the nurses and attendants in the asylum.

Lying in bed the night before the journey, Emily dreamed of Joe and wondered again what he was doing and whether they would one day be able to see each other. She would love to write to him but it seemed that any chance of that was now beyond her reach, not having an address for him. She hoped that Nurse Paxton might help with that. At this time, the nurses were so busy, but maybe once they'd settled in Brighton, there might be a chance to speak to her about getting a letter to Joe. At the moment though, it all seemed far beyond the realms of possibility. She had more chance of hearing from her brothers on the front line than she had of hearing from Joe again. And she hadn't heard from them since she'd been in the asylum and could only wonder if they were still alive and still writing to her Pa. It was with a heavy heart that she settled down to sleep that night.

Chapter Forty-three

Emily

The journey was a long, uncomfortable one and the Brighton asylum wasn't even in Brighton. Out in the countryside, near Haywards Heath, it was disappointing to know they were so far from the coast. Emily had imagined she would be able to write to May about seeing the ocean from the windows but that wasn't to be. The ambulance approached from the north side, passing a lodge and along a narrow drive. It was yet another building surrounded by a high wall, but this one was of yellow stone, beautiful in its own way, with red-brick banding around the round-headed windows. It was vast, bigger than the asylum in Portsmouth and loomed over them as they alighted from the ambulance and were led into the building. Inside, the long corridors were familiar and the layout seemed to be in the same design that Emily knew from Portsmouth.

Emily wondered if she would ever leave this place. It was such a long way from home. She felt the walls closing in on her like a labyrinth with no way out. The

Portsmouth asylum was bad enough but at least she'd been within walking distance of the streets and the sea-front that she had grown up so close to. Life just seemed to get worse and worse. Unable to bear the thought of working indoors again, she could only hope that there would be a job on the farm here.

Sitting in the day room in her new ward, she gazed out of the window. They were on the second floor which looked out across the South Downs. Such a wonderful view even though she was locked in. It seemed almost cruel to think that all those fields were spread before her and she was unable to get out to enjoy walking in them. But what could she do? She tried hard not to let her spirits drop and wondered how long it would be before she returned to Portsmouth.

Before the war, she was told, they held dances in the ballroom here, just like they had in Portsmouth. Since the moving of patients from other asylums though, the ballroom had been used as a massive dormitory. Emily was told she was lucky that she'd been given a bed on this ward. At least there were some home-comforts here and although it was crowded, it wasn't as bad as sleeping in a huge draughty hall with over a hundred others. There seemed to be noise and chaos everywhere.

Similar to the Portsmouth Asylum, this one was self-sufficient. She'd been told that there were workshops for the men to work in and a sewing room, a laundry and a courtyard for drying the washing. She was glad when they told her that she wouldn't be sent to work in the laundry.

She still had bad feelings about working in that place at Portsmouth. The sewing room would have been better but with all the extra patients on the wards there was no room for more to work in the sewing room. Any sewing work would have to be done on the wards.

On the second day, Janet Smith arrived. She looked around the ward and soon spotted Emily. She marched across the room and sat in the chair opposite. 'Well, well, you've come down a peg or two, haven't you? Thought you'd be looked after, didn't you?'

'Janet, it's good to see you.' Emily smiled, wondering what the woman meant.

'You want to talk to me now, do you? After all those weeks in Portsmouth of ignoring me, you've got a nerve.'

'I don't know what you mean.' Emily shifted in her chair.

'I know what's been going on, don't try and pretend you don't know.'

'I don't.'

'Picked out as special by the nurses, given preferential attention by the do-gooders who come to visit? Flirting with the farm boy? I thought you were my friend but suddenly you'd better things to do other than spend time with me. I was your first friend in that place and then you went off on your own.'

'I'm sorry. I didn't think you wanted to talk to me. You had so many other friends in the ward and on the farm group. I thought you'd dropped me as a friend. I didn't think you'd want to spend time with me after all I've done.'

Janet stood up. 'Pah! Don't give me that rubbish. You're just a stuck up madam, trying to make more of yourself than you deserve. I've seen the nurse talking to you, spending time with you. You're just a snobby bitch but now you've got your come-down, being sent here.' She was shouting now.

Emily looked at her in horror. 'Please, I don't want to fall out with you. It's not like that. The nurses are kind to everyone, aren't they?'

Janet moved towards her with one swift stride and took a swing at Emily's face. The slap was hard, sending Emily falling backwards and she landed on the hard floor. Janet was screaming, foul words coming from her mouth as she leapt on top of Emily. It happened so quickly and was over in a flash as two nurses were pulling Janet off and dragging her away.

Emily was stunned, sore and confused as she sat up and watched the nurses locking the door to a side-room, Janet safely out of harm's way. Where had that come from she wondered. Nurse Paxton was by her side within minutes, helping her up and seating her on a nearby sofa.

'What was that all about?' The nurse inspected Emily's head for cuts. 'Are you alright?'

'My back hurts. Just bruises I think.' Emily shook her head. 'I have no idea why she did that. She said I'd been ignoring her, snubbing her. I thought she didn't want to speak to me, not the other way round. I'm sorry. I don't know how to make this right.'

'She'll be in that room for a while now. Hopefully she'll be calmer when she's back in the ward. I'll talk to her. But not today.'

'The thinks I've been given better treatment. She feels neglected.'

'Hmm. I can't talk about other patients, but I will talk to her, don't worry.'

Emily soon healed and before long Janet was back in the main ward. Emily tried to speak to her a couple of times, but Janet just looked at her in disdain and moved away.

Time passed with no changes for Emily with no work for her to do. Everything seemed to be in a muddle with the wards over-crowded, the nurses forming two groups, one group looking after the Brighton patients, the other focussed on the Portsmouth ones.

There didn't seem to be any kind of pattern to the daily routine. Emily missed her work on the farm. She was eventually given sewing tasks to do again like she had in the early days of her recovery. Keeping herself to herself, she resisted making any new friends. Each day was a monotony of boredom.

Life was easier to bear once she was allowed out into the grounds. At first she was taken out with a nurse escorting her with a small group of other patients. They walked in the gardens near to the building. Emily longed to be able to work outside again but at least she could breathe in the fresh country air and she enjoyed stretching her legs as she wandered the paths around the asylum. Of course the women were segregated from the men, as they were in Portsmouth. Walls divided the area the women walked from the other half of the asylum where the men were allowed. Sometimes she could hear them from the other side, although could never see what they looked like. She just heard occasional shouting. It was strange to hear a male voice that wasn't that of the superintendent or one of the male hospital visitors.

Emily's thoughts often strayed to the men that had been so central to her life in the past. She missed her Pa, her brothers, and Billy, hoping that she would see her brothers again one day. Then she thought about her baby, Billy's son, who'd been taken away from her so cruelly. She tried not to linger too long in thinking about him. There was no point and it only made her feel so terribly sad. And then there was Joe. Sweet Joe, who had promised to keep in touch with her. Yet as time passed, she had heard nothing from him. She'd heard nothing from anyone at all. Despondency seeped into her like mould in the walls of the scullery at home. She should write to May but couldn't bring herself to put anything down on paper that wasn't gloomy. Why would May want a letter from her with the way she was feeling?

Chapter Forty-four

Emily

Emily tried to put all thoughts of Portsmouth behind her. It was a surprise therefore when she received a visitor. It was Marjorie Simpson, the hospital visitor who had been so kind to her but was the last person Emily thought she'd see again. And she had some news for her.

'I have two pieces of good news for you, Emily.' she said. 'First of all I have been to see Mrs. Cartwright in Southsea and she has agreed to give you your old position back, this time as a live-in housemaid. Your wage would be slightly less but you will have your own room and it will include all of your meals and a uniform. I know you said you would prefer to work outside but this will be a start for you. If you are happy to take it of course. I have spoken to the doctor and he assures me that you are well enough to be discharged. Going back to Portsmouth would be better for you, don't you agree?'

'I don't know. I mean, yes, It would be wonderful to be back in my home town.'

'How do you feel about working indoors again?'

'Well, I would be very grateful for anything at the moment. Obviously, I would have loved to work outside again, but to be free of the asylum and working for Mrs. Cartwright again would be wonderful. She was always a good employer. I can't promise I could do it forever, but it would be a good stepping stone. Thank you.'

'Good. That's settled then. The hospital will arrange for your discharge and transport back to Portsmouth.' She paused. 'And the other news.' Reaching into her bag she pulled out a letter. 'I have this for you.' She handed it to Emily and watched as the young woman tore open the envelope.

'A letter from Joe.' She looked up at Marjorie. 'I wonder, I hope it's good news about his father and that he's going back to his old lodgings in Portsmouth.'

'I went to see him myself,' said Marjorie. 'I know it's against all that I'm told is right. We shouldn't get involved with our patients. But I felt somehow a connection with you when we met all those weeks ago and there's too much sadness in the world today. I thought if I could help you find a little bit of happiness, then it was my duty to do what I could.'

'Is he back in Portsmouth already? I wonder what happened to his Pa. Do you know?'

'He is back, yes. And still lodging with Mrs. Johnson. But he won't be there for much longer. You should read the letter, and then we can talk.'

Emily opened the letter and read:

'Dear Emily,

I do hope that you are well. I was shocked to learn that you are so far away now and am truly sorry that I didn't see you to say goodbye when I was called away. My Father was suddenly ill and now he has sadly passed away. My Ma is struggling to cope with the farm now there are no men to do the heavy work so I have to go back to Droxford to help. We have a land girl helping but she has no experience of farm work even though she tries to pull her weight. I have briefly come back to Portsmouth to collect my belongings and to let them know at the asylum farm that I won't be back and I was hoping I would see you.

Mrs. Simpson came to see me and explained what had happened to you and that she was trying to find you a position back in Southsea. I am hopeful that you will be free of the asylum soon. I do hope life is not too difficult where you are. I think of you often.

I have included my address in Droxford in this letter in the hope that you will soon write.

Your dear friend (I hope I may call myself that)

Joe'

She looked up at Marjorie and wiped the tear from her eye.

'Oh dear,' Marjorie said. 'Joe has told me he would like to write to you once you return to Portsmouth. Do you think that you will?'

Emily smiled. 'I'm not sure I could wait until then. Perhaps I could write to him before then. There's little for me to do here.' She paused and looked around the room at the other women who were restlessly moving about. 'Not that I have much to write about apart from my hopes and dreams for the future and it's surely too early for me to share those with a young man?'

'You could write and tell him about your new position in Mrs. Cartwright's perhaps? Tell him about your journey here and how different it is to the asylum in Portsmouth? What you see from the windows and any friends you have made.'

'I haven't made any friends since I arrived here. My friend May left the asylum when I was moved here. I do miss our chats. It's difficult making friends in a place like this. And now I know I'll be leaving soon I don't want to make new friends with people I'll probably never see again. May and I had little in common and I doubt that she'll want to see me once I'm back, even though she told me she would. I'll be a servant and she will always be a lady, a naval officer's wife, so life will be very different for us both.'

'The war has made some interesting changes to the world. You may be surprised at how things between classes are different.'

Emily was not convinced but smiled all the same.

Chapter Forty-five

Emily

Early autumn was upon the landscape as Emily finally left the asylum. She walked down the long drive kicking up the first leaves that had fallen, her heart bursting with hope. The bus waiting at the lodge house was already full of visitors who had been spending a few hours with their loved-ones. Emily felt sad that the only person who had bothered to visit her was Mrs Simpson. None of her own family had come, or even bothered to write to her. Apart from Joe, of course. She thought of him with such a fondness. It was a good feeling knowing that there was at least one person who cared. The bus drove through the country lanes to the railway station in Haywards Heath. This time Emily travelled in the train back to Portsmouth now she was no longer an inmate and was free to travel wherever and however she wished. It was such a different journey to the one she'd taken a few weeks previously. Going home although not going home, Emily's mind was full of thoughts of what might be, of what life would be like now that she had broken her ties with her Pa. And was she foolish to hope that there might be a future for her with Joe?

Her thoughts drifted to her elder brothers. She wondered what they were doing? Where were they now? She supposed that they were still in Belgium although she'd not heard from either of them. She hoped that they didn't feel bad about her. Surely they would understand how things can happen in times like these. Prior to this awful war, people often married in haste with a child on the way and no-one thought anything wrong in it. It was only now, with so many young men lost, that there were more women like herself. But why did people think so badly of her? It was unfair. Then again, there were a few women like Marjorie and Nurse Paxton, too, who had a more open mind about these matters. She hoped that Mrs. Cartwright would welcome her without thinking too badly of her. She must be sympathetic, Emily thought, or she wouldn't have offered her the job back, and a room to live in as well. She thought about Percy. He would be leaving school soon and then it would be his turn to go to war. She hoped that the war would be over before that day came but knew realistically that was not going to happen. It seemed to go on forever.

Emily gazed out of the train window at the countryside passing by. The trees were starting to turn from summer green to the golden colours of autumn, not a season that she usually found promising but today there was only hope carrying her forward. The warm browns and oranges of the leaves glistened in the light rain. Whatever happened in the wider world, she was determined to make her life better.

Her thoughts went back to Joe. In her pocket was his letter. She drew it out and read it again for the hundredth time. "Dear Emily", and "Your dear friend Joe", he'd written to her. And he hoped that she was well and would write to him. She was sad for him that his Father had died although she remembered that Joe had been estranged from him before he'd become ill. She hoped they'd been able to resolve their differences before he'd passed away. Emily still felt a deep sadness about her own Pa and their last meeting. Maybe they would be able to be friends again one day. She would never give up hoping for that, despite what she'd said to him.

Looking at the letter again, Emily thought about all of those people who had helped her. She was grateful that she'd had a good nurse at the asylum and remembered their parting earlier that day. Nurse Paxton had to remain in the Brighton asylum until the patients from Portsmouth were all returned after the war was over, whenever that may be. The nurse had insisted that Emily write to her and let her know how she settled into her new position and said that she should call her Maud now. 'We shall be friends,' she'd said. 'You can't keep calling me nurse.' Emily remembered when they'd first met and the thought of Maud being Mad without the U. She smiled to herself, thinking about how far she'd come since then.

Maud had also advised Emily to keep in touch with Mrs. Pullman. She wasn't too sure about this, May had been a good friend to her whilst they were both patients in the asylum but there was a barrier between them, a barrier of class. How could she overcome this?

Of course, Emily knew that the person who had helped her the most in getting her freedom was Marjorie Simpson, the hospital visitor. In the past, Emily had hated the thought of those "do gooders" who thought they were better than the likes of her. Of course Marjorie was nothing like that and had given Emily so much confidence to start a new life for herself. Emily suspected that Marjorie had her own story to tell which perhaps wasn't so different from her own. Emily hoped that one day she could help someone herself in a similar way.

It was late afternoon before the train pulled into the station at Fratton. Emily alighted from the train and made her way down the platform and out into the street. The bustling of Portsmouth hit her senses, suddenly she was afraid. What had she been thinking? It was all far too much. Coming back to a busy city was a shock after being in the relative quiet of an asylum after such a long time. Even the long train journey and the people milling about on the train had not prepared her for the busy streets around the station.

Emily sat on a bench to catch her breath before she moved on to make her way to Southsea and Mrs. Cartwright's house. She decided that she would walk to the sea front first and to take her time along the promenade just to try and get her thoughts in order before embarking on her new life. She longed to see the sea again. As she walked through the streets, she kicked up the leaves again that had begun to fall. It reminded her of the times she'd walked with Billy. It was less than two years ago but seemed to be a lifetime. So much had changed for her since those days of laughter and hope for the future. During the earlier days of the war everyone was so optimistic for a swift end to hostilities. It would be all over in a flash, they said, and all the boys would come home, waving flags and celebrating.

Emily remembered the night of the air raid. How terrifying it had been to know that the vast Zeppelins had flown over them in the darkness and had even dropped bombs on the city. Of course, it had turned out that it was only one Zeppelin and only one bomb which had been dropped, almost indiscriminately and had missed doing much damage. But it was the thought of being attacked from the skies that made the ordinary person living in the town so afraid. You would never know when it could happen again, and if they sent one, they could send more. The constant sound of guns firing into the skies at night brought many a sensible person to their knees in fear. Emily had seen the result of that fear whilst she was in the asylum. It was ironical, she thought, that those in the asylum were shut behind a wall to keep those outside safe from them. Only whilst you were inside you could see you were actually safer away from the mad world outside. She fleetingly wondered whether she would be happier if she should go back and live in there instead of out here in this uncertain world.

This was only a fleeting thought, however. Emily could see that she had a future now, even if she wasn't sure where that future would take her.

With all this thinking, she reached the shore before she'd realised. Sitting on the beach, she gathered up some pebbles and one by one threw them into the waves as they lapped on the shore. The sea was calm today. Emily loved it best when it was stormy and the waves rushed at her, sucking back the pebbles as they withdrew. Remembering that this was the place where Billy and she had first made love, she stared out to sea and wondered again whether Billy would still be alive if she'd agreed to marry him that day. She had to stop thinking about those times.

Emily turned away and gazed out across to the Isle of Wight, the one thing in her life that had always been there, never changing. She sighed, telling herself it was no good dwelling in the past. This was the start of her future, and it was wonderful to be back in her home town with something to look forward to at last. Finally, she pulled herself to her feet, brushed off her skirts and made her way with purpose to Mrs. Cartwright's house in Granada Road.

Chapter Forty-six

Joe

Standing in the field at the bottom of the lane, Joe looked about him and thought about the task in hand. His father had struggled in the past year whilst he'd been away. He could see that now and wished he'd come back before. Now it was too late for his Pa. Still, Joe was glad that he'd had the chance to say goodbye. It had been a hard parting but they'd settled their differences in the end and Pa had made it clear that he wanted Joe to carry on the farm. He wondered not for the first time whether he was man enough to do it. He also wondered about the war. All of his mates were signing up, some were going voluntarily, others called up, and he felt guilty. Guilty that although farming was an important occupation and he was exempt from being forced into the army, he still felt he should be doing his bit.

Casting his mind back several weeks to when he'd left Portsmouth, he remembered sitting on the back of the cart, looking down from Portsdown Hill. He could see in the distance the fields that he'd worked on around the asylum in Milton. It seemed such a long way, looking down from the height of the hill and he wondered if he would ever go back. Emily was on his mind too. He thought about her face, her voice, the way she smiled shyly at him and the touch of her hand in his as they'd danced. His face burned as he remembered what he'd written to her and he'd wished that he could have seen her in person before he'd left. But that had been impossible. She'd been sent away to Brighton and he'd not known when or if ever she'd be back. It had been a surprise when he'd been contacted by Mrs. Simpson who'd agreed to take the letter to Emily from him but he'd heard nothing back. He'd hoped that Emily would write to him but realised that it was probably a hope too far.

Now he had to stop thinking about her and get on and make sure that the farm got back to how it used to be. The wheat in this field was ready to cut but he needed more workers to help. It would be a task that he couldn't do alone. The one Land Army girl who'd been working for his Pa had left when her soldier sweetheart returned from France. He couldn't blame her. In these days you were stupid if you didn't grab at any chance of happiness and her young man would be going back to the front soon enough. Even had she not left, they still would have struggled to get the crops in. With her gone it only left old Fred who'd help. He'd worked with his Pa for many years and knew his way around the farm. In fact, Fred was the one who'd guided his Pa and he hoped he would do the same for Joe. Fred told the lad not to worry, that he'd put the word out among the village families that there was work in the fields. There were plenty of young lads who'd be more than glad to escape a few days away from the school room. Joe just needed to work out what was to be done.

'You planning to stand there dreaming all day, lad?' Fred was shouting as he tramped across the field.

'Bloody hell, Fred, you creeping up on me now?'

'I weren't creeping. You were miles away. And watch your language.'

'Sorry Fred. I'm worrying about getting the crops in. I don't know if I can do it.'

'Course you can. I told you. It's not difficult to work it out, you just need to get a few hands in and work damned hard until it's done.'

'Pa didn't think I was good enough to do it. He told me I weren't up to being a good farmer. I'll never forget those words. What if he was right?'

'Bah! That was a long time ago, before you went away. He was stuck in the old ways that's for sure and it was only you coming up with your new-fangled ideas that put him out. No-one likes to be told that their old ways aren't so good any more.'

Joe looked down at his boots.

'I wish I'd not stayed away for so long, I wish Pa was here now to tell me what to do.'

'Yes, well he's not and there's nothing you can do about that, is there? You'll just have to use your brains and get on with it. Of course there's nothing wrong with the old ways either. Things have worked well on this land for thousands of years and I don't doubt they'll carry on much the same for some time yet.'

'Maybe. It's just so soon after losing him. My head's not straight any more. I sometimes think I'm going mad. After seeing what it's like in the asylum, I'm scared it's going to happen to me if I'm not careful.'

'Don't talk like that. You're only going through normal grief. It happens to all of us and it does get better. If everyone who lost anyone ended up in the madhouse, they'd all be filled up soon enough.'

'But I can't work out what to do. I feel lost.'

'You'll have to listen to this old man instead then. I still know how to plan and manage a harvest even though I'm not as strong as I was.' He broke off and began to cough, a long wheezing cough.

'You alright? You sure you're going to be well enough to come into the fields. The dust will be the ending of you with that cough.'

'It's nothing. I've had this for years and it's no worse than it ever was.' He took out a flask from his trouser pocket and took a swig.

'What's that you've got there?'

'It's medicinal - purely medicinal. A drop of brandy. Sees me through the day.'

Joe smiled at that. 'Well you'd best take it easy. I don't want to lose you as well.'

'I'm going nowhere, lad. Not for some time anyway. Now. Let's go and get sorted, shall we?'

Together they strode across the field, Joe feeling a huge weight lifting from his shoulders now that he knew however hard it would be, Fred was by his side.

Chapter Forty-seven

Joe

It was late afternoon, Joe was in the barn feeding the rabbits they kept in hutches. During these times of war, breeding rabbits was a good way to make sure there was always meat on the table. His Ma was calling him from the farmhouse garden gate.

'Joe, we have a visitor. You need to come to the house, lad.'

He had no idea as to who this might be. Someone from the Ministry of War probably, he thought. He hoped that they didn't want more horses. He couldn't bear to lose anything else now and relied on his horse for the farm work and for getting into town. The war had taken too many horses already. Washing his hands under the tap in the yard, he took his boots off and went into the house in his woollen socks.

Ma was sitting in the parlour with the lady who'd helped him before by taking a letter to Emily. She was dressed in a pale pink dress and coat with one of those impossibly large hats perched on her head. He wondered fleetingly how she'd got in through the door without knocking it off. She stood as he entered and held out her hand.

'Hello Joe. I'm sorry to call you away from your work, but I felt I needed to let you know the news about Emily. I know that you'll be keen to hear how she is, won't you?'

'Is she alright? I haven't heard anything from her. I had hoped...'

'She is well, and the reason you haven't heard is that you forgot to put the return address on the letter you gave to me before. There is good news too.'

'Good news?'

'Emily has been discharged from the asylum and is no longer ill. She is working in Southsea, living in as a maid to Mrs. Cartwight.'

'That's where she worked before, isn't it?' His heart was thumping.

'Yes, Mrs. Cartwright is very kind, a good employer and was happy to take Emily back and to give her a room of her own as well. I went to see Emily a few days ago and we talked about your previous letter. She's hoping that you still want to write. So I thought as I was on my way back from Winchester this afternoon that I'd take the opportunity to pop in and see you. I hope you don't mind me being presumptuous about this. I just felt I needed to do something to help.'

Joe looked across the room to his Ma who was looking a little uncomfortable. He smiled at her before answering.

'I am grateful,' he said. 'You are very kind and shouldn't have taken so much trouble, really.'

'It is no trouble. Like I said, I was passing this way to-day anyway. I'm sure Emily would have written eventually, only she was feeling that you would want to forget her once you'd come back home, and be too busy with the farm to even think about her. Of course, I couldn't believe that could be true. I am just an interfering woman I'm afraid. I only hope I've done the right thing.'

'You have, from my point of view anyway.' He turned to his Ma again. 'Ma, Emily is a good woman. I know she's had a bad time of her life so far, but you will love her, I know you will. I don't want to waste any more time. Life is too short.'

His Ma looked at Mrs. Simpson and back to him. 'I wouldn't disagree with that, Joe. Perhaps you could write to each other and see how things go. Now, I will pour some tea. And there's a seed cake in the kitchen. Excuse me a moment.'

Joe perched on the edge of the chair by the window. 'I'm so glad you called today. Please tell Emily that I do want to see her again, and to write to her.'

'If you want I can take a letter for her today. Only please remember to write your address on the top of the paper.'

'Thank you. I will.'

It was as Mrs. Simpson was leaving and he stood with his Ma watching her walking along the lane towards the edge of the fields that he realised. 'There is no way that this farm is anywhere near the road from Winchester. She must have walked miles.'

Chapter Forty-eight

Emily

The mornings were getting darker now that the autumn days were firmly set in. Clouds covered the late moonlight and the trees were rustling angrily in the wind. Emily shivered as she rose from her bed, flung on her clothes and made her way quickly down the narrow stairs to the house below. There was plenty to be done before the mistress was woken with her morning tea and inside the house it was quiet. Quieter than she'd been used to in the asylum. There were no restless women in this house, the floors were either richly carpeted or highly polished and it was her job to keep them clean with not a speck of dust on the floorboards or anywhere else for that matter.

The kitchen range was the first port of call. Emily had to ensure that the fire was still lit and to stoke it up enough to heat the vat of water that she'd put on for the mistress's morning wash. Beside this she placed the heavy filled kettle which would be used to make Emily's first cup of tea.

Mrs. Price, the cook would arrive later ready to cook the breakfast.

Waiting for the water to boil, Emily laid the tray for the mistress's early tea, to be taken up later. She winched down the airer and took down the linen that had been drying there in the warmth of the kitchen. Folding the linen ready to be ironed later, she then placed the tidy pile on the ironing table in the corner of the room.

The kettle boiled and the very welcome cup of tea taken, Emily moved from room to room, laying the fires in the dining room for breakfast, in the morning room, to be lit in an hour's time, and in the drawing room ready for later that day. She carried in coal from the store in the kitchen yard, heavy work, straining her back. She didn't mind hard work. It took her mind off her thoughts about what would happen next in her life.

Emily had read and re-read the letter from Joe. Each time, she read it differently. At first it had lifted her spirits, but as the time had passed and she'd heard nothing more from him, she began to doubt herself. She convinced herself that she'd been no more to him than a distraction, a dream of something that never could be. Then she looked again and her hopes lifted. He did have feelings for her and would never forget her. She laughed at herself for even imagining that. She'd not heard from him, she'd not heard from Marjorie, nor from May. How can she ever have imagined the barriers between classes and situations could ever be lifted.

Mrs. Cartwright was kind to her but there was always plenty to keep her busy and no time to spend long in thinking about what might be. So Emily was surprised when she was called to the drawing room one afternoon. She'd been in the vegetable garden cutting a cabbage for dinner, her thoughts going back to those days in the asylum working in the fields there and she'd not heard the front door. Thinking that it would be a call for more tea for the mistress, she smoothed her apron and made her way to the room.

As soon as she entered she realised that Mrs. Cartwight was not alone. 'Ah, Emily, we have a visitor,' her mistress was saying.

It was Marjorie. 'Hello Emily,' she said.

Emily bobbed a curtsy, not sure how to behave in this situation.

'Please,' Marjorie said as she held out her hand. 'Do sit down for a while. I have some good news.' She looked to Mrs. Cartwright for approval. 'It's alright for Emily to sit, isn't it?'

'Of course.'

Emily looked about the room, wondering where would be most appropriate for her to sit. Mrs. Cartwright rose and walked to the writing desk, taking the chair and offered it to Emily. 'Here, Emily, sit here,' she said.

Emily's heart was beating like a drum as she sat, feeling very awkward, wondering what the news was about and who it had come from. A million thoughts flew through her head; was it her father? One of her brothers coming home? A letter from May perhaps? That would be wonderful although most unlikely. But the news was the least expected and the most welcome.

'I have been to Droxford,' Marjorie said. 'I know I should perhaps not have done, it takes me completely outside of the parameters of my position as visitor to the asylum, but something touched me in your story and I have decided to try and help you as much as I could.' She stopped and looked at Mrs. Cartwright. 'I trust first of all you are happy here?'

'I am happy here, and very grateful to you Mrs. Cartwright, for taking me on and in giving me a home.'

Mrs. Cartwright smiled. 'You are a good worker,' she said.

'Well, to the point,' Marjorie went on. 'I decided to visit your friend, Joe, at his farm in Droxford. He was surprised to see me, I have to say. And he's in the middle of possibly one of the busiest times on the farm. It had been left to run down somewhat, with his father being unwell and the young men all going off to war. His Mother was struggling too. Now his father has passed away, he has been assisted by an elderly farm hand and some of the young lads of the village.' She smiled. 'And a few of the local women too. All hands to get the work done, eh?'

'Poor Joe, I do hope he'll make a success of his farm. I miss working outside, I have to confess. As much as I love working here, of course,' she added hastily, glancing at Mrs. Cartwright.

'I know you enjoy being outside. I have watched you in the garden in the afternoons and seen how you light up in the open air.' Mrs. Cartwight shook her head. 'I wanted to help you by giving you somewhere you could feel safe, and work and be welcomed after all you've been through, but I know you won't want to stay here for ever. There is a life out there for you. I would hate to think you felt you had to be tied to this place indefinitely.'

'Well said Mrs. Cartwright,' Marlorie said. 'And I am sure that Emily is very grateful for what you have done for her.'

'Oh, I am grateful,' Emily said. 'It is hard work though and I hope I've given satisfaction in my work.'

'Oh you have, my dear and I too am grateful.'

'Well, I am sure we are all grateful but the point of my visit is to give you this letter from Joe. I was remiss before in that although I brought his letter to you, there was no returning address on it. When I explained to him you had nowhere to write back to he was relieved, thinking that you wished to have nothing to do with him, perhaps he would be a reminder of your time in the asylum and how painful that must be. I did reassure him you'd be more than happy to hear from him again and that I would ask you to write back to him, should you have something to say, of course. I do hope I haven't be presumptuous.'

'No. Not at all,' Emily said. 'You have a letter from him?'

'I do.' She took the folded envelope from her bag and passed it to Emily. 'I'm sure you would like to read it to yourself when you are alone, but I would be more than happy to sit and talk for a while after we have taken tea. Is that alright Mrs. Cartwright?'

'Of course. We will take tea together and then you may join Emily in the garden for a while.'

Emily stood and nodded. 'I will fetch the tea,' she said and made to leave the room, turning at the door and bobbing a quick curtsy.

Chapter Forty-nine

Emily

Emily stood in the kitchen waiting for the water to boil. Mrs. Price was rolling pastry for the evening's supper. Looking up as Emily took the letter from her pocket, she tutted. 'What's that you got there, girl?.'

Emily blushed. 'It's a letter from my friend, Joe. Mrs. Simpson has been to see him.'

'Well you'd best put it away and get the tea.'

'I will, I am. I'm waiting for the kettle.'

Emily looked at the envelope again. Joe's strong hand stood out in bold ink. She gently sliced open the envelope with the bread knife and drew out the single sheet of paper. Her hands were trembling as she read.

Dear Emily,

I trust that you are happy for me to address you by your first name. It seems too formal to call you Miss Harris. It feels as though I know you so well even though we have only spoken on three occasions. Your friend Mrs. Simpson tells me you were pleased to receive my previous letter but that I had not put a return address on it. I thank the heavens she took it upon herself to visit me at the farm today. I was sure you had forgotten me but she tells me you would welcome another letter. So, I am writing again. Life on the farm is very busy and now my Pa is gone, I have more on my plate with everything. Still, I think of you every day that I am in the fields and long to see you again.

I have written enough but hope you will write back soon and let me know how you are getting on.

Your friend,
   Joe.

He had written the address at the top of the letter. Emily's spirits lifted a little. Still she was in a state of disbelief. Surely he couldn't have meant those words. What could he mean? He wanted her to write back to him and let him know how she was getting on? She supposed she was getting on alright but would have been happier if she could have seen him in person. Would that ever happen? It was all very well writing to each other but what would a future be? Droxford seemed such a long way from Southsea and a life on a farm so far removed from working in service in this refined household. And of course there were all the other differences between them.

Carefully folding the letter and tucking it into her pocket, she made the tea and carried it through to the parlour.

Emily passed the next hour preparing the vegetables for Mrs. Cartwright's supper, working alongside Mrs Price in silence. Her head was full of what ifs and maybes and she found it hard to keep her mind on her work. Finally, the vegetables done, she left the kitchen and went into the garden. A bit of weeding always soothed her mind. She felt the letter in her apron pocket and sat on the garden bench to read it again, wondering what she should do. Her heart was telling her to write back to Joe but her head was holding her back. 'We could never have a future,' she convinced herself.

She'd not noticed the kitchen door opening until Marjorie sat down beside her.

'My dear, I do hope that I haven't upset you by interfering in your life.'

'No, of course not. It's just I have so much to think about,' Emily looked up at the autumn clouds scudding across the sky. 'I was sure I would never see Joe again. Our lives are so different and there's so much to be overcome. It seemed impossible to me, until today, and even now, I find it hard to see how we can overcome our differences.'

'Anything can be overcome if you want it enough.'

'That's not always true. So much has happened already in my life that I had no control over. I've lost so much that I thought would be there forever.'

'Alright, you have had some bad experiences and there have been times when it has seemed nothing would ever be good again. I do understand it's been hard for you and things have seemed against you at every turn. But maybe it's your time now. Perhaps with help, you can overcome many of the obstacles that seem to be stopping you from being happy.'

'I hope so.' Emily looked at the letter again. 'Joe has asked me to write to him. Droxford seems such a long way. Even if we wrote to each other, how can we have a future together?'

'Is that what you want? A future with Joe?'

'It's far too soon to know after only speaking to each other on a few occasions.' She paused. 'But I would like to get to know him better. It was like a dream when I was in the asylum, meeting him, something that kept me hoping. Now that time is in my past I don't know whether there was anything there, or what I felt about him. Now I have his letter, my thoughts are upside down. I don't know what I think any more.'

'Perhaps you need some time to let it all sink in. My advice would be to leave it for a few days and then write back to Joe. Let him know what you're feeling and whether you would like to continue to write and receive his letters. But remember in these days of uncertainty it's important not to waste a moment of your life. You may regret not at least giving Joe a chance.'

'I will write to him. Thank you for all you're doing. I don't know why you think I deserve to be helped, but I am grateful.'

'You are welcome.' She stood up. 'Of course you deserve to be helped. If only someone had helped me when I needed it, I would have had a happier life now.'

'Oh, You appear to have no problems, but I suppose we all have our stories.'

'You are right, Emily, but my story is an old one and yours is at the beginning. I believe we all deserve a chance at a happy ending. I hope you will think of me as a friend and one day perhaps I will tell you a bit about myself. Just remember there is no need to be grateful to me and don't waste your chance at happiness. I have done little.'

Emily smiled and bobbed a curtsey. 'Thank you any-way.'

'Enough thank you's. Now I must go. And please, no more curtseying to me. I hope I'm right and you see me as a friend now.'

Emily watched as Marjorie stepped back into the kitchen and was gone. She sat back down and looked again at the letter. She could feel the sunlight warming her, or was it the words on the page that made her feel like this? She held the letter to her heart and sighed before placing it back in her pocket.

Looking at the cabbages in the garden, she smiled at the memory and her hope for the future then went inside to collect the tea things.

Chapter Fifty

Joe

Joe was exhausted but the harvest was in at last. It hadn't been easy but the young lads in the village and many of the women had rallied round and helped. There had been little money to pay but he'd offered them what he could and promised ale and food once it was all safely gathered in. He was worried it couldn't be done, but soon saw that although hard work it was so rewarding. He'd never felt like this before when he was working with his Pa. Everything had seemed such a hard slog before as he fought with Pa at every turn. He'd not realised how this could be so satisfying. On the final day, the workers were singing in the field, knowing the task would soon be over and they would enjoy the celebrations at the end of the day.

Dusk was falling when they arrived back at the farmyard. The workers sluiced under the tap against the stable wall and made their way to the barn where the wonderful aroma of mutton stew was drawing them in. Two benches were set out with bowls and a huge pan of the hot meaty stew, next to hunks of fresh bread piled up and a whole block of creamy cheddar.

Ma stood behind the bench with Annie, the dairy maid from the farm next to theirs. She was helping Ma as she ladled out the food into the bowls and cut the cheese into portions. A wooden cask of ale was set on the other bench and Joe watched as the workers took out their own tankards and poured themselves a draft of the amber sweet nectar.

The ale was much needed and plentiful to quench the thirst of the workers, men and women, with even enough for the children who were allowed some too. Bales of straw had been set around the barn for seating and once the food had all been eaten, Fred took out his fiddle and began to play. Soon the workers were all on their feet, pushing back the straw bales to make room for dancing.

Joe loved to dance but this music and laughter reminded him of the ballroom at the asylum and his time there, dancing with Emily. How he missed those days. He wondered again if they would ever meet in the future and how long he'd have to wait to find out. He had such hopes when Marjorie had visited him but the days had passed slowly, it seemed, and he'd heard nothing. Best put her out of your mind, he told himself as he looked around at the villagers who were all laughing and singing to the music as they whirled past him in a delightful polka.

Eventually, the evening came to a close, many of the workers wandered off down the lane back to their homes in the village. Those who'd drank more than they were used to settled down amongst the hay in the barn and slept. Joe wondered how many sore heads there would be in the morning. All in all, he was happy and content that a good job had been done and the harvest was in.

The house was dark. His Ma had made her way to bed some time earlier with the remark that some people still had to get up in the morning and get the breakfasts, feed the chickens and rabbits and muck out the pigs. This was normal for her, she loved to grumble about her lot in life. Joe knew how much she loved it though, and always smiled to himself whenever she had a good old moan about things.

He lit a candle, sat in his Pa's chair beside the fireplace and looked at the faded photograph of his parent's wedding which was in its place on the mantlepiece. 'Well, Pa,' he said. 'I've done it. We got the harvest in and it was a good one. I think things'll be alright now, Pa. I know it'll never be easy but I'm going to do my best to make a go of this place. I hope you'll be proud of me at last.'

It was then that he noticed the letter. It was tucked behind the photograph. Why hadn't his Ma told him there was a letter? He snatched up the envelope and looked at it by the light of the candle. It had to be from Emily but would it be what he wanted to hear? He turned the envelope over and held it up to the light, trying to see what was inside without actually opening the seal.

Telling himself not to be a fool, he gently tore it open and took out the sheet of paper. Her writing was small and fine, the ink was pale as though it had been written a while ago and left in the sun to fade. He read.

'Dear Joe,

I was so happy to receive your second letter. Memories of you at that place were the only things that kept me half sane whilst I was so far away in Brighton. I honestly didn't think I'd ever see you again.

I have given much thought to the words you have written to me and it makes me happy to think of you wanting to be my friend.

My heart tells me that I should hope we can overcome obstacles but in reality there's so much holding us apart. I am a damaged woman as you know. I've been branded 'mad', I'm many years older than you, and you know I have had a child which was taken from me at birth. I know I have said these words over and over again until I am sick of hearing me saying them. But you could have any young woman who'd be more suitable for you. Your life is in Droxford and mine is here in Southsea. We are so far apart in many ways.

Still I would love to see you again. My life here is good enough, working for Mrs. Cartwright. She is kind to me and although the work is hard, I don't mind as it keeps me from thinking too much about the past.

I had better go now and get on with my duties but I hope to hear from you soon.

Your friend,

Emily

PS. I am sorry that I have taken so long to reply. I did write as soon as I got your letter but hesitated to post it. I am hoping that finally sending this was the right thing to do but if I don't hear anything back from you I will understand.

Joe read the letter, then re-read the letter. His heart felt like it was going to burst. She did care about him. Yes, she was right, there were obstacles that could have held them apart, but obstacles could always be overcome if you wanted something badly enough. He didn't care that she'd been in the asylum, he didn't care that she'd had a child before marriage. He didn't care that she was older than him. His fear had been that he wasn't good enough, experienced enough, for her. He wondered about talking to Ma about it. She knew there was someone, as she'd been there when Mrs. Simpson had come before. But she didn't know the whole story of who Emily was and what she had done. Surely she would understand. But then, if she disapproved of him courting an older woman, one such as Emily who had suffered so much already in her life, that would be another obstacle he'd have to overcome. He didn't think he could actually bear it if Ma didn't approve.

Carefully folding the letter he placed it back into the envelope, tucked it into his shirt and made his way up the narrow stairs to his bedroom. As he lay awake in bed, he could hear his Ma's gentle snoring in the next room. 'But I can't break her heart, either,' he told himself before he tried to get to sleep at last.

Chapter Fifty-one

Joe

A week had passed and still Joe hadn't written. He'd
kept it to himself and when Ma had asked him the next
morning if he'd found the letter, he couldn't find the
courage yet to talk to her about Emily.

'Yes, Ma, thank you.'

'You're not going to tell be about her, then?' she'd said.

'There's no point. It's not important any more. We were
friends in Portsmouth and we're too far away from each
other.' He'd shrugged his shoulders and left the room.

Later Ma had asked him about the letter again. 'She
must still like you, this friend, it's Emily isn't it? You never
talk about her but she must think there's a point to have
written to you.'

'I told you, it isn't going to go any further.'

His Ma just nodded and went back to her work in the
kitchen.

Joe wondered why he'd not told his Ma. 'I should have
just told her the truth. I do want to have a friendship with
Emily. I want more than friendship if I'm honest, but

I'm just afraid it won't happen without hurting Ma.' He was in the White Horse that evening with Fred. Always a bit uncomfortable about sitting in the pub knowing that most of the young men had all gone off to war whilst he was safe at home, he hoped that other farmers would be in there. He was only just old enough to join up although was aware that many young lads had lied about their ages and gone as young as fourteen. The country needed farmers, he knew, and he was a farmer now, so he was within his rights to sit here and enjoy a pint with Fred after a hard day out in the fields. All the same, some people would give him looks and tut at him behind his back. In some ways it had been easier when he was working at the asylum. That place was set away from the rest of the world. Even though near the City, it was still countryfied and a safe haven in a way.

'Should I sign up and go to the front, Fred?' he asked.

'What?' Fred spluttered over his pint. 'What's brought this on lad? You know the farm wouldn't carry on without you. We need you to keep it going. Your Ma needs you, and someone's got to feed the troops and the country. That's your role in life now, not to put yourself in front of some cannon somewhere in a foreign field.'

'Blimey, that's a lot of words from you, Fred.'

'And you'd better take notice of them,' Fred glared at him. 'I won't be repeating them either.'

'I always feel bad when I come in here, enjoying my pint when the other lads from the village are away at war.

I don't know, I sometimes think that people see me as a coward.'

'Only fools would think that, and you're no fool. No-one has said anything in my hearing, they wouldn't dare. If you have heard that then take no notice, lad. We all do our bit. Look at me,' he said. 'Old fool that I am, I should have stopped work years ago but I know I'm needed and so I just get on with it. This war won't last for ever and then I can rest and let you get on with what you're good at. That's farming, lad.'

They sat quietly supping for a while, then Fred looked at Joe again.

'What's on your mind, boy? It's not just the war, I know. You miss your Pa?'

'I suppose, although we never sat down like this to talk. No. It's not Pa but I do have a problem. It's a woman.'

'Ha! It had to be. I knew it. Felt it in me bones from the moment you came back from that asylum. Who is it? Some nurse I suppose? You have to watch those women, they'd eat a lad like you alive.'

'No. She isn't a nurse. No. It would be easy if she was a nurse. No. I don't know how to tell you.'

'You don't have to tell me.'

'But I want to. I need your advice. I can't tell Ma.'

'Oh, well I suppose you'd best tell me then.'

'Ma does know there's someone. Her name is Emily and she is...'

'Is what?'

'She's a housemaid to a lady in Southsea.'

'And what's wrong with that? Have you got her with child? Is that it?'

'No! We've never, you know, we've not done that.'

'So what is the problem then?'

'So many things, I'm not sure how to start. It feels like we'd never be able to get together. There are so many things about her that Ma would disapprove of and I don't want to break Ma's heart again after losing Pa but I don't want to break Emily's heart either.'

'Slow down, lad! All these broken hearts is too much for an old man to take. P'raps it'd help if you told me a few of these things on your list.'

'She is a good ten years older than me for one.'

'That can be a problem sometimes but if you love each other it won't matter. The only problem I can see is that she may not be able to have children.'

'She is able to have children, I know for a fact. She's already had one child.'

'Ah, is she a widow, then?'

'No, not a widow. But she was betrothed and her sweetheart was killed at the front.'

'I see.' Fred thought for a moment. 'So she has a child. How does she manage to care for a child and work as a housemaid?'

'The child was taken from her at birth. It was very cruelly done and she had an episode of madness. But she is well now.'

'Let me be clear about this. She was a patient in the asylum? Is this how you met?'

'Yes, but like I said, she is well now. No longer a patient but a hard working woman with friends who care for her.'

'How did you get to know her if she was a patient?'

'She was working in the fields on the asylum farm. I saw her in the fields. We spoke a few times. Then we danced at the asylum dance. We danced together twice. It was wonderful. But then she was sent to Brighton when the American's took over the asylum for their troops and we lost touch for a while. One of the hospital visitors, Mrs. Simpson, befriended her and has been very kind, helping her. She acted as a go-between for us and now we've been exchanging letters. Mrs. Simpson came to the farm and gave me a letter from her but I could see that Ma wasn't too happy with it. I want to see her again and I know she feels the same, but I am worried about Ma and how she'd take it.'

Fred supped his beer, deep in thought.

'What do you think I should do, Fred?'

'I been thinking about what you've said and there ain't an easy answer. What I know, though, is you won't get this sorted unless you talk to your Ma. You won't be breaking her heart if you tell her how you feel. She might think you're a fool, but I know her well, and whatever she thinks or feels, she will support you.'

'I don't know if I can tell her.'

'We all have things in our past we'd rather not have happened. Your Ma knows that and she'd do anything for you to be happy. We're in hard times and she would understand that. You have to tell her.' He drained his glass.

'Your round, lad,' he said as he pushed the glass across the table to Joe.

Chapter Fifty-two

Joe

Another week passed before he saw the chance to talk to his Ma properly. He'd tried before but each time he'd plucked up enough courage something had happened to put him off. There never seemed to be the right moment.

It was on a Saturday. The letter in his pocket was almost worn away from his constant taking it out and reading it over and over again. Sitting on the log in the yard, he spread it out and looked once again at the words, 'I hope to hear from you soon.' Joe sighed.

'That's a big sigh, Joe.'

He hadn't noticed his Ma had been standing there, watching him. He jumped as she spoke, then laughed at his embarrassment as he quickly tucked the letter back into his pocket.

'What you got there?'

'Nothing. Just a letter from a friend.'

'Joe. I know something's been bothering you for the past few weeks and you haven't been yourself since you got that letter. You can talk to me, you know. Whatever it is can't be all that bad and I might be able to help you.'

Joe said nothing. He turned away and looked across at the barn as if he was trying to find the answer written there on the wooden slats.

'I don't think you'll find the answer there in the barn, lad.' She touched his shoulder gently. 'You're still my boy and I'm always here if you need me to talk to. Me and your Dad always talked through our troubles and I do miss him. Don't shut me out of your life.'

'Sorry Ma, I know we both miss Pa. I just don't know how to start.'

'I'm making a cuppa in a minute. Come in and sit with me for a while.'

Joe watched as his Ma went into the house, her shoulders stooped, wondering still if he had the courage to tell her everything about Emily and his feelings for her. He was still thinking about it when the kitchen door opened again and his Ma called him in.

The tea was poured.

'I think this occasion calls for a slice of that seed cake I made yesterday. It's a bit dry and short on sweetness, but there is a war on, you know.' She laughed as she cut the cake and passed him a slice.

'Thanks Ma. You know I love your cake. It's a real treat, even with the sugar rations. I don't know how you do it.'

'Never mind all that. I want you to tell me what's troubling you.'

Joe munched his way through a mouthful of cake before replying.

'I don't really know how to tell you, Ma.'

'Just tell me about the letter. That's what's been troubling you by the looks of things, and then we can go on from there.

Joe's hand went to his pocket. He drew out the letter, now crumpled from his hastily hiding it there earlier. Slowly unfolding it, he spread it on the kitchen table, gently smoothing out the creases once more. The ink was starting to fade a little from all the times he had ran his fingers across the words. He looked up at his Ma, took a breath and began.

'The letter is from Emily. We care for each other, but I'm afraid you might not approve of her. We have so many things to keep us apart you see. Not just the distance, I know it's not so far in miles to Southsea from here. It's just we are worlds apart.' He kept his eyes on the tablecloth whilst he told Emily's story.

'Where is she now?'

'She's cured of the madness now and works as a maid to a lady in Southsea.'

'Oh, Joe. It's such a sad story. I won't pretend I'm not afraid for you, that you risk being hurt by this woman. You're a good-looking lad and there are so many girls here in the village who'd have made you a good wife one day. Yes, and it's true, you are too young to marry yet. We need you here on the farm as well, so courting someone who lives outside of the village would effect all of us here. The farm is your responsibility now, you know that, don't you?'

'I have no plans to leave the farm whatever happens, Ma.'

'Good, I'm glad to hear it. I hope that you were a gentleman with her. I take it your friendship started when she was still a patient at the asylum. They must have rules against that?'

'They do and of course I was always a gentleman, as you call it. Some of the patients worked in the fields. It's part of their treatment, to work. That's where we first met although we didn't talk to each other more than a few words each time. It was at the asylum dance that we met properly. We danced with each other on two occasions, that's all. I know it's not much, but there was something between us. I knew it straight away. Then Emily and many of the patients were sent away to Brighton. I thought I'd never see her again and probably wouldn't have had it not been for the kindness of Mrs. Simpson, the lady who came here to visit a while ago. I was worried about telling you about Emily. If you are against it, I won't take it any further and will stop writing to her. I don't want to hurt you.'

'Oh, Joe, you won't hurt me if you're happy. That's all a mother ever wants for her child.'

'Oh Ma, I will be happy. I don't know what I'd do without you.'

'You'd better take care though and don't rush into anything, get to know each other properly if you can, not just through writing letters. It's not such a long way to Southsea. I should like to meet her myself of course.'

'I would love you to meet her, Ma.'

'Well then, you must invite her here for a visit.'

'I will, soon. And perhaps I could take you to Southsea for a day out. We can go by train from the village, have a look at the sea and even have tea beside the pier if you like.'

'You don't need to make plans to take me on days out. I'm more than happy to stay here on the farm. Please don't worry any more about what people might think. Perhaps she has had a troubled past but I'm not one to judge people. We all have a past we would rather not talk about, believe me.'

'What does that mean?' Joe frowned at her. 'Secret past, Ma?'

'Not for your ears lad. It's all in the past, like I say. Long before I even met your Pa so nobody's business but mine.' She smiled and nodded to Joe. 'Now stop grinning like an idiot, get some paper and a pencil and write back to your young lady before she finds someone else. A woman won't wait forever, you know.'

Joe stood and hugged his Ma. 'I love you, Ma,' he said.

'Oh get on with it.' And she took up the cups and plates to the scullery where he heard her clattering about loudly.

Chapter Fifty-three

Emily

A letter came and life was wonderful at last. Joe had invited her to visit the farm and wanted her to meet his Ma. Emily read and re-read the letter, not really believing it was real. But it was real and today she was taking the train all the way to Droxford. It would take forever to get there with a change at Fareham Station but he would be waiting on the platform for her in Droxford and they'd travel from there to the farm together on the cart.

Mrs. Cartwright had been so kind, giving her an extra day off so she could stay overnight at the farm. It wasn't until she was safely on the train, sitting in the carriage, looking out at the city that she began to feel anxious. What if he saw her and realised she wasn't what he'd remembered? What if his Ma hated her? What if she'd made a mistake and Joe wasn't what she'd remembered either? They only knew each other from letters and two dances some months ago. They were still worlds apart in every way, even though in his letter he'd said that they could overcome anything. So many things to worry about and the journey was going to be long and slow.

The train pulled away from the station, steam, smuts and noise gushing through the open window. Emily stood and pushed it closed and sank back into her seat. She watched as the houses passed, the long gardens full of vegetables now as the people had been encouraged to grow crops since the war started. How much longer would this go on for, she wondered.

She watched as they passed over the bridge at Cosham and the train left the island of Portsmouth. It seemed such a long time since she'd left the island before - not since going to Brighton, and she'd been a patient then, an inmate of the asylum. Such a terrible time and one she wanted to forget. But if she hadn't been in the asylum, she'd not have met Joe. These thoughts only made her more nervous.

They passed along the coast, the sea on one side and Portsdown Hill on the other. Emily had never been this way before, had never even been to the top of the hill. She'd been told about the wonderful views from there which was the way the road went to get to the villages of Hampshire. 'That's the way Joe probably would have travelled,' she thought.

Fareham station was busy. It was market day and the platforms were filled with country folk carrying baskets of produce: apples, pears, cabbages and a wide range of other goods. Crates of chickens and rabbits were being loaded onto the train as she alighted and made her way to the other platform at the direction of one of the porters. She stepped around a group of children being herded by a tired looking woman and climbed the steps over the bridge, finally sitting down on the seat outside the ladies room and waited for the Alton train to arrive.

Eventually on the train, it was even slower than the one from Portsmouth. She was being given too much time to think and didn't want to worry whether it might all go wrong or not be what she'd hoped. Still, the countryside from the train was helping to take her mind off it. Everything was so fresh and new to her. The trees were lovely shades of brown and gold, the fields now were ploughed and being made ready for the winter crops. Emily thought about the cabbage fields at the asylum and smiled. There were some happy memories still in her mind.

They passed flashes of a river. It must be the Meon, she thought, and there on a hill was an imposing red-bricked building, another asylum. It was even bigger that the one in Portsmouth and the clock tower loomed over the front of the building. She'd heard about the Hampshire Asylum at Knowle, near Wickham. Some of the women in the ward she'd been in had talked about it. They'd hated it there, so far away from anywhere. Looking across the fields she realised how isolated it was. So much more so than the Portsmouth Asylum and she'd thought that was bad enough. She gazed at the elegant but awesome building and wondered what it must be like to be taken there, so far away. They passed Knowle Halt, the train slowing but not stopping as they passed. Emily shuddered at her memories and tried to shake off the dark thoughts that had descended. Not for the first time in the last few weeks she realised how lucky she'd been, having people around her who were quietly helping her.

Finally they arrived at Droxford. He heart was thumping far too loudly now as she took up her overnight bag and stepped from the train. The platform was empty.

Now what to do? She wondered which way she should go as she watched the train draw away, leaving behind trails of steam, the noise fading into the distance as it disappeared around the bend. Hoping that he must be on his way, Emily took a breath and walked towards the exit. There was still no sign of anyone let alone Joe. Cursing that there was not even a station master she could ask, she went through the gate.

Stepping into the lane beside the station, she looked about, her spirits dropping more and more by the minute. She would have to just sit and wait as she had no idea which direction Joe's farm was in. Perhaps she'd made a mistake and come on the wrong day? Or maybe he'd got cold feet and decided meeting again was a bad idea after all. She took his last letter from her bag and opened it. Had she made a big mistake, mis-interpreted his words somehow? But no, the letter was clear. She was invited to stay at the farm today and to travel back the next day. The date was right. But what was wrong? Why wasn't he here? She told herself to stop worrying, to be patient and wait. He would surely be on his way.

Twenty minutes came and went and still no sign of him. Looking around, Emily tried to stay calm and think it through. She needed to be logical about this. There must be a village store nearby where she could ask directions. Having come all this way she wasn't going to be put off now and had to know one way or another what was going on. The short lane from the station led to the main street so this was the way she walked. And yes, there was a little village shop just a few steps up the main road.

The shop door bell tinkled as she entered and she was faced with a smiling woman from behind the counter.

The shop keeper was a jolly-looking woman of about forty years, her grey hair tucked into a cap that could have been worn by someone from the Victorian era. Her long apron was spotless with pockets that appeared to be stuffed with pencils and a notebook on one side, and a bag of boiled sweets on the other. 'What can I do for you?' she asked.

'I'm trying to find my way to Blacklane Farm,' Emily said. 'Joe, Mr. Berry was supposed to meet me but he seems to have been delayed.'

The woman looked her over before replying. She took out a paper bag of sweets and offered one to Emily. 'Have a sweetie, dear. You look like you need something to perk you up.'

'Thank you.' Emily took a humbug from the bag and waited.

The woman popped a sweet into her own mouth before she continued. 'It's a busy time of year for farmers,' she said. 'No doubt he's been waylaid with something or other.' She stepped from behind the counter and opened the shop door. Pointing up the road, she continued. 'Take the lane beside the pub there and follow the path along the river bank. Once you reach the edge of the first field you'll see the farmhouse.'

'Thank you. I'm obliged.' Emily moved away.

'You're welcome, and good luck.'

Emily was thinking she would need all the luck in the world. Perhaps he'd got cold feet and decided she wasn't for him after all. Otherwise why would he have let her down? No doubt she'd find out one way or another and if he was leading her on then she'd give him a piece of her mind.

All of these thoughts were running around her head as she walked. The autumn leaves were damp under her feet, the colours of the countryside dazzled her eyes. She was amazed at the oranges, reds and deep greens of the meadow as she walked along the lane beside the river. Taking a deep breath of the clean air, she felt an uplifting of her spirits and told herself all would be well.

When she reached the edge of the first field, now dark with burnt stubble, she could see the farmhouse which was set in the centre of another vast field, the winding track leading to the cluster of buildings, barns and out-buildings. Blackberries were still on the hedges and she stood a while to get her bearings, then reached out to pluck a juicy berry, staining her fingers. She popped the berry into her mouth, looked at her stained fingers and for a moment wished she'd worn gloves, only to berate herself as she would now have had stained gloves and not fingers. Using the handkerchief in her reticule, she wiped at the dark stain then shrugged her shoulders. Turning towards the middle of the field and the farm, she walked.

Chapter Fifty-four

Joe

Everything had to go right today. He'd got up early with a wonderful feeling of what the day would bring. His Ma was fussing in the kitchen when he came down for breakfast.

'Don't get under my feet, lad,' she snapped. 'I've got so much to do to make the house ready for your young lady.'

'Don't fuss so, Ma,' Joe chided. 'She won't expect to find a palace. She knows we are farmers.'

'I know, but I don't want her to think we don't know how to keep a house clean. She'll be used to living in the city where life is so different. I won't have her looking down on us.'

'She won't look down on us, I'm certain of that. People who live in the city don't all live in big houses and have fancy ways. Emily is a housemaid and is used to working hard. And don't forget she's suffered and where she's been in the past. She will love the farm, I know she will.' He looked around the room. 'This will be like a palace to her, I'm sure.'

'I hope that she likes her room. I've aired the back bedroom next to mine, put clean linen on the bed and given the room a good cleaning. It's been shut up for so long and I had to dust out a few cobwebs from the corners. It's a nice room, but she'll think it too small.'

'She will love it Ma. It's a cosy room, and she's only here for one night.'

'But I want to give a good impression. First impressions matter you know. We want her to be comfortable and feel welcome, and I'm sure you want her to come back again, don't you?'

Joe helped himself to a piece of bread and taking the knife, buttered it. Sitting at the table to eat, he smiled at his Ma. 'Of course I do. At least, I think I do. We'll have to wait and see won't we? This will be the first time we'll have met outside the asylum. I want her to be comfortable but she'll have to take us how she finds us. What are you baking anyway?'

'Apple cake. Do you think she'll like it?'

'She will, I'm sure. It smells good, How could she not love it.' He got up and hugged his ma. 'Stop worrying. The house is spotless, you haven't stopped cleaning since I told you she was coming. All you need to do is be yourself, smile and make her feel welcome. That's all I ask.'

'I'm sure your probably right,' she agreed. 'Now let me get on. Go on, finish your breakfast and get on with what needs to be done in the yard before you go to fetch her. Let me get on in here. There's still lots to do.'

'I'm on my way. Just a couple of things to do then I'll come back in for a wash before I go.' Joe stood and donned his boots, slipped on his working jacket and left the warmth of the kitchen.

It was a chilly breeze that swept through the farmyard as he made his way to the barn. The plough still needed oiling, ready to turn the earth for next year's crop. The cart that had carried the hay bales to the barn needed a repair or it wouldn't be any good for the next season. These jobs would have to be done before long. He checked the stacked up hay, safely in the warm barn for the winter feed. There was little money for buying food for the horse and Joe relied on what had been stacked in the barn. All seemed well, then he noticed a wooden roof slat was flapping. Letting the rain in would spoil the hay. It would have to be repaired, and there was rain on its way by the looks of the sky.

Up on the roof with hammer and nails, Joe could see across the whole of the farm. Fields stretched away across the hills around the village. There was a good feeling in his heart knowing that this land was his and he'd successfully brought in the harvest just as his Pa had for so many years before. And today, his Emily would be coming to see him, meet his Ma and hopefully, there might be a future for them both here.

Joe shook his head. 'Don't get so ahead of yourself,' he said out loud to the sky. 'It's early days and I'm probably jumping the gun.'

Grabbing hold of the loose plank and some nails, he hammered it back into place. 'That's a good job done,' he thought and looked around once more at his home from this perfect view point. He couldn't remember afterwards what exactly happened, but felt himself sliding to the edge of the roof. He heard the hammer splash into the water-butt below and clung for a moment onto the wooden gulley before he fell with a feeling of despair as he knew this wasn't going to end well. His last thought before he passed out was that Emily would be arriving at the station soon and there'd be no-one there to meet her.

Chapter Fifty-Five

Emily

The farm looked so peaceful as she trudged along the lane towards it. Emily could feel the trepidation in her stomach, a knot she wished wasn't there. Feeling perhaps she was being ridiculous, she should turn back now before she made a complete idiot of herself. But she'd come a long way and a part of her was telling her she needed to know one way or another whether she was wasting her time. 'Just enjoy being out in the countryside,' was one of the thoughts passing through her mind as she walked. These fields did remind her of her time in the asylum. The fields she'd worked in had been filled with cabbages rather than stubble but the open spaces and the wide sky was the same. And there were crops beyond the hedge in the distance that looked as though they could be some type of vegetable.

As she neared the farm buildings there was the sound of a cockerel crowing, and then she could see chickens scratching about in the farmyard garden. But where was

Joe? He obviously wasn't on his way to meet her - she'd have met him by now. What should she do? Knock on the door of the farmhouse? Look in the barns, or just turn around and go home again. Joe could be hiding from her, not wanting to face her to tell her it was all a mistake.

She hesitated at the gate to the farmhouse kitchen garden, vegetables growing in neat rows amongst the fruit bushes, now empty of fruit. Then telling herself how stupid she was being, she opened the gate and took the last few steps to the door, bravely rapping her knuckles on the wood before she could change her mind again. She heard noises coming from inside and soon the door was opening.

Mrs. Berry was a small woman with a round face that looked as though she'd spent a lot of time in the sunshine. Her grey hair was in a neat bun, the lines on her face added to her comfortable look. Dressed in an ankle length woollen skirt in a dark shade of green, a crisp white blouse, topped with a knitted shawl, she wore a long apron over the skirt. She could have been from the last century and was looking up with at Emily with a strained smile as she took off the apron.

'You must be Emily. Please come in.' She paused. 'You are so welcome.' Looking over Emily's shoulder, she added, 'but where is Joe? Is he putting the horse away?'

Emily held back, unsure now of what to say. 'He, erm, he didn't meet me at the station, so I walked.'

'What? He made you walk all that way? I thought he'd left to collect you in good time. And you didn't pass him on the way?'

'Well, no.' Emily shifted uncomfortably, glancing around the garden. 'I wondered if he'd changed his mind but thought I'd come anyway having taken the trouble to come all this way on the train.' She straightened her back and looked at the woman as she spoke. 'I need to know either way whether I've made a mistake but I hope I've done the right thing to come. He did invite me after all.'

'Of course you are right and I'm sure you haven't made a mistake. Joe was looking forward to you being here. He never stops talking about you. But now I'm worried about what's happened to him. If you didn't pass him on the way here, maybe he's still on the farm. Excuse me my dear, but I need to go and check in the barn. That's where he was planning to be doing a few jobs before he set off to meet you.'

'I'll come with you,' Emily dropped her bag and stepped aside to allow Mrs. Berry to lead the way back through the gate and headed towards the barn.

As soon as they'd turned the corner, Mrs. Berry gave a gasp. 'The cart's still here so Joe must be around somewhere.' She called out as she ran into the barn, 'Joe. Where are you? Joe?'

Silence was the only answer. Emily looked about the barn. He could be anywhere. She shuddered as she saw the shiny metal farming implements, the plough and something with many sharp-looking spikes sticking up. What if he'd fallen onto something like that?

'He was supposed to be cleaning the plough and checking on the hay bales. I can't think where else he might have gone.'

Mrs. Berry dashed out of the barn, Emily following her close behind. They didn't need to go far. As soon as she'd turned down the side of the barn, there he was, lying awkwardly on the ground, his head had landed close to a stone kerb. Emily felt sick at the sight of him like that, a dozen terrible thoughts flying around in her mind. But his Ma took over and knelt beside him. 'Joe, Joe, wake up Joe.' She shook his shoulder gently until slowly he began to wake up.

'Got to get to the station,' were his first words. 'Emily will be there.'

'Oh, Joe,' Emily sank to her knees and took his hand. 'I'm here already. What have you done?'

He was trying to get up.

'Don't move yet,' his Ma was saying. 'You might have broken something.' But he wasn't listening to her as he struggled to a sitting position and reached to embrace Emily.

'You walked from the station? Oh, Emily, you're a sight for sore eyes.'

'You never listen to me, do you?' His ma smiled at him through her worried eyes. 'Well we'd best get you up then and into the house for something to eat. It's all ready.'

They helped him along, one on either side, taking him back to the farmhouse and into the parlour where the smell of something wonderful filled Emily's senses. It reminded her of her own Ma's kitchen before the war when everything in the world had been good.

They sat around the wooden table which was laden with cheeses, a jar of chutney and a bowl of apples. Mrs. Berry was serving large portions of meat pie onto each plate. Joe had washed himself clean in the scullery and was now looking smart, wearing a white shirt tucked into his corduroy trousers which were held up with black braces. He passed around a dish of potatoes and cabbage. Emily couldn't remember when she'd last sat down to such a spread. She'd served up enough good meals at Mrs. Cartwright's and had been allowed to have what was left after they had eaten their fill, but not prepared especially for herself, not since long before the war.

'Thank you so much for inviting me, Mrs. Berry,' she said. 'It's very kind of you.'

'You are most welcome. I know how much Joe wanted you to come and meet me and see the farm.'

Emily blushed.

'Now eat your food and then I'll show you to your room. You'll want to get settled in before you go out again. As soon as you're ready, Joe can take you outside to look around properly. Hopefully without any more unwelcome surprises. That is if you're not too sore, Joe?'

'I think I'll live,' he said. 'Luckily just a few bruises.' He looked at Emily. 'I'm just relieved that you managed to find us without me being there to meet you.'

'Thank you,' Emily said. 'And what a lovely spread. A feast.'

It was delicious. After the plates were cleared and Joe had fetched a jug of cider that he announced was home-pressed, they sat and supped their drinks to wash it all down.

'Can I help you to clear everything away?' Emily asked.

'No need. I'll show you your room now. Take your time to settle in. Joe can help me clear up.'

The staircase was narrow and dark, similar to the one in her old home, but the room was so quaint, tiny with low windows. A narrow bed half-filled the room and the windows were draped with pretty curtains in pink and yellow. A washstand stood beside the bed and was topped with a bowl and jug of fresh water for washing.

'Please make yourself comfortable in here my dear. If there is anything you need, if I've forgotten anything at all, let me know.'

'The room is beautiful, thank you.'

'I'll leave you to settle in. Come down as soon as you're ready.'

Emily sat on the bed and looked around the room. A warm glow was spreading through her. This was more than she could have dreamed of. Although the room was small, and the window was tiny, the light was shining through onto the patchwork bedspread. The bed was soft with a large feather pillow. If she hadn't been so excited to be seeing Joe, she'd have wanted to lie on the bed and enjoy the peace and comfort of the place. Instead, she unpacked her overnight things, hanging her change of clothes on the hook behind the door and placed her hairbrush and mirror on the wash stand. She was smiling when she came back down the narrow staircase and found herself back in the farmhouse kitchen. Joe was waiting for her just outside the kitchen door.

Chapter Fifty-six

Joe

Joe was more than happy. What a wonderful day this had turned out to be. Although it started with what could have been a disaster, the day improved as soon as Emily arrived. He remembered being on the roof, sliding off and feeling that everything was going to go wrong, but when he opened his eyes, it was like a dream. It had taken him a few moments to believe that he wasn't still dreaming. But there she was, exactly as he'd remembered.

He was planning to take her across the fields, to show her the beauty of all the land and they did indeed walk down the lane through the blackened stubble. Joe's leg was bruised and he couldn't help limping although he tried his best not to.

As they walked he told Emily of the crops he planned to plant for the spring. He could smell the cabbage fields even before they reached the hedge that marked the boundary. Not exactly a romantic thing but for Joe it was a strong reminder of the first day he'd ever set eyes on her, all those months ago. Suddenly Joe felt afraid. Surely she wouldn't want to be reminded of those days which must have been so hard for her. He remembered the look on her face when he'd seen her that day. A look of fear and mistrust before their eyes had met across the field. It was as if the sun had come out. His world had turned upside down that day and was never the same again afterwards.

Emily's arm was linked in Joe's and he felt her squeeze his arm. 'Cabbage fields,' she said. 'Oh I have such wonderful memories of cabbage fields.'

'You do? I do too.'

'I love cabbages,' she said and looked at him.

'Emily,' Joe started even before he could think about what he was doing. He'd spend so many hours thinking about this moment so the words slipped out so easily. 'Emily, I know it's maybe too soon, and you may not want to be a farmer's wife, and I know I am far younger than you so you will probably want to wait for a more mature man, but I love you, and I want you to be my wife more than anything. Do you think I stand a chance with you? I mean, will you marry me?'

As soon as the words were out of his mouth he wished he'd held back. How could he ever dream that she would want him?

Emily

This was the last thing that she'd expected out of this day. A day that had started so many hours ago, with hope and with fear too. When she'd arrived at the station and stepped off the train to an empty platform, she'd wondered again whether she'd made a mistake. Had she only imagined he would ever be interested in her now he was back at his home village, where all the people he knew lived? There must have been many girls of his own age he'd rather spend time with, girls more suited to a young man with a farm to run. And how would she ever fit into such a different life? She was used to living in the busy town of Portsmouth, her friends worked in factories or in the dockyard now. Yes, she had loved working on the asylum farm and although it was hard work, the hours weren't long, not as long as if the farm were your own and you had to work in the fields from dawn until dusk.

When she'd reached the farm and he was no-where to be seen, Emily'd had a bad feeling, almost like a confirmation the world was against them ever being together. Joe's Ma had greeted her with warmth but she sensed there was something there, a hesitation in wanting to welcome Emily. Had she been imagining it? By the time they'd found Joe, lying on the ground by the barn, those feelings had shifted away, replaced by love and concern for Joe, but Emily still doubted herself and had wondered whether Joe's Ma really did welcome her or was she just being polite?

The dinner had been more than she could have expected, delicious food and a warmer atmosphere, and her room was perfect. It had been his Ma's suggestion that they go out together to look at the farm, so Emily hoped that maybe she did approve of her after all. But to be proposed to? She hadn't expected that. Was it the cabbages in the sunshine that had prompted Joe to be so rash?

It had been a long time since Emily had been proposed to and the last time she'd hesitated. She'd held back and this had led her through so much that was painful and hard. Now she was being asked again and this time she didn't hesitate. Of course she knew there were obstacles between them, but obstacles can be overcome couldn't they?

She smiled at him. 'Yes, yes, yes, I would love to marry you.'

Chapter Fifty-seven

Emily

He had kissed her. Their first time and something she had never thought would happen. She wasn't expecting the proposal, not this soon and not really at all. But she had said yes and he'd taken her in his arms and kissed her. She immediately could tell he hadn't done much kissing before in his life and this made her feel awkward, wondering if he'd find her too forward, too experienced. This was just the first of the many things they needed to overcome. She tried not to let it put her off and soon relaxed, telling herself to take things as they happened, to not worry too much about their differences, however hard it might be.

As he leant towards her to kiss her again, she'd moved her head and he'd missed her lips, kissing her on the nose first. Laughing at the clumsiness, they'd stepped back and looked at each other.

'Look at us,' she said, grinning at him. 'Like a pair of children.' Then she wished she'd not said anything, thinking he would be offended at her implying he was a child. 'Sorry, I didn't mean...'

'Stop,' he said, taking hold of her again. 'I may be young, and perhaps I haven't kissed many women before, but I know what I want. And that's to kiss you. So just be quiet and come here.'

He pulled her closer and gently their lips met. This time it was right on target, his inexperience no longer a problem. Emily felt the warmth of his love flowing from his lips to spread throughout her as she relaxed into the embrace and kissed him back.

When they eventually parted, both were smiling.

'You are lovely, Emily,' Joe took her hand in his. 'I've dreamed of this for so long. I honestly can't believe you're here.'

'I know, I feel the same. But I am here, Joe. This is me and I am real.'

'What do you think of the farm? And Ma? She's been longing to meet you.'

'The farm is wonderful, Joe. I love it so far anyway. Your Ma seems very nice too. But are you sure she approves of me? She's been very kind and made me feel most welcome, but I'd understand it if she took some time to get used to someone like me being in your life, I really would. It can't be easy for her. What does she really think about me? Have you told her my background?'

'I have told her all I know, of course. I couldn't keep things from Ma. I thought she'd have a problem with us and yes, I hesitated to confide in her but when I did she was more than understanding. Of course, it might take her time to get used to you but no more than if I was bringing home a local girl or someone younger. She knows about your baby and how you had a breakdown but she wants me to be happy and her only fear is that I may be hurt, I suppose.'

'Perhaps we shouldn't tell her just yet about you proposing, do you think?'

Joe frowned and looked up at the sky. A few clouds were building on the horizon but the sun was still warm for the time of year. He turned back to Emily. 'I think I know why you're hesitating but I want to tell the whole world about us. I don't think I could keep it from Ma anyway.'

'Please Joe, I just would like to keep the happiness to ourselves for a while. I think we need to give your Ma time to get to know me and to be used to the idea of us courting first. She'll think it's too soon and I'd hate to start off on the wrong foot.'

'I don't think that's very likely but alright, if that's what you want I'll go along with it.'

'Thank you.'

'I'll show you the rabbits and chickens if you like.'

'That will be nice.'

They walked back to the farm hand in hand together. Mrs. Berry was looking out of the kitchen window as they passed. Emily noticed the woman's frown which changed quickly to a smile. She wasn't sure but maybe she'd been worrying about nothing after all.

The afternoon passed quickly with so much to see. The

rabbits were kept in the upstairs part of the outhouse, above an area that was used for keeping the chickens in at night, safe from the foxes. Emily knew about urban foxes in the town, that lived on Milton Common and drifted into the streets to forage for food whenever they could, and had heard about them destroying whole coops of chickens if they got in. Joe's chickens were allowed to roam around the farmyard during the daylight hours and were always locked in at night into the security of the farm buildings which were kept in good repair. Joe's Ma looked after the chickens and also fed the rabbits.

There was a ladder up to the floor above where the hutches stood. She counted twenty wooden oblong boxed shapes, stacked one on top of the other in two rows of ten. The fronts of half of each box were open but covered with chicken wire, the other half enclosed to give the rabbits a cosy nesting area for sleeping in. Emily watched as Joe cleaned out the dirty straw and replaced each hutch with clean bedding. He put fresh water into each and gave every rabbit a bowl of meal. Each was also given a handful of hay. Emily loved to see the rabbits munching away at their food. When Joe told her that he was breeding them for meat, she frowned.

'I can't believe we actually eat these lovely creatures,' she said.

'This is what farming life is all about,' said Joe. 'We rear cattle to provide milk but to get the cows in milk, we have to breed them. When they have male calves they're raised for the beef. It's the same with the chickens. We let some of the eggs hatch so we can raise more chicks, but the ones we don't need, we sell on at the market to other farmers. A lot of those chicks are raised for meat. Not so many are kept for eggs but at least those that are layers, they have a good life. Our chickens are happy anyway.'

'So you take the young rabbits to the market as well, do you?'

'From time to time. They breed quickly.' He showed her a hutch with a doe and her kittens, all snuggled together in a heap. 'These will be sold as soon as they are grown in about three or four months time. Some will be used for breeding, many will be going straight to the pot.'

'You get hardened to it eventually, I suppose.'

'It's been part of my life ever since I was a boy. I've never known anything else. Come down and you can meet Arthur.'

'Arthur? He's one of the farm hands?'

'You'll see.'

He led her down the ladder and out through the barn back into the sunshine. Chickens scuttled away as they walked.

'This way,' he said as he led her through a gate which opened into a walled yard with cobbles underfoot. The ground was still wet from the earlier rain and slippery. 'Mind how you go.'

Emily cautiously stepped across the yard, looking down at the ground ahead and was only drawn to a stop at the sound of a loud whinny which came from the half open stable door ahead. As they approached, the large brown head of a horse appeared over the door. As he spotted them, he lifted his head, and whinnied again, almost as if he were saying hello.

Joe laughed. 'Meet Arthur,' he said. 'I think he's fed up with not having his outing this morning. He was supposed to be taking me to the station to meet you. How are you with horses?'

'Pleased to meet you, Arthur.' She stepped forward. 'I don't have much experience with them, to be honest. I used to love seeing the milk-man's pony when they delivered in our street, but I've always been a bit scared of horses. I'm frightened I might get kicked or they might bite me. All those big teeth make me a bit wary. I've never ridden a horse either and wouldn't know how to start.'

'We don't often ride Arthur now. He's far too old. But he's good with the plough and can still pull a cart. Before the war there were more horses here but they took the younger, stronger ones to work with the army on the front line. I often wonder where they are now. I don't even know if they're still alive.'

'That's sad.'

'That's war for you I suppose. Come and say a proper hello.' He stepped closer to the door and stroked Arthur on the nose. 'Don't be afraid, he's as gently as a lamb, and he likes the ladies.'

His long nose felt soft under Emily's touch. She was sure he'd sense her fear and nip at her and it took all her courage to reach out to him. When he nuzzled into her hand she felt a kind of happiness flooding through her making her wonder what she had ever worried about. Even so, she was happy that there was a stable door between them. Those long legs and heavy feet looked far too dangerous for her to trust being that close to him without the barrier keeping them apart.

'See, he likes you. You'll soon get used to being around him, I hope.'

Emily smiled.

Chapter Fifty-eight

Joe

That evening they sat in the front parlour, the three of them beside the fire, he and Emily on the little sofa with its back to the window, and his Ma in the easy chair opposite. Although it was still warm enough during the daylight hours, the evenings had a chill about them. Ma had laid another spread of bread and cheese with a ham which she sliced for them. Joe was so proud of his Ma, she had done her best to make Emily welcome. He wondered how Emily could have thought Ma wasn't happy to meet her.

The day had been wonderful, more than he could ever have hoped for and he wanted to tell his Ma that Emily had agreed to marry him. He was sure she'd be as happy as he was. However, as Emily felt it was best they give it some time, he had agreed to go along with it. He was completely sure of his feelings but Emily of course had been right and they needed to take things a bit slowly, not just for others to get used to it but for each other too.

He looked into the flickering flames of the fire and thought about his Pa. If he hadn't become ill and died when he did, life might have been different. But then, if Pa hadn't been so ill, he'd possibly have stayed away longer and things might not have moved on to the stage they were at now. Joe probably would have still been at the asylum. He regretted the rift they'd had between them although if that hadn't happened and he hadn't gone to work at the asylum, he would never have met Emily. How strange life was. You never knew where it would take you or how things would turn out. Looking across at his Ma he wondered how she would feel when Emily was living with them here, helping his Ma in the house and garden, and helping him on the farm, being his wife.

'Penny for them,' his Ma looked back at him.

'Oh, nothing worth paying for Ma,' he said. 'I was just thinking about how life takes so many unexpected turns sometimes.'

'You are far too wise for your years, Joe. It's true, we never know quite where life will take us. Sometimes it can be almost too hard to bear, but then something changes and everything seems to go right again.'

Emily sat quietly, looking from one to the other. She felt somehow comfortable here and hoped that she wasn't just dreaming and it wouldn't all fall apart before long.

'You're very quiet, too, Emily,' Joe reached and took her hand in his. 'Are you alright?'

She squeezed his hand. 'I am more than alright. You have both made me feel very welcome and I'm having a pleasant time, more than I'd hoped for to be honest. I can't thank you enough, Mrs. Berry, for making me so at home here.'

'I'm glad you feel comfortable here my dear. I hope you'll visit us again too.'

'I would love that.'

Mrs. Berry stood up. 'I'm going to put some milk on for cocoa. Would you like some before you go to bed?'

'That would be lovely, thank you.'

Mrs. Berry smiled to herself as she left the room. 'She likes you, Emily. I've never known her offer her precious cocoa to a guest before. Although we haven't had many guests in the past few years, and never a lady friend of mine anyway.'

Emily laughed. 'So I've passed the cocoa test? I am honoured. I must say, good cocoa is scarce and has been in the past three years. Or is it four years since the war started? I've lost track of time I must confess.'

'It's over four years now. But it must be nearly over surely?'

'I hope so. Everything is upside down now. It's been so long that we've been living in this state of war and uncertainty, not knowing when or if ever we will see our loved ones again. So many people lost. I wish I could know whether I'll ever see my two brothers again. It's been so long. And I'd love to see my younger brother too, but even seeing him seems to be something out of my reach. Still,' she paused. 'There's not a lot of point in wishing and hoping. I'll have to do something about it. I'm determined not to be stopped from succeeding in what I want in the future. And the first step towards that would be to write again to Percy and attempt to see him.' She looked at Joe. 'And, of course, making plans for more times to see you, to get to know you better and to plan our future.'

Chapter Fifty-nine

Emily

Waking the next day, at first she wondered where she was, then gradually it dawned on Emily that she was in the tiny bedroom in the farmhouse. Joe was probably asleep just a few feet away from her, under the same roof. She felt so completely happy, knowing she was now sure of his feelings and his Ma had been so nice to her.

Emily scrambled out of bed and poured some of the icy cold water from the jug to the bowl beside her bed. She hurriedly washed herself and threw on her clothes. The little mirror looked back at her reflection. Her hair was tangled and needed a good brushing but she didn't want to take too much time getting tidy. The fact that she was at Joe's farm made her want to get downstairs and start the new day, to make the most that she could in the short time left before she had to go back to Southsea and her working life. Her hair was swiftly plaited and pinned up into something resembling a neat coil, even though it still looked like it would tumble down at the slightest sneeze. But she didn't care. Joe was here, in this house, his house, and she wanted to be with him for as much time as she possibly could.

They spent the morning walking around the farm again, and sat for a while on the wall looking across the fields, happy to be together, both wishing it would never end.

The ride in the cart down into the village went far too quickly and soon Emily and Joe were at the station. The train would be arriving before long. Joe helped her down from the cart. 'I'm sorry it's not a better carriage,' he said. 'You must be used to riding in hansom cabs in town.'

Emily laughed. 'Not at all. I'm used to walking everywhere or riding on the tram or the omnibus. One of the joys of living in a town is that you can walk almost everywhere and we have public transport. We have a little time left. Shall we sit here?' She indicated the bench just outside the station.

'Just give me a moment. I'll tether Arthur over there and join you.' He led the horse and cart across the road and tied the rein to the rail that had been placed there just for that purpose.

Emily sat and watched.

There were few other people about and she wasn't thinking of much whilst she watched the passing of a small family group, the children skipping along behind the mother. Then there was a woman pushing a perambulator, its big wheels bumping along the stoney path. They came to a stop beside where Emily sat. A baby. Emily tried not to do it but couldn't resist leaning in to look at the child.

Her heart seemed to stop for a moment. Surely she was imagining things. Was it her own little baby? How could she think that? She'd only seen him fleetingly, long enough to decide to call him Billy after his father, but not long enough to be able to recall really what he looked like. But she'd seen other babies since leaving the asylum and not felt like this. Babies changed so quickly didn't they? Her's would have been five months old by now and not look anything like he did at birth. Even so, there was this strong feeling that they were connected. She was drawn to him.

Emily realised the woman was staring at her. 'I'm sorry, I don't mean to be rude. Your baby is beautiful. What's his name?'

'His name is Thomas. We've named him after his grandfather.'

'Thomas. That's a nice name. I'm sorry if I seem strange, but he reminds me of a child I knew. I know that will sound silly, all babies look alike really don't they?'

'Not at all.' She looked closely at Emily. 'Are you feeling quite well? You look rather pale.'

'I think so. Thank you, but I feel perfectly well. Please excuse me.' Emily stood and moved across the street towards Joe.

'What is it?' Joe took her arm and held her close. 'You look like you've seen a ghost or something.'

'I'm alright. But the train will be here in a short while. Can we wait on the station platform?'

'Of course. Are you sure you are well?'

'Perfectly.'

It was difficult saying goodbye but they made promises to see each other again soon. Joe had told his Ma that he'd take her to Southsea for an outing and they would meet with Emily for tea near the seafront. Emily would have preferred to have Joe all to herself but they needed to include his Ma as well, to get her used to seeing them together. She realised their courting wouldn't be straight-forward, with the distance between them now. It would have been easier, so much easier, had Joe been living and working in Portsmouth, or if she was living in Droxford near the farm. Then they could have seen each other more frequently, possibly even every week. As it was, they'd have to be patient and rely on writing to each other. Then she thought about all those sweethearts who were separated by the war and scolded herself, counting her blessings.

Sitting on the train, watching the countryside pass by and the steam from the engine sometimes clouding the view, Emily's thoughts went back to the baby she'd seen. It had shaken her to the core. She asked herself why she'd reacted in the way she did. Perhaps it was because it had brought back to her the pain of having her child taken away. She'd always tried to push memories of him away, sometimes even denying to herself he'd existed in the first place, knowing she had scarce chance of ever seeing him again. She'd blocked him out of her thoughts and the mad-ness had taken over. Maybe this little baby had just opened the wounds she'd sealed and allowed the painful memories back into her life. It was too much to bear.

As the train moved further away from Droxford, so Emily tried to push away such thoughts from her mind. It was too much of a co-incidence and was probably brought on by the feelings of love and hope in her heart after seeing Joe.

Chapter Sixty

Joe

After waving her goodbye from the platform, Joe walked back to where Arthur stood waiting patiently for him with the cart. He wondered about what had upset Emily. She'd been talking to the young woman with the baby. His thoughts shifted to Emily's own child. That must be it. Seeing the baby would have upset her, he should have realised. He turned to look at the bench where Emily had been sat. The woman had gone of course. Joe tried to recall if he knew who she was but couldn't think of anyone in the village who'd had a baby in the past few months. He decided that he would ask his Ma as soon as he got home and moved his thoughts onto his future with Emily.

There was so much catching up to do on the farm, with him spending time over the past day with Emily, so it wasn't until supper that he had the chance to talk about it.

'There was a woman at the station this morning with a baby. She spoke to Emily while I was seeing to Arthur and something about her upset Emily. I guessed it was seeing a young baby but she said there was nothing wrong when I asked her. Do you know of a mother in the village with a baby?'

'That would be Mrs. James. She lives behind the schoolhouse, in that little cottage there. She's new to the village so you won't know her.'

'And she has a small baby?'

'She arrived with the child at the end of June. There was a bit of gossip about her, to be honest. I heard that her husband was a cousin of the schoolmistress but he's away in Belgium. He's a doctor apparently working on the front line with the wounded. But no-one has seen him yet, not that that's unusual these days. Only people like to gossip, don't they. There was talk that she didn't even have a husband and the child was fatherless, if you know what I mean.'

'Really Mother? But that's only gossip. You don't know?'

'Of course it is, and I wouldn't judge her if it were true anyway. Only, I was sure I'd seen her around the village earlier in the year and could have sworn she wasn't even showing. There was no bump there at all. It did cross my mind the child may not have been hers. I didn't say anything to anyone though. It's none of my business after all.'

'You say her husband is a cousin of the schoolmistress? Miss Woods? My old school teacher. I might ask her about the woman.'

'Why would you want to do that? What on earth are you thinking?'

'Nothing. Perhaps you're right. I shouldn't go prying into things. Still, I can't help wondering.'

'Wondering what? What's going on in your head?'

'I'm not sure. It did cross my mind that it's odd Emily had such a reaction, that's all. I'm sure it's nothing. She couldn't possibly have remembered what her own baby looked like after all these months, she only saw him briefly before they took him away.'

'You're not seriously thinking it might be her own child are you?'

'No, of course not. It's just, strange, that's all.'

'Well just be careful, Joe. You don't want to get into trouble do you? Prying into other people's business is not right.'

'I will be careful, don't worry.'

The next day he was walking the cows back to the fields to graze when he saw Annie, the dairy-maid, in the distance. He made up his mind to speak to her and once the herd was safely in the field he walked across to the dairy which was shared with the neighbouring farm. Annie was an old friend from his schooldays. She greeted him with a smile.

'Hello there Joe, what brings you here? I haven't seen much of you lately.'

'Hello Annie. I've been busy on the farm and actually I have a bit of news too.'

'I know. You're courting at last.' She grinned. 'I'd thought once it would be you and me, but I can see that's never gonna happen. And anyway I'm sweet on Johnny.'

'I knew you always had a soft spot for him. Good for you. How's it going?'

'We're getting along well enough,' she said. 'You never know, he may even pluck up the courage to ask me to marry him before long.'

'That's good news. Let me know when it happens won't you. Johnny is a good man.'

'He is, he's a fine man. Since he came back from France, he's changed a bit but he's much better than he was when he first got home. I know it's wrong, and I shouldn't say it, but I'm glad he got his injury and was discharged.'

'How is he coping with it? Losing an arm must be a terrible thing. It makes me feel ashamed I haven't joined up when I hear about men like Johnny.'

'He's coping well, losing an arm is better than losing your life or your mind. That happens to too many young men. You'd be surprised what you can do with only only arm.' She laughed.

'Really? I'm not sure I want to know. Anyway, I'm glad he's coping.'

'He is, and I'm there to help him too. Come on, tell me all about what's happening with you. What's your news?'

'Yes, I am seeing a young lady who lives in Southsea. It's a long way I know, although not as far as Europe. She came to meet Ma and stayed overnight. They got on well, I think. I'm going to take Ma to Southsea for a trip sometime soon so we can meet up with her again. In the meantime we're going to write to each other and she may get the chance to visit us again soon, God willing.'

'That's wonderful. I hope it all goes well for you.'

'Actually, I wanted to ask you if you knew anything about Mrs. James who lives in the cottage behind the schoolhouse? She's related to Miss Woods, I think.'

'Mrs. James? She's the one with a baby, isn't she? Just turned up one day and had the baby with her.'

'That's her. Have you met her. My Ma told me that she'd seen her around the village before she moved in, earlier this year, I mean.'

'I don't know her really. Although now you mention it, I think she was around at Easter. Wasn't she staying with Miss Woods? Yes, I'm sure she was. But I don't remember her being pregnant.'

'Oh, well, don't worry about it, I'm probably over-thinking things.'

'Why are you so interested in her anyway?'

'No reason really. Just forget I asked.'

Annie stood. 'I have to get on,' she said. 'Actually, I do remember there being some talk about Mrs. James in the post office. She came from Portsmouth apparently. Or was it Winchester? Sorry Joe, that's not much help really, but I can't understand why you're interested in her.'

'I'm not really, just forget I asked.'

'Alright, if that's what you want. Better get back to work then.' And she walked away and entered the dairy.

Joe sat for a while wondering if he'd done the right thing in mentioning Mrs. James and the baby at all.

Chapter Sixty-one

Emily

The next week passed quickly enough with each day blending into the next. During the day it was easy to work with thoughts of Joe and herself and their future to dream about. She remembered the moment they stood in the field and he'd asked her to marry him. And then the first kiss. Thinking of those moments made her feel warm and loved. But the face of the child kept forcing itself into her mind too.

She was so tired by the time she crawled into her bed and hoped that sleep would come easily, but it didn't. As soon as she'd blown out the candle and snuggled under the covers, thoughts of the child pushed their way into her head. Each time it was like a new wound being opened.

She couldn't stop wondering. What if it was her own little Billy? What if Kate had given her baby away to that woman? It was certainly possible. Droxford was far enough away from Southsea for the child to have been taken without much risk of Emily ever finding out. Maybe it was just a strange twist of fate that Emily had even found herself going there. And a baby is a baby, they all look the same, don't they? How could she even think this one could be her own? Emily told herself over and over again she was being fanciful, imagining things that weren't likely, that she hadn't properly accepted her baby had been taken, and she'd never see him again. During the daylight hours, she made herself believe it was all her imagination, but at night, in the dark, the thoughts would not leave her alone.

She wrote to Joe. A long letter thanking him and his Ma for making her so welcome, describing the journey home on the train and how life was for her back in Southsea. She had walked to the seafront on her half day and sat and looked at the sea. She wrote about looking out to the Isle of Wight and seeing dolphins leaping in the waves. Joe would love to hear about those, with him living so far from the ocean. She wrote about looking forward to seeing him again, and how nice it would be for him to visit with his Ma.

What she didn't mention was the baby she'd seen in the perambulator outside the station, nor the young woman who was with him. It was best not to mention that again to him, as he would only think she was going mad again. But in truth she longed to talk to him about her thoughts, even if it was just a fancy of hers, it was so hard holding it inside, not being able to talk to anyone about it. Her biggest fear was of having another breakdown and being taken back to the asylum so she tried her best to keep sane and to focus on her work and her future with Joe. She told herself she must leave the past behind.

Meeting up with Mabel again at the pier on a Wednesday afternoon, she hadn't meant to talk about it. It had been so long since she'd seen her friend and it was a pleasure just to spend time together, hearing all about Mabel's stories working in the Post Office.

'I don't know what's going to happen to my job when this war is over, Emily. It does worry me.'

'Won't you be glad when the men are all home and things start to go back to normal?'

'I will be glad about that, of course, but they'll want their jobs back won't they? Then what's to become of me?'

'I know it's what you said before, but I expect you'll soon find a young man and get married and do what women always did before the war, have a family?'

'You used to say that was the last thing you wanted. To be tied to a man with kids.'

'I know, but things have changed since then. I've been through so much in the last year, I was bound to have a different view on things.' She took a spoonful of sugar and stirred it into her tea.

'What was it like in there?' Mabel shifted in her seat, leaning forward.

'At first, it was a nightmare. Only I don't remember much of it. I don't think I want to remember either. Later, I suppose I just got used to it. You can get used to anything I suppose.'

'I can't imagine what it must have been like.'

'You don't want to either. Are we having cake?'

'Yes, cake would be nice. My treat though.'

They ordered the cake and sat in thought for a while, Emily staring at the windows, unable to see through the condensation. The sound of gulls was muffled through the glass and rain beat against the panes. She shivered.

'You don't have to tell me about it,' Mabel finally said.

'I don't mind. It's just there are so many gaps in my memory. I think I've shut out the worst of the times. We had to work whilst in there. You didn't just sit in a ward doing nothing. Even when I didn't go off the wards to work, there were jobs to do. The place wouldn't run without the inmates all doing their bit. I did a lot of sewing and cleaning on the ward. Then they put me in the laundry. I had to do the ironing. Masses and masses of sheets, and dresses, shirts, everything. It was hard work, hot, heavy work. At first it was alright, I don't mind hard work and the people in the laundry were nice enough. The laundress was quite kind to me actually and took a letter to Percy. But then she left and a new head laundress started working there and we didn't get on.'

'What happened?'

'Nothing. I got moved.' She frowned and looked away.

'Nothing? They wouldn't move you for nothing would they?'

'You have no idea what they could do.' She looked up. 'Here's the cake. Can we change the subject please?'

They were on their second pot of tea when Mabel broached the subject again. 'You said you got used to it. I suppose things must have got better after you left the laundry?'

'Yes, after a while, I was given a job working on the farm group. We were taken out into the fields every day and were given light work to do. It was still quite hard, hoeing and weeding mostly, but was nice to be out in the fresh air and sunshine. Well, sometimes it was in the rain. I didn't mind, it was a relief to be out of the building and the noise of the ward. Some of the women were nice. I didn't make many friends to be honest but I did make one special friend. Her name is May. I've lost touch with her now. I don't expect to see her again. Her husband is a naval officer. A little out of my class, you know?'

'I expect being in a place like that is a leveller of classes? But different once you leave.'

'It is rather like that. When she was discharged she said she'd like us to continue being friends but I can't see it happening and I haven't heard from her since. We'd promised to write but it all seemed a waste of time. I don't see the point of writing to her. Why would she want to write to a housemaid like me.'

'I suppose you're right. It seems a shame though.'

Emily shrugged her shoulders. 'There is something else I was going to tell you.'

'Really? Is it a young man?'

'How did you guess? Is it that obvious?' Emily smiled and lifted her eyebrows.

'Well, it had to be didn't it? We've been sitting here through two pots of tea and cake and you haven't mentioned a man yet, what else would it be? Come on, tell me all.'

'I'll start from the beginning. When I was working in the fields there was a young man, a farm worker at the asylum. We weren't supposed to talk to each other and said very little. It was mainly just looks and smiles at first. Then we danced together at the asylum dance.'

'They have dances in the asylum?'

'Yes, for the patients. Lots of other people come as well, mainly local dignitaries, and the staff, of course. It's a privilege for the patients to be allowed to go to the dance and I was lucky enough on two occasions. The young man was there and we danced together, under the eyes of the nurse attendant of course. Then he left the asylum and I didn't think I'd ever see him again. Any relationships between staff and inmates is forbidden but a kind hospital visitor, Mrs. Simpson, helped by taking letters to and fro for us. She probably would have got into quite a lot of trouble had she'd been found out. She's been a good friend and has visited me at Mrs. Cartwright's house. In fact, it was Mrs. Simpson who helped me get my position back too.'

'So, what's this young man called? Tell me about him?'

'His name's Joe. He had to leave the asylum as his Pa died and he went back to work on his farm in Droxford. I've been to see him there and met his Ma, too.'

'That's wonderful. Has he proposed yet?'

'It's early days and, well, yes, he has and I've said yes but we want to keep it to ourselves for a while. It's been a bit of a rush and we don't want people to think we're being hasty.'

'Emily, that's wonderful news. You've sat there all this time and said nothing! I don't think anyone would think you were rushing things. Not these days with the war still on. Although I've heard rumours it'll be over soon.'

'I hope so, although they've been telling us that since it began. Anyway, there are other reasons to wait a while. He's much younger than me. I think people will frown on our match, not just because of the age difference. There's also my history, with a label of madness upon my name. My family have disowned me, I have so much shame in my past.'

'Nonsense, Emily. You mustn't think like that about yourself. You said you've met his Ma. How did you get on with her? Does she know your past?'

'She does. Joe told her all about me. I was afraid she would be against me but she was so kind when we met. We just don't want to put too much on her yet. She only lost her husband a short while ago. It's all so new and raw still. She doesn't show it but I think she must find everything quite difficult.'

'Well, I am sure it will all turn out well in the end. I am very happy for you.'

'There's something else. I've been in a turmoil over my lost baby. I saw a woman in Droxford who had a child and I started imagining that he might be my own babe.

You know they took him away from me on the day of his birth so it's possible, if unlikely. I just can't get it out of my mind.'

Mabel reached for her hand. 'You need to forget all about that, Emily. Wondering and longing for what is past won't do you any good.'

'Perhaps you're right.'

'It's stopped raining. Let's walk to the common.'

Chapter Sixty-two

Emily

Emily tried to forget but couldn't stop herself seeing the face of the child in the perambulator. His sweet face, with the dark lashes on his cheeks and then the deep brown eyes that had met hers as she'd gazed at him was a sight she couldn't put out of her mind. She knew thinking this way was driving her nearer and nearer to madness again. There was only one way to face up to this. She made up her mind to find out once and for all so on the following Sunday she made her way along Aylesbury Road to her old home.

How strange it felt walking along this street again. So much had happened in the short time since she'd live here. She had been through so much and had lost so much too. As she neared the house, Emily felt fear rising within her like an old enemy. Was she doing the right thing or should she do as Mabel had advised, and leave it all in the past? A part of her felt this was the right thing to do, but it was no good, something was driving her on to try and get to the bottom of where her child might be.

Knocking on the front door felt wrong but it also wouldn't be right to just enter as though she still belonged in the house. She knew she no longer belonged and doubted if she would ever again. They'd always kept the door unlocked during daylight hours so she could have just gone in and surprised her Pa but something held her back. She knocked and waited.

It was her Pa. On seeing her, immediately his face lit up, but a wary look shifted to his eyes almost straight away.

'Aren't you going to ask me in Pa?' Emily stood on the doorstep, waiting.

'Emily.' He hesitated a moment more before opening the door wide. She stepped into the hallway. 'Here, give your old Pa a hug,' he said as he reached for her and took her into his arms.

The old familiar smell of him, the warm feeling of his strength as he held her was enough to make Emily want to cry. A few tears did flow, but she wiped them away, determined not to let him see her upset. She stepped back and smiled.

'I'm so glad you came by,' he was saying. 'Come through and sit down.' He led her through to the back parlour where the fire was lit. It was cosy but there was no sign of Kate, nor Percy. 'Kate's visiting her friend, Ruby.' He looked away. 'You might know her, Ruby Ledbetter.'

Emily felt cold suddenly. 'Ruby Ledbetter. I certainly do know her. I'd rather not be reminded of her though if I'm honest and I don't think she would want to be reminded of me either. I suppose you heard what happened, did you?'

'I did, but didn't believe you could have done something so bad.' He looked away again then his eyes were back on hers.

'You can't imagine what life was like in there Pa. And I don't want to remember it either. Where's Percy? Is he in?'

'No, he spends a lot of time at his pal's house, or they go to the park to play football. I don't see much of him other than in the shop. He's only a lad and needs to be outside as much as possible. He might be home soon, but doubt he'll show his face before dark. Did you want to see him?'

'I would have liked to but that's not why I came. I came to see you, of course, but I had hoped to speak to Kate.'

'You two parted on bad terms. Have you come to make amends with her?'

Emily hesitated to answer. Her hand resting on the arm of the sofa, she felt the roughness of the material and remembered what it had been like sitting here with her own Ma before the whole world had gone wrong. There was a loose thread which had been hanging there like that since she was a child herself. She'd fiddled with the thread when she'd talked to her Ma about Billy and now felt stupid when she thought about the things she'd said then about not wanting to get married or to be saddled with a husband and children. How she wished she could turn the clock back now. But then, she wouldn't have met Joe if things had been different.

'Pa, I don't want to live with a rift between you and me, and want you to be happy and for us all to be like a family again. I accept that being with Kate is what makes you happy. But I spent a lot of time in the asylum trying to block out the pain of losing you and Billy and of course, losing my child. I think shutting it all out helped to make me mad. It was the only way I could get through it at the time. Now although I'm well, and I'm making a new life, there are things I cannot forget.'

'I want us all to be happy, too. But Kate...'

'I need to talk to Kate about my child. Or you. Do you know where my baby was taken, Pa?'

The look on his face was one of disappointment but also fear. His eyes wouldn't meet hers as he spoke. 'I don't think it's a good idea to go searching for something you can never have back, Emily. Don't ask me, please don't.'

'I haven't got any choice Pa. I can't move forward to any kind of future until I know where he went and if he's happy and safe. You can't deny me that. I am his Mother and it's my right.'

'You don't have any legal rights, you know that.'

She glared at him as she picked at the thread on the sofa. 'I am well aware of my legal rights Pa, and any rights that were taken from me when I was at my lowest point. I'm sorry, I don't mean to upset you but he is your grand-child after all. I only want to know, then I can rest.'

Pa stood up and moved to the door. 'I don't know Emily. Even if I could help you, I just don't know. It was Kate who organised everything.'

'Where are you going, Pa?'

'The kettle will have boiled. I was making some tea. Would you like some?'

She sighed. 'I suppose. I'll come and help.'

'No need. Just wait in here and I'll bring it.' He left the room and closed the door behind him.

Emily stared into the empty fire-place, thinking about what to do next. Should she wait and try to speak to Kate who would surely be returning soon? The woman had no right to keep from her the whereabouts of her child. Emily was convinced the woman hadn't gone through the proper procedures for putting a child up for adoption, but if she had Emily would want to see the paperwork, if only to put her own mind at rest that her son was safe and happy in a good home. Surely no one could deny her such a simple thing?

Still mulling over these thoughts, she hadn't noticed the front door opening and then the parlour door. She jumped as she heard her name being spoken.

'Emily, child.' It was Kate standing there, looking down at her with a look of disdain on her face. 'Whatever are you doing here? Have you seen your father?'

Emily stood and faced Kate. 'Hello Kate, she said. 'Pa's making the tea, but I've actually come to see you really. I wanted to ask you something.'

Kate frowned. 'Ask me what? I thought we had said all we were ever going to say to each other.'

'Yes, but that was when I was unwell and unable to speak out for myself. Even if I had, you wouldn't have heard me nor taken the trouble to listen. No, I may be wrong to try but I need to know what happened to my baby and it appears you're the only one who can answer that question. I'm hoping you will find it in your heart to take pity on a mother and help me.'

'You're asking the wrong person.' She moved into the room and stood with her back against the fireplace. 'You seem to be a little upset. Are you sure that you have fully recovered from your madness? Should we be looking to arranging more treatment for you?'

Emily smiled. 'I can assure you I am quite well, Kate. I would like some answers that's all. I am very well, in fact. I am no longer under the care of the asylum, having been discharged as fit and sane some time ago. I came here to visit my Pa but also to find out something about my child. I only want to be reassured that he is safe and well. Surely you, as a mother yourself, can understand and respect that. Or are you so hard-hearted?'

'I am sorry you think I'm hard-hearted, as you say. Everything I did was for your own good. And for the good of your Pa of course. I could see you were breaking his heart and he was making a mistake in supporting you keeping the bastard.'

'Don't call my baby that! He would have been loved and if Billy hadn't died, we'd have been married soon enough.'

'But Billy did die, didn't he? You can't change that. Your life would have been miserable, bringing him up without a father.'

'And my life was so much better in the asylum after you took him away, wasn't it? Although you wouldn't have known what my life was like then would you, since you stopped visiting me straight away and Pa only came once, and that was to tell me I wasn't welcome in my own home.'

'It was for the best for everyone.'

'Like it was for the best when you beat me with the poker?' She stopped talking, realising that the conversation wasn't going at all how she'd hoped. 'Look, Kate, I'm sorry. Please can we be friends, draw a line under the past for Pa's sake if not for mine? I didn't come here to upset you or make things worse between us. I only wish to know if my baby is safe and to know where he might be now. I have no intention of fighting to get him back if he is well looked after and happy. Please, Kate.'

Kate stood, her back rigid. Finally, she spoke. 'Very well. Let us start again. I love your father and don't want to see him upset by you. I will be civilised whilst you are here, I can't be dishonest and say I am glad to see you, but if it makes him happy I will welcome you into his house. But only as a guest you understand. This is no longer your home. You're a grown woman now and must make your own way in the world.'

'I understand. And the baby?'

'That will be difficult. I'm not sure if it would be the right thing to do, however much you pester me. I will have to think about it.'

'That is all I can ask. Thank you.'

Chapter Sixty-three

Joe

Ma was calling from the farmhouse door. 'Joe, the war's ended! Come in and listen. It's on the radio. They stopped the fighting at eleven this morning. Oh thank the Lord.'

It was hard to believe. The past four years had seemed more like ten. All of Joe's years in growing up were through the war, he was only thirteen when it had started. He'd seen so many of the older men he knew go away and some of them would never come home. There was so much to celebrate but still so much sadness too.

'You should go to the pub and celebrate tonight.'

'I'm not sure Ma, I feel bad that I never went. I know you say I shouldn't but I do and so do others in the village. It'll be hard facing some of them. The ones who've lost their boys and who'll never come home.'

'Don't think like that. You've done your bit and you're still only a lad anyway. We couldn't have managed the farm without you these few months and I'm sure the work you did at the asylum was just as essential too.'

'Maybe you're right. Still I hate it when people give me dirty looks. It does happen you know.'

'You just have to ignore it, Joe. You deserve to celebrate as much as anyone else.'

'I suppose. It would be good to have a pint.'

'Well as long as you don't have too much. I don't want you rolling in here and being sick.'

'Oh, Ma, I won't.'

'You'd best go and finish off out in the stable then and get washed up. I'll serve supper early so you can get down there before they've run out of beer.'

'That'll be the day. There's always plenty of beer what with the brewery just down the road.'

Fred was in the front bar, drinking a pint with Johnny Taylor, Annie's young man. It was strange watching him holding his pint in his right hand; his left sleeve was empty and pinned to his jacket. Seeing him like that made Joe hesitate, feeling awkward that here he was, fit and able-bodied, standing in front of Johnny, who had experienced the war and all it's horrors and had lost an arm. Joe couldn't imagine what life would be like for him if he was maimed in such a way. It would be almost impossible to be able to continue with farming, he thought. Although Annie had said he was getting used to it and managing to do most things with just the one arm.

Fred called across to Joe. 'Hello lad, you going to join us?'

'Evening Fred. Johnny.' He stood at the bar and ordered himself a pint. 'Another pint you two?'

'Thanks, I will,' they both answered in unison. Johnny put down his pint and thumped Joe on the back. 'How are you doing on the farm, Joe? Glad the war is over, eh?'

Joe knew he was going red in the face, feeling ashamed again. 'The farm's doing well, thank you. But yes, it's good to know the men will be coming home. I'm sorry about your arm, too. It must be hard.'

'This old thing? I manage well enough. I'm lucky aren't I? I came back and I've got a good woman now. Yes, I believe I am very lucky.'

'Annie is a good woman,' Joe agreed. 'I saw her only a few days ago, well, last week it must have been. We were talking about that woman who moved into the cottage behind the school. She'd got a child and we were wondering about him. Whether it was her own or maybe someone else's?' He stopped and looked bashful. 'I don't mean to gossip about her, it's not what I would normally do. I just wondered, that's all. I just wondered because someone told me she hadn't seemed to be pregnant and then suddenly she has this child.'

Fred spoke. 'Is this to do with your sweetheart, Joe? Your young lady, that came to see you and your Ma recently?'

The new pints arrived on the bar and Joe took a long drink from his, then passed the other two to his companions.

'Alright,' he said. 'I'll come clean. It's a strange thing but anything can happen I suppose in these times. My Emily, she spoke to Mrs. James when she was waiting at the station and was convinced she'd seen the child before. She told me he reminded her of her own baby that was lost. It may have been she was just being fanciful, her imagination taking over. I didn't take any notice at the time. But then I heard that Mrs. James, who had been seen around the village earlier this year and didn't look like she was with child, had moved in with the baby. She's related to Miss Woods at the school. I wondered if I should go and speak to her about it but don't know how to start. What could I say to her without offending her?'

'You should just ask her straight out,' said Fred. 'Why beat about the bush?'

'It's not the kind of thing you can talk about to a woman,' Johnny took a swig of his beer. 'In fact, I can't really believe we're talking about this so openly. It's not the done thing is it? Talking about women's business. I don't think your Emily would want us to know about her past and the lost baby either.'

'I wouldn't normally. I do agree with you, but I don't know where to start and need to try and help Emily somehow. She's having trouble getting over it and I don't think she will until she knows for sure what happened to the child. What should I do, Fred? You've been around for a long time. What would you do?'

'I'd probably just go and talk to Mrs. James. I'd go and speak to her, ask her outright. Tell her what I think, but that's not necessarily going to be the right thing to do. We're still in uncertain times aren't we? Anyway, get that pint down you lad, you need to catch up with us. Come on, we are supposed to be celebrating.'

Chapter Sixty-four

Joe

It didn't take Joe long to find out more. The next afternoon, Annie wandered into the farmyard, looking for him.

'Afternoon, Annie. Don't usually see you at this time of day.'

'Hello Joe, I've got some news for you. I've been to see Mrs. James, did a bit of nosing around.'

'Really? Come and sit down for a while.' He led her into the barn. 'Ma's in the kitchen but we can talk out here if you like. It's a bit cold but it might be best not to let Ma know just yet.'

'I'm used to the cold. It's warmer than the dairy anyway.'

'So, what have you found out? What's this Mrs. James like?'

'She seems to be nice enough but there's something about her that I'm not sure about. The way she was with the babe.'

'What do you mean?' Joe frowned.

'The baby was crying when I arrived and I know babies cry a lot, especially at that age. It was hungry I guessed but Mrs. James didn't seem to know how best to nurse it. She said her milk had dried up and she was feeding the baby with a bottle. Not the best of feeds for such a young baby, but I suppose if she had no milk of her own there wouldn't be a lot of choice.'

'I've never heard of a baby being fed with a bottle before.'

'Well, Joe, I don't expect you to have any experience in feeding a baby. Bottle feeding is more common than you'd think. Maybe not so much in village life out here in the country, but if a woman has to go out to work then she might have to use one. If you leave your child to be cared for whilst you're out at work, the babe needs to be fed somehow.'

'I don't know of any women with children who work. I don't know of many women with children at all actually.'

'Anyway, that's neither here nor there. The point is, she didn't seem to be natural around the child. And she was awkward around me, too. I offered to help her but she snapped at me and wouldn't let me near the babe.'

'It must be hard having a child so young and being on your own. Her husband's away isn't he?'

'So I've been told. But that's another odd thing. There were no photographs of him anywhere that I could see. Everyone has at least one wedding portrait, don't they? And no pictures of him at all in uniform. I did ask her how her husband was, had she heard from him lately, was she expecting him home soon now the war was over, but she managed somehow not to answer my questions. She busied herself with the child, and when I asked again, her face was flushed.'

'Did she say anything?'

'Eventually, after a long pause, she said that he wouldn't be coming back. That he'd been posted to India of all places. I don't know, but somehow I didn't believe her.'

'Why should she lie about something like that?'

'I know you'll think me fanciful but I'm almost certain there is no Dr. James. I think she may have invented him, or maybe there is a Dr. James but she isn't his wife? That sounds shocking doesn't it?'

'It does. But I thought that this Dr. James was a cousin of Miss Woods. Surely she can't have invented him. We would have heard wouldn't we?'

'You'd have thought so, and yes, I'd heard he was a cousin of our old schoolmistress as well. Perhaps we should ask Miss Woods about him? Get to the bottom of it.'

'Maybe, although I'm not sure how to go about it without upsetting her.' I don't want people to think I'm prying.'

Annie stood up and walked to the barn door. She turned and walked back before continuing. 'That's not all. I wanted to distract Mrs. James so asked for a glass of water. She hadn't offered me any tea, which I thought odd in itself but wondered if she hadn't wanted to leave me alone in the room with the child. She was reluctant, it seemed, to even leave the room to fetch the water but it did give me a few minutes to have a close look at him.'

'And? What was he like?'

'A bonny child indeed, although by that time he'd quietened down and was looking up at me. His eyes were glazed. I told myself that it was normal for his age, but he didn't seem able to focus on me even though he was looking up at me. I uncovered him to allow his arms to be freed of the tight blanket and noticed dark shadows on his arms. I think they were bruises. Then the woman came back in the room. She looked alarmed that I was so close to the crib and spilt the water in her haste to get across the room.'

'You think she's been harming the babe?'

'I don't know. It could be anything, only she seemed so agitated seeing me there. I moved back to my chair and she gave me the water, then she sat down glaring at me. I wasn't sure what I could say to her, to be truthful, but I felt all wasn't as well as it should have been.'

Joe was now on his feet and pacing up and down. 'This is not good,' he said. 'But what can we do? We're still no nearer to finding out whether the child might be Emily's. Am I being ridiculous to even think it might be possible?'

'I think it's possible. In fact, I did ask her some more questions about herself and the baby. I asked her how she'd come to live in Droxford and she told me the story, and I believe it might be a story, of her husband wanting her to live near his cousin so she could help, that the house had come up just at the right time after he'd been called up and the child had been born in their old home which was in Petersfield. She said they had to move out of their old home as it was attached to the local hospital and was needed for the new superintendent now that her husband was leaving.'

'All of that sounds unlikely but it could be true I suppose. Why would a hospital evict a young mother from her home whilst her husband was away at war?'

'That kind of thing probably happens more that you realise. I don't know, we live fairly isolated, sheltered lives out here in the countryside, but the world can be a hard place can't it? You must have seen more of this, living in the town, and working in the asylum.'

'I suppose you're right.' Joe stopped pacing and looked back at Annie.

She went on, 'I also asked her if she had any other family. Perhaps someone who would come to stay and help her. She told me she had no other family. It all seemed so vague and left me with an uncomfortable feeling altogether.'

'What else can we do. I feel I can't leave it at that. What if she's harming the child? Should we do something?'

'I don't think we can assume she's harming the child. We don't have any evidence apart from the bruising and children do bruise easily. I think maybe a good way would be for me to befriend her if I can, and keep an eye on the child, see if anything else happens or, I don't know really. I don't feel I can walk away and ignore my suspicions now but if we start to accuse her of anything, she's most likely going to run away, or at least keep the baby hidden from any prying eyes.'

'It is frustrating but I agree. I don't want to upset her. I'm very grateful to you for wanting to help me in this. You're a good friend, Annie.'

'You'd do the same for me. Anyway, it's for the child's sake as much as for anyone. I couldn't bear to see a baby suffering. Not only that, but I think Mrs. James is struggling as well and if I can help another woman, I will. I don't think she's a bad sort, but there is definitely something not quite right there, I'm sure of it.'

Joe sat down on the bench again. 'I'm wondering about going to speak to Miss Woods as well. Do you think she'd talk to me? Like you say, I don't want to frighten off Mrs. James, but if Miss Woods knows something more I think it's worth trying to talk to her.'

'I did think about that myself, but it would be better coming from you. Will you tell her about Emily, or just keep it general about Mrs. James and the child?'

'I might just keep it to telling her about Emily at first. It would be fairly easy to try and catch her one day and get into conversation. Then I can see where we go from there.'

'You've thought a lot about this, haven't you?'

'I have. I've gone over and over it in my mind, trying to work out how I can get into conversation with her without it seeming forced. I don't want to put her off talking to me.'

'I think it's a great idea. I hope it works. You must let me know how you get on.'

Chapter Sixty-five

Emily

She was woken by the sound of bells ringing. The war had been over for a week now and there was suddenly noise everywhere. Not only the church bells ringing but people in the streets at all hours of the day and night. The celebrations never seemed to cease.

Still her work had continued each day. All the same jobs had to be completed in the house, but now more people came to visit Mrs. Cartwright. There was more tea to serve each afternoon, more suppers to clean up after each night and more washing and cleaning it seemed than ever before. Emily was happy though. She knew that soon she'd be seeing Joe again and as each day passed she was getting nearer to a better future.

Emily was glad that she'd seen her Pa and knew he still loved her, even though it wouldn't be easy to see him often. She was glad, too that she'd spoken to Kate and knew how she stood with her. They would never be close, but there was a slim chance Kate would let her know what had happened to her child. Emily accepted it would be too late to have her baby back but each day she lived in hope that he was being well looked after and maybe one day she would see him again.

Knowing the war was over at last was a relief, although Emily regretted so much about the war. All those men and women who'd had been lost. She still hadn't heard from her two elder brothers, Harry and Edward, had no idea whether they'd survived and were coming home, or were lost somewhere in a distant place she could only imagine. She would always regret losing Billy of course, although was happy in the thought of a future with Joe.

Travelling across town on the tram to North End one Wednesday afternoon she'd looked out from the top deck at the busy streets below, people milling about, the shops as busy as they ever used to be before the war. The tram was filled with happy people too, laughing together, no longer looking so pinched and worn. It was so good to see. The conductor was a woman. It occurred to Emily that soon the woman would lose her job, when the men came home. She thought about Mabel and her work in the Post Office and wondered how her friend was going to get on when or if she was made to give up her job. It was certainly a time of change and uncertainty for everyone.

There were some men about in the streets, perhaps only recently sent home, many with injuries. They certainly didn't seem like the same young men that had so recently gone off to fight and to keep the country safe. Now they were home and looked thinner and broken somehow, even those without obvious injuries. Some were being pushed along the pavement in bath chairs, the crowds seeming to be avoiding eye-contact with them for whatever reason, embarrassment, or shame that the onlookers themselves were still able-bodied and had no experience of being on the front line. Emily had heard of some men still being given white feathers if they hadn't joined up, even those who had important occupations like munitions workers or even medical men. She hated the thought of women doing that. How could they judge? Nobody had the right to judge another and the thought of this made her think about Joe again, as she wished they could be together.

Emily stayed on the tram all the way to Gladys Avenue and although she'd planned to get off and wander around the shops, her heart had gone out of her plans so she stayed on the tram and travelled all the way back to Southsea again. Once again, she found herself walking beside the sea. It made her think about moving away to Droxford, which she supposed could be her future life now. How she would miss the sea, walking on the shingle beach, and looking across to the Island, a view that had been with her for all of her life. But she'd be with the man she loved and working on a farm would surely compensate for her missing the sea. Deep in thought, she didn't notice that Mabel had stopped beside her.

'Emily. What a nice surprise.'

'Mabel, it's so good to see you. I hadn't planned to be here this afternoon otherwise I'd have written you a note and we could have arranged to meet. Honestly, I didn't think you'd have a day off again so soon.'

'I know, time seems to either go too quickly or not move at all. Still it's good news that the war is over, isn't it?'

'I think so. Everyone looks happier and the world has come alive with colour again. But I wondered how things would be for you now. You said you might lose your job when the men started coming home.'

'I know. That's going to happen soon enough. But so far, and it's only been a few days hasn't it, so far they still want me to carry on as before. I imagine many of the men who used to work in the depot might not be coming back. Sad though that is, it may be to my benefit. I feel awful saying that, but it's true and I can't deny it.'

'How are things with you anyway? I mean is there a young man in your life at all. The last time we spoke there wasn't anyone was there?'

'No and there's still no-one. I did have hopes but that was a long time ago. I look at the men coming home and feel so sad about them all. The ones I've seen so far all look lost and damaged. I'm not sure I want to give up my life to caring for some man.'

'Surely they aren't all like that?'

'The ones I've seen have been. But I'm no expert in men am I? I've been thinking it's not a bad idea to stay a spinster. To be really honest, I prefer the company of women anyway.'

'Do you think a woman can live without a man looking after her in these times?'

'Of course we can! We've been doing it for the past four years haven't we? Well, some of us have anyway. And your experience hasn't been good has it? Your Pa didn't step up and look after you when Billy died.'

Emily looked at her, then kicked at the pebbles beneath her feet.

'I'm sorry,' Mabel went on. 'I didn't mean to upset you. I open my big mouth without thinking sometimes.'

'No, it's perfectly alright. I agree with you about my Pa although I suspect he would have stood by me if he'd not been with Kate. And I'm sure we'll have to get used to women looking after themselves. There will be many more women than men for some time now with so many killed and lost in the war. I think you should follow your heart and if you don't want to find a man, then don't. It won't be easy though, with women's wages being so much less than what a man can earn. How would you manage to live?'

'Perhaps I will live with a woman!'

'As a companion?'

'Yes, of course, I suppose that's what I mean. If we are bringing in two wages, it should be easy enough to manage.'

'Living with a woman? It's been done for many centuries and at least you won't have to answer to a man. Not every man is kind and considerate. Wouldn't you miss having a man though? You know, for, you know.'

'I do know, and no, I probably wouldn't miss that part of life, but who knows, I could change my mind one day. I only know this is how I feel now and I'm not alone in thinking like this. I know a few women in the Post Office who are not at all interested in men. Kind women who are funny and strong-willed.' She blushed.

'I'm sure there are women like that everywhere. Only we expect to get married and follow the normal way of life, having a family and bringing up children, looking after a man. It doesn't have to be like that I suppose.'

'No, it doesn't. Anyway, enough about me. Have you found anything more about your child yet?'

Emily picked up a pebble and felt the smooth surface in her hand. 'I haven't got very far. I did go to see my Pa and Kate. It was good seeing Pa and I hope that Kate and I have built some bridges. I asked her outright to let me know what happened to my baby but she said she didn't know. I tried to persuade her to find out. I think she knows really but won't tell me. Eventually she agreed to think about it. I'm not sure whether I'll ever find out.'

'Well don't give up hope. You never know what could be around the corner. Have you heard anything from Joe?'

'Not this week yet. He usually writes to me on a Thursday so I might get a letter by Friday. I don't know what he's making of all this. I wish I could see him and just ask. He lives so far away.'

'Keep strong, Emily. I'm sure it'll all work out how it should in the end. But if you find out the child is happy and healthy, will you give up? You wouldn't want to take him away if he was happy, would you?'

'That's what makes me hesitate in wanting to know. I'm saying to myself I wouldn't jeopardise a good future for my child, but I don't know how I'll feel once I know for sure. As well as all that, how would I be able to take my child back? Legally, I mean. The law would surely be against me and I'd stand no chance in court to have him back. I wouldn't be able to prove it anyway would I?'

'Probably not. It wouldn't be easy that's certain. Perhaps you should rethink what you're doing. Stand back and take time to think about it for a bit longer?'

'I would but I can't stand back. I can't let it go. I just have to know either way. I suffered a madness when he was taken and recovered in a fashion, but now I'm well again, the thought of him being brought up as another's child, being given the love I want to give him, and not knowing where he is or whether he is being treated well, is starting to make me feel like I'm slipping back into some kind of madness again. I don't want that to happen, so what else can I do?'

'Oh, Emily, I am sorry life is so troubling for you again. It's not fair, I know. You deserve some peace in your life. Is there no way you can put it behind you, accept that you've lost him, like you lost Billy, and look forward to your new life with Joe? You should fill your lives with children, Joe's children, and be happy with that. Is it possible?'

'Perhaps but I can't let this go yet. I'm determined to at least know if my little Billy is safe and well and happy. I promise though, I will know when to give up and let him go finally.'

Chapter Sixty-six

Joe

He saw his chance to speak to Miss Woods on Thursday afternoon as he stood outside the village shop. He'd written a letter to Emily, but hadn't let her know of any of the things that Annie had told him, not wanting to raise her hopes, nor worry her about the child should he in fact, be her own little one. It would be too cruel, he'd realised, to say anything before he knew either way. In his heart he wasn't sure whether he hoped it was Emily's child or not. It would be easier if the baby wasn't hers. Then perhaps she could move on with her life.

He'd posted the letter as Miss Woods passed the letter box. He raised his cap. 'Afternoon Miss.'

'Good afternoon. It's Joe isn't it?'

'Joe Berry, Miss.'

'Of course, I remember you. Are you keeping well? And the farm? Your father passed away recently I believe. I'm sorry for your loss.'

'Yes, Miss. Thank you. I've come back to run the farm with Ma. Been back a few months now, since Pa died.'

'Well, it's good to hear that you're back and doing well here. It must have been a difficult time. How is your mother keeping?'

'She's well too, thank you.'

'Good, I'm pleased to hear that. Life must be hard for farmers in these times, although it is good news about the war being over, isn't it?'

'Very good news, Miss. Farming is hard but we're doing alright. We've got the harvest in and should be set for the winter now.'

She smiled. 'I'm glad to hear it. Well, I should make my way back. It was good to see you.'

'I wonder, I mean, I don't wish to intrude but was hoping that I could have a talk with you about something.'

'Something? I am intrigued but I don't see why not. I can't promise I can help you, but I'm happy to listen. Shall we walk together to the schoolhouse and we can talk on the way.'

As they moved down the road, away from the post box and the shop, Joe wondered how he could find the words to broach the subject. 'I'm not sure how to say this,' he finally said. 'It's probably just a stupid thought and I don't want to upset you or anyone. It's about Mrs. James, actually.'

'Really? What is it about Mrs. James that you're worrying about? Before you answer, I have to say I'm not obliged to discuss her at all. It may not be appropriate.'

'I do understand and I hope our conversation will stay between just the two of us. Perhaps it would help if I start from the beginning.'

'Very well.' By now they had reached the school-house gate. 'You'd better come in Joe, I'll make some tea and we can sit down and talk properly.'

Joe felt uncomfortable sitting in the school-house parlour, but determined to get to the bottom of things.

Miss Woods passed him his tea and he began. He told her the story of how he'd worked at the asylum farm and how he first met Emily. She looked away when he told her about how Emily had became a patient in the asylum after her child was taken from her. Joe paused in his story and waited until she looked at him again.

'Please, go on,' she said.

'Is everything alright?' asked Joe.

'Yes, of course. Please go on,' she repeated.

'Emily's my sweetheart. She's no longer a patient. I say that because I don't want you to think ill of her. She's recovered well but when she visited me here in Droxford, she came across Mrs. James and her baby. I know this may seem strange and maybe it was just her longing to have her child back, but she seemed to recognise the baby. We didn't talk about it but I actually wondered if she was thinking he was her own boy.'

He stopped talking, wishing that he'd kept to his plan to befriend Miss Woods first before blurting out what he was thinking. He was sure now he'd most probably ruined the plan to find out more about Mrs. James. She would not confide in him now, would she?

After a long silence, Miss Woods spoke. 'I am sorry to hear all this, Joe. It is most unfortunate. As to Mrs. James, she is married to my cousin and I owe it to him and to her to keep what I know about her confidential. I cannot help you I'm afraid.'

'I thought you'd say that but had to try, didn't I? Can't you tell me anything about the child? Is the baby her own, for a start? I have heard rumours that people don't think she was actually ever pregnant.'

'I can't comment on this at all, Joe. Please don't ask me again.'

'Very well. I thought you might be able to help, but I understand. Family must come first. I will respect your wishes, of course. Only, please may I ask you to let me know if ever there is anything you think I might be told. If only to help Emily?'

'If ever that happens I will.'

'And if you think at any time that the child is unhappy or neglected, or anything...'

'What are you saying? Are you implying the child might be in danger? Little Thomas is a well loved child. I can't imagine he would ever be unhappy or neglected as you put it. In fact, I find the suggestion quite absurd and distasteful. Now I think I should get on with my duties. I have to prepare for tomorrow's school lesson. Perhaps our little chat should finish now.'

She stood and showed Joe to the door.

'Thank you anyway, Miss,' Joe said. 'And I'm sorry if I've offended.'

'Goodby Joe.'

Chapter Sixty-seven

Joe

He didn't sleep at all that night. The thought that he'd ruined any chance of finding out more about Mrs. James and the baby was eating away at him. He cursed himself over and over for being so rash. He wanted to write to Emily again but felt it would be better to keep her in the dark about his meddling until he had some proper news for her. It would only upset her if she knew about the conversation he'd had with Miss Woods. What a fool he was.

The next few days didn't get any easier. He worked ploughing the fields from dawn until the darkness fell. The days were getting shorter and shorter. Soon they'd be planting next year's crop. Farming life never eased up, he knew that and was grateful to be busy. It did help a bit to take his mind off things.

He was looking forward to seeing Emily again. They'd planned for him to take his Ma to Southsea by the end of November and he couldn't wait, although it would have been good to spend time on his own with Emily. They had so much to talk about. He just wished that he had good news for her.

Another day passed. It was the end of the day and a long walk back from the bottom field. As he neared the house in the late afternoon light he could see his Ma waiting for him at the door of the farmhouse. She waved.

'I'm just finishing off for the day, Ma,' he called to her. 'Let me rub down Arthur and bed him down for the night.'

'This won't wait,' she said, crossing the yard to where he was standing. 'I've got some news about Mrs. James. I think you'll want to hear this.'

'You'd better come with me then. I need to get the horse stabled before I do anything else.'

Ma hurried along behind him, chatting as she moved. 'Everybody is talking about her in the Post Office,' she began. 'There had been a tremendous noise, shouting and crashing, coming from the cottage. Mrs. Harrison lives just down the lane from the school and she could hear it all the way from her house. Her son went down to see what was going on whilst she went to get help from Constable Evans. Her son said he could see through the window into the cottage that the furniture had been turned over. There was an awful mess everywhere as far as he could make out. It was dreadful.'

'What about the baby? And Mrs. James? Were they hurt? What had happened? Was it an intruder that got in? What, Ma?'

'I don't know about an intruder. Mrs. Harrison said when Constable Evans arrived, he went into the house and brought out the child first. The poor little mite was crying so hard they couldn't settle him. She said she was handed the baby and told to take him into her own house, to make sure he was safe and in the warm. She rocked him in her arms until he slept but then she told me this.'

'What? Oh, Ma, you are being annoying. What did she say?' He was furiously brushing the horse now, taking his anger out on the job he was doing.

'Steady with what you're doing to poor old Arthur, Joe. Slow down, I am telling you what she said.'

'Sorry, Ma.' He patted Arthur's flank. 'Sorry, Arthur.'

'Never mind. What she said was that she noticed some marks on the child's forehead and that made her want to have a closer look. She uncovered his arms and chest and they were covered in bruises. It was pitiful, she said.'

'I knew we should have done something about this before.' Joe put the brush away and gave Arthur a net of hay before closing the stable inner gate. 'You'll be fine now, Arthur,' he said then turned to his Ma. 'Annie said she thought she'd seen bruising on the babe but we did nothing. We agreed we should wait and see because we didn't want to upset anyone. What a couple of fools we've been. The baby could have been killed and it would have been our fault.'

'I think he'll be alright, now he's safe in the hands of Mrs. Harrison. Come indoors now, we'll have some supper and hopefully all will be well for the baby.'

'What about Mrs. James? Was she hurt? You say there wasn't an intruder? Surely there must have been someone else there?'

'No. Mrs. Harrison told me the woman was taken away by the constable. I have no idea why but it seems that she was alone in the house at the time, apart from the little babe that is. Mrs. James was screaming as they led her away.'

'Where did they take her? Where could they take her? Was she arrested? I don't understand.'

'She's being kept in the Police House. Hopefully locked safely in there until they can take her away. They're saying she may be suffering from a madness. I don't know any more than that. I just hope they do keep her safe and unable to do any more harm. I don't like the idea of her being let loose in the village.'

'Do you really believe Mrs. James harmed her own child and smashed up her own home?'

'I don't know what to believe. I only know what I've been told but am sure the truth will come out sooner or later. I hope we find out sooner. I know you told me about your speaking to Miss Woods and how Emily had been when she saw the child. It may well be she was right after all and it wasn't just that seeing a baby, any baby, was part of her longing for her own child. I was wondering perhaps when Mrs. James met Emily that day, it may have started her down the road to this madness today. If she thought she was going to lose the child, I mean. I can't believe she's wicked but when a woman longs for a baby and has had difficulty in having their own naturally, it's possible they may be reckless enough to do anything to be a mother.'

Joe followed his Ma into the house and sat down in the kitchen.

'I find it hard to believe that a woman could harm a child.' Joe said. 'But then, in the asylum, there were women who had done terrible things whilst in their madness. And had terrible things done to them too. What a world we live in.'

'I'm sure we'll see and hear much more madness as the world starts to return to some kind of normality. Fetch me some water, now, Joe. I need to get the potatoes on to boil. I'm all behind with the supper.'

After they'd eaten Joe sat down to write to Emily. He was still torn between whether to tell her the news about Mrs. James or not. Until he knew all the facts about what had happened, it would be wrong to raise her hopes. There was no proof yet whether the baby was actually Mrs. James' own child, and even if he wasn't there was no reason to believe he was Emily's lost son. In the end he wrote a short note asking if he could bring his Ma to visit on the following week.

Chapter Sixty-eight

Emily

Emily was impatient. She didn't really expect Kate to get in touch with her with any news about her baby but she believed the woman knew exactly what had happened to him and where he was now. It was so frustrating, having to wait for something she knew would never happen without further persistence.

A letter came from Joe asking if he could visit with his Ma on the following week. Emily wrote back straight away and was excited with the thought of seeing him again. It seemed a long time ago that she'd been with him in Droxford. At least now she had something to look forward to.

All the same, she was impatient. The next day, on the Sunday afternoon, she donned her coat and hat and left the house as soon as the lunch things had been washed up and cleared away. She had the rest of the day free.

The front window of her Pa's house showed a faint glow. They'd always lit the lanterns early at this time of the year. It wasn't usually dark until five o'clock but this afternoon, with the clouds glowering above, the light was fading and it was only half past three.

She didn't hesitate to knock this time and was happy to see the smiling face of Percy as he opened the door.

'Emily, what a surprise. It's good to see you.' He opened the door wide and putting his arm around her shoulder, he pulled her in.

'Percy. I'm so glad you're here.' Hugging him back, she stepped away to have a good look at him. 'You have grown into a young man while I've been away. Where's my little brother?'

He laughed. 'I haven't grown much, have I really? I can't have in the few months since we saw each other.'

'Well I think you have. And you are a sight for sore eyes.' She could feel herself welling up.

'You should have come earlier and shared dinner with us. When are you coming home anyway?'

'Ah, Percy. Pa hasn't told you then?'

He shook his head. 'Told me what?'

'I've grown up now, Percy, so won't be coming back to live here now. You know I'm working back at Mrs. Cartwright's house, of course. So I am living there now. It won't be forever, but one day I expect I'll have my own home to care for.' She paused. 'At least I hope so anyway. I will always come and visit you though, and hope to see my other brothers too. Is there any news about when they'll be coming home?'

'Not yet. We know they are safe and well, but no idea when they'll be home.'

'Really? That's wonderful news. I can't wait to see them both too. Good times indeed. Do you think they might write to me now?'

'They might. Hopefully it won't be too long before they're back here. But about you. I hope you're not working too hard, and, you are well?'

'I'm very well. It's hard work, no doubt about that, but Mrs. Cartwright is a good employer. She's kind to me, and I have a lovely little room all to myself.'

'That's good but it must be strange living in someone else's house. Shall we go in. I expect Pa and Ma will wonder who's here.'

Emily cringed inside when she heard Percy call Kate Ma. She wanted to say something but held back and took a breath before following him into the parlour.

Pa stood as she entered. Smiling at her, he reached to take her hand. 'Emily, dear girl,' he said as he squeezed her hand. She kissed him on the cheek and turned to Kate.

'Kate,' she nodded to the woman and gave her a smile.

Kate's smile back to her was a little strained but her voice sounded warm enough. 'Emily, dear, this is a nice surprise. I'll fetch another cup and you must join us for some tea.'

'Thank you, that would be nice.'

Her Pa stood and offered her his chair. 'Sit here, Emily. Percy and me have some jobs to get done out the back before it gets too dark. Come on lad, and get the yard broom from the scullery on your way. We'll have our tea when we're done.'

As soon as they were left alone, Emily could waste no more time in asking Kate. 'Have you decided yet whether you can tell me what you did with my child?'

Kate's shoulders stiffened. She still had her back to Emily but the young woman could see this wasn't going to be easy. She went on. 'Kate, I am sorry but I need to know. Please, I am begging you to take pity and just tell me. Where is my child? If he was adopted properly within the law, then I need to see the papers. If not, then I want to know exactly where he is so I can make sure he is in a good home, and loved. You can't deny me that.'

She saw the slump of Kate's stature before she turned to face Emily. 'Very well, I will tell you. He was adopted legally and there's no returning him. That would be impossible and cruel, both for him and for his new family who had wanted a child for so long and your baby was a gift for them.'

'A gift for them? You steal my child and gift him to another family. Now, that is cruel, but you didn't think about my feelings did you?'

'You were unwell and unfit to care for him. It was for the best.'

'Very well.' Emily could feel her heart was near to breaking point. 'If it was done legally, there must be some paperwork.'

'There was but it's been destroyed unfortunately.'

'Destroyed? Why would you do that?' Emily stood up and walked across the room.

There were cobwebs still hanging from the curtains. It made her think about how her Ma would never have let the room get like this. She swiped the cobwebs down and turned to face Kate. 'Well?'

'I didn't. It was your Pa. He threw them in the fire some time ago now, after he'd been to see you at the asylum.'

'When he told me I wasn't welcome in my own home any more? But I still don't see why would he destroy them.'

'It was for the best. The past is the past. That's what he said on that day anyway. It wasn't me that pushed him to do it if that's what you think.'

'It was for the best? The best you say? I think I'm the only person who can decide what's for the best for my child. I know I was unwell at the time, but it was him being torn from me that made me mad. I am well now, fully recovered and I want to have my child back. If you had been doing it for the best as you say, you'd have cared for him for me until I was recovered. Now, you say the legal documents are destroyed but you must know where he was taken. You must know who you "gifted" him to. Where is he, please Kate, please tell me.'

'I cannot. You must forget him, Emily.'

'I won't ever do that. I will look at every child I see and wonder if he is mine. Please.'

'You won't ever find him. He isn't anywhere nearby. His new mother doesn't live in Portsmouth now. It will be better for you to put it all in the past and try to get on with your life.'

'You will never understand will you? He is my life. Please tell me where he is.'

Kate banged down the teapot she'd held in her hand. It slammed onto the table, splashing hot tea onto the table-cloth. 'I understand more than you'll ever know, girl. I do know what it's like to lose a child, to have your baby taken from your arms. Yes, Emily, it happened to me a long time ago. I know what it's like to live with a broken heart, believe you me.'

Emily was shocked. She looked at Kate and saw in her face the truth of what she was being told. 'If you know how it feels, surely that's more reason to not do it to me?'

'I kept my baby for as long as I could but it was too hard to manage on my own and when he was taken away we had already bonded. I didn't want to lose him but had no choice as there was no money and no food. We were starving. I thought it would be better for you if I took the child away before you had the chance to love him. I was doing what was best.'

'But it was too late. I loved him from the moment he was born. You were wrong, Kate. So wrong to do what you did, whether or not you believed it was for the best as you put it. I am sorry that you went through the same pain that I have, but it doesn't excuse you and I won't ever rest until I find him, whatever you say. Have you ever tried to find your son?'

'No. There would have been no point. He was better off without me.'

'Things are different for me. You had a choice and made that choice. I didn't.'

'It wasn't my choice to lose my child. But he wouldn't have lived had I been so selfish as to try and keep him.'

'Things are different now. It wasn't the same for me. We weren't starving, were we?'

'No. We were not.' She went to the dresser and took down another cup and saucer to put on the tray. 'I am sorry, Emily. I am truly, but I don't see what I can do about it now. What's done, is done.'

'I will never stop looking for him.'

'I feel sorry for you, but you must let it go.'

'I can't do that, Kate.'

'Really, Emily, I would not advise you to keep pursuing this. It'll do you no good at all in the end.' She picked up the teapot and poured the tea.

Pa came in from the cold, rubbing his hands together to get warm, Percy following closely behind. They filled the room and the tension between Emily and Kate was soon hidden beneath the sound of their chatter.

Chapter Sixty-nine

Joe

Another day had passed and Joe couldn't stop thinking about the child being cared for by Mrs. Harrison, and about Mrs. James. He wondered what had happened to her since being arrested and why she'd behaved the way she had. There must have been a reason, but no one in the village seemed to have known her well enough to know her past. Apart from Miss Woods, of course. That was it, he decided. She would be the one person to ask.

It was late morning and the school day was in progress. As Joe walked through the gate to the classrooms, his mind cast back to the days when he was a pupil here. It only seemed to be like yesterday and was, in truth, but a few years ago. How quickly he'd been made to grow up from those times.

Feeling a little awkward at preparing himself to confront his old schoolmistress, especially after the way she'd behaved towards him the last time he'd tried to speak to her, he hesitated at the window and looked in. He could see Miss Woods sitting at the high desk at the front of the class and the children on their benches with their heads down over their work. Something made her look up, perhaps it was his shadow blocking the light, and she looked straight at him. He watched as she stood and spoke to the class before leaving them to go out into the corridor. Joe made his way through the outer door and stood face to face with her inside. The air was warmer in here and the smell of the coke fire took him straight back to his first day here when he was a mere tot of six years old.

'Joe, I was wondering how long it would be before you'd seek me out again. You'd better come into my office.'

He followed her in, eager to hear what she would say this time.

'I owe you an apology, Joe,' she said. 'I should have been more open when you spoke to me before, but Mrs. James is family and what I know about her was told to me in confidence. Now the situation has changed, I feel I should let you know the truth of the matter.'

'So you do know more than you would tell me before?'

'Yes. I'm sorry. I couldn't tell you then. Mrs. James has now been taken to the Hampshire asylum to be cared for but I am sure you will understand I wouldn't want you gossiping about her?'

'Of course not. But is she in a madness, then? Why else would she harm her own child?'

'The term madness isn't very helpful. You must know better than most people in the village how easy it is to lose one's mind, and it isn't necessarily something that can't be recovered from.'

'I suppose that's true. Is the baby her own, though? That's really what I want to know.'

Miss Woods stood up and paced the floor as though fighting with herself before she spoke again.

Finally she continued. 'Joe, when you told me about your Emily and her child and how she'd behaved when she saw little Thomas, it made me stop and think about what Mrs. James might have done. I hadn't even thought before that the child may have had a living, loving mother of it's own. I had assumed he was orphaned. I thought and thought about it and eventually spoke to her. I asked her about the adoption process and I have to say truthfully she was unable to explain clearly how she'd come to have the child. I could see that I was being fobbed off.'

'Why didn't you tell me this sooner?'

'I wasn't sure, and I thought I owed it to Mrs. James to say nothing. I would have done something if I'd been sure. I was waiting for my cousin to come home from the frontline so that he could deal with it, but of course, things have taken over since then.'

'I understand the child is with Mrs. Harrison still? Will Dr. James be returning for him? I'd heard he's been sent to India.'

'No. He is still in Europe. I don't know if he will come back yet. I believe they are starting to bring home many of those that are wounded but he is needed there and as long as the child is safe and his wife is being cared for, he might not be home for a while yet. I have heard nothing, to be truthful. What I can tell you is that before she was taken away, Mrs. James did let it slip she was given the child as a gift from a lady in Portsmouth. She was bitter about it when she told me, saying she'd been tricked into taking a baby that was damaged. She then told me she'd paid a good sum of money to the woman who'd handed the child over to her. I think she imagined in her state of madness the baby had been taken over by the devil and needed to be punished.'

'Dear God!'

'I didn't believe she would ever hurt him though, otherwise I'd have done something about it. Now I feel I am as much to blame for any harm she's done to him as she is herself.'

'You could have stopped this.'

'I am so sorry, Joe. I am sorry that I didn't do anything before and I truly wonder, like you did, whether the child could be Emily's. She is a Portsmouth girl isn't she? And when you told me her step-mother took the child away without her blessing I should have told you what I suspected. I wish I had now.'

'What's done is done and there's no point in thinking about what should have been done. I need to find out the full facts about the child so that I can put Emily's mind at rest.'

Chapter Seventy

Emily

Emily was busy in the kitchen preparing the tea tray ready for the afternoon guests when the doorbell rang. She took off her apron and wiped her hands before running up the stairs into the main hallway. Glancing at her reflection in the mirror before she opened the door she saw a face she barely recognised looking back. The worry was surely taking its toll. Turning away with a sigh, she opened the door.

Emily wasn't surprised to see Marjorie Simpson there, but she wasn't expecting to see her step-mother Kate standing beside her. 'What are you doing here?' she blurted out before realising how rude she'd sounded. 'I beg your pardon Marjorie, please do come in.'

'Thank you Emily. I have brought Mrs. Harris along with me today as we have some news for you. But please let Mrs. Cartwright know we are here. Then I will explain everything to you.'

As soon as the women had been shown into the sitting

room, and Emily had fetched the tea, Mrs. Cartwright asked her to sit down. 'Mrs. Simpson and Mrs. Harris have something to tell you, Emily. It's rather delicate.'

Emily felt her stomach churn. She sat on the edge of the chair that had been placed there for her and looked at Mrs. Simpson, Marjorie, the woman she'd considered to be her friend. 'Delicate?' She glanced at Kate. There was only one reason why she'd be here, surely. Unless it was Pa. 'Is it Pa?'

'No, it's not your Pa. He is keeping very well isn't he, Mrs. Harris? Don't be alarmed, Emily. This will be a shock for you but it's good news really.' Marjorie reached across to Emily and took her hand. 'We have a lot to tell you.'

'Is it about my child? Please tell me whatever it is. I need to know where he is.' She looked at Kate. The woman wouldn't meet her eyes.

'I am sorry Emily,' Kate said. 'I couldn't tell you before. Only things have changed since the last time we spoke. I meant it when I said I was doing it for your good and for the good of the child, but it hasn't worked out so well for him after all. The thing is, his new mother has now had a breakdown. You will understand what that's like, won't you?'

'How do you mean, she's had a breakdown? Look, I need to know, where did you take my baby? Who did you give him to? You told me before you arranged it through the law, that he was adopted. Is this true?'

'I only said that so you wouldn't pursue it. I said it before, it was for your own good that you didn't know. Only I may have been wrong, I see that now.'

'Of course you were wrong. You had no right to make decisions for me without my permission. You say you're sorry now but I still can't believe you. Did you take money for him? You said you gifted him to her, but I know you better than you think. Well, did you sell my baby?'

'Does that really matter now? We have come to tell you we know where he is. Please let Mrs. Simpson explain.'

Emily looked at Marjorie. 'Well? Are you going to tell me?'

'That's what I've come here to do. It has been a whirlwind of a few days. The constable at Droxford telephoned me because he'd been approached by your young man, Joe.'

'Droxford? My baby is in Droxford? So I wasn't imagining things. And Joe is involved as well?'

'Let me continue. It seems that a Mrs. James, who was fairly new to the village, was taken into custody by the police officer after she'd had an episode. She had smashed up the whole of her sitting room. The young baby with her was taken from the house by a neighbour during the upheaval and it was discovered by the neighbour that the child had bruising on his body.'

'Where is the baby now? Is he alright? Is he with this Mrs. James?'

'That's just the thing. She isn't actually his mother. She admitted that she'd bought the baby from a woman in Portsmouth.' Marjorie looked at Kate. 'The little boy is your son, Emily.'

The room began to spin. Emily grit her teeth and shook her head. 'But how did you know? How could you have realised that?'

'Joe remembered how you reacted when you saw the baby at the train station and he'd started to ask questions about the woman. She's related to the school mistress so Joe went to speak to her. He didn't get any answers but he'd confided with his friend Annie, who tried to help by going to speak to Mrs. James. She didn't find anything much, just had some suspicions. But it seemed to bring on Mrs. James' brainstorm moment, or mental breakdown, or whatever you would call it. When Joe was told about the bruises on the child, he decided to speak to the Police Constable. Once the police started looking into the matter, it came to light she had in fact bought the child. Joe told the officer about your story, and how I'd befriended you and they contacted me on the telephone. As soon as I heard, I went to see your step-mother and she has told me what Mrs. James said was the truth and the baby is yours.'

Emily tried to stand up but her legs seemed to be made of jelly. The room swayed and she felt herself sliding to the floor.

When she opened her eyes she was on the sofa, Marjorie was sitting on the chair with a concerned look on her face.

'Is it really true? My child, she had him all the time? That little baby I saw in the perambulator was my little Billy?'

'It seems so.'

'Is he safe now, though? Where is he?'

'He is being cared for by a woman in the village, Mrs. Harrison is her name. She's a neighbour, living in the same road as Miss Woods, who is the school mistress. 'The constable would be very happy to know the child's real mother has been found. There are too many children without parents in these times.'

'I can hardly believe this. What should I do now though? I should go and fetch him but where would we live? I couldn't have him here, could I?'

Mrs. Cartwright had been sitting quietly until that moment. 'I think having a child here probably wouldn't be the best solution, Emily. I am sorry my dear, but I don't think it would be suitable at all.'

'I don't know what to do.' Emily was in despair. 'I only know I need to have my child with me. What can I do, Marjorie?'

'I may have the solution, if you would consider it, Emily.' Kate had been sitting by the window on the other side of the room and for a moment, Emily had forgotten she was there. She stood as she spoke. 'Emily, I can only say how sorry I am. I was wrong, I knew almost straight away but I couldn't admit it even to myself. I've spoken to your father about this and told him the right thing to do would be for you to come home. We still have your room.

It's small, as you know, but there's room for a crib, if you want, that is.'

'And does Pa want me home, too?'

'He does, of course. What do you think?'

Emily didn't know how to answer at first. This was what she'd hoped for for so long but now she wasn't sure. How could she trust this new Kate for a start? Would life be any different at home? Kate had made her life a misery before, resenting her and had been so cruel, even before the child was born. But what was the alternative? Until she and Joe were ready to wed, she'd need a roof over her head and she couldn't have her baby with her here. There was no choice, she knew that.

She looked at Kate and spoke at last. 'You've made my life and probably my Pa's and Percy's miserable, Kate. I don't think I have any choice but to move back home as much as the idea of living under the same roof as you makes me feel sick to the core. I will never forgive you for what you did, but for Pa's sake and for my son, I will do my best to keep my thoughts to myself.

Chapter Seventy-one

Joe

Emily came in a carriage all the way from Portsmouth. She was with Mrs. Simpson. Joe was to meet them at the constable's house so they could collect the child. Mrs. Harrison was carrying him in her arms, walking towards the police house. Joe waited by the gate, wondering what time Emily would arrive and when he heard the sound of the carriage coming along the road, his heart leapt. There she was, sitting inside, her face showing anticipation through the window. It was delightful to see her again, and looking so full of love and hope.

Mrs. Harrison had reached the gate as the carriage drew to a halt and Emily leapt out before it had even fully stopped. She ran to the woman holding the baby and took him in her arms, weeping now and laughing too. Joe stood back for a moment, hoping she would notice him but her eyes were on the child. So he stepped forward and touched her on the shoulder. As she turned to look at him, her face lit up and she was smiling through her tears.

'I love you Joe,' she said. 'So much. And I love my little Billy too. Thank you for helping me to find him.' Then she turned to Mrs. Simpson. 'And thank you too, Marjorie, for being such a good friend. My life is complete now.'

Mrs. Harrison touched the baby on the cheek. 'I am so glad that we've found his real mother. I can see he will be well cared for now. I'll miss having him in my care but am so happy for you.'

'Thank you, too, Mrs. Harrison. I am obliged.'

The constable was standing in the doorway to the police house. 'I think you'd all better come inside. There is some paperwork to complete and I expect a cup of tea would be welcome.'

Tea taken, Marjorie was to return to Portsmouth but Emily would be staying overnight at the farm with Joe. It was an opportunity too, to talk to his Ma, introduce the baby to her and to discuss their plans for the wedding. It seemed that although they'd decided to take it slowly before they announced their engagement, things had been taken out of their hands and to marry sooner rather than later would be the best thing.

Emily spoke to Marjorie before the carriage pulled away. 'I can't stop thanking you, Marjorie. Without you I might have still been in the asylum.'

'Nonsense, young lady. You would have recovered, you are stronger than you think.'

'But you have helped me so much, and I am grateful.'

'I am pleased that things are going your way at last. Make sure you keep strong and write to me. Let me know how you're getting on. And I hope I will be invited to your wedding when it happens.'

Emily blushed. 'You will, of course, you will.

Joe appeared beside her. 'We should make our way to the farm before dark, Emily. Goodbye Mrs. Simpson, and thank you for everything.'

As soon as the carriage had pulled away they said their goodbyes to Mrs. Harrison and the constable, climbed up onto Joe's cart and with the baby Billy in her arms, Emily sat whilst Joe clicked his tongue and Arthur the horse began to walk on, pulling the cart behind him.

'What will happen to Mrs. James?' Emily asked.

'She's in the Hampshire asylum now but Miss Woods told me that they think she stands a good chance of recovering soon. Her husband is due back in a month's time, she says, and hopefully that will help her.'

'I feel sorry for her being in that place. I saw it from the train when I came to see you before. It looks a bit like the Portsmouth asylum only it's more isolated, I think. I know what she did was wrong, but still, I feel sorry for her.'

'Miss Woods is very sorry too, for not telling me when I asked her about the woman. I expect she'll speak to you herself soon enough. Today wasn't the right time though. I'm glad she stayed away, but she's not a bad woman. Did I tell you she was once my teacher?'

'No I don't think you did. And I am sure you're right about her. Oh, Joe, we have so much to tell each other about our lives, but we have so much time ahead of us haven't we?'

'We certainly do, my love.'

'I was worried that you might change your mind about marrying me now that I have a child to care for. I wouldn't blame you if you wanted to back out now.'

'Well you can stop worrying about that. I love the idea of a complete family and I know my Ma is delighted too.'

'You are a good man, Joe.'

'And you are a good woman.'

Chapter Seventy-Two

Emily

She knew it would be hard to move back into her old home. Nothing would be like it was before, there had been too many changes. Marjorie had arranged for a cab to pick her up from the station the next afternoon and she'd spent the journey home with so many conflicting thoughts attacking her mind. When the cab finally reached the house, it was late afternoon.

Emily hesitated at the door. The past few times she'd passed this threshold, she'd had to wait to be let in, not feeling welcome at all. Today, she held her child in her arms and carried a small bag which contained all she owned in the world. Determined not to feel like a guest in the house, she placed the bag on the path and opened the door with her free hand. She looked back at the cab driver who'd dropped her at the gate and smiled.

Little Billy was stirring awake as she stepped inside the house. Emily wished that her own Ma was still alive and there to welcome her home. How Ma would have loved her first grandchild. But then if Ma had been alive none of Emily's past nightmares would have happened. She scolded herself for thinking such things. 'A fresh start, Emily,' she told herself and acknowledged the joy in her heart.

The door to the kitchen opened and Kate appeared. The pleasant smell of cooking was in the air. 'Emily, dear, welcome home.' The woman's voice was strained. 'Come on into the warm, and we'll settle you in.'

'What time is Pa due home?' Emily followed her through and stood looking around the room. She noticed that it had recently been cleaned. No cobwebs at the windows, and the kitchen range gleamed.

'He'll be home at five-thirty.' She stepped towards Emily. 'Shall I take the babe whilst you take your things upstairs?'

Emily snapped. 'No need. I can settle him upstairs.' She looked at Kate. 'You might as well know, Kate. I don't trust you and don't think I ever will. I'm only here because there's nowhere else and I'll be gone as soon as I can leave.'

'Please, Emily, I want to make amends.'

'If you really want to do that, you will leave this house, leave Pa and let him have his life back.'

Kate winced. 'You don't mean that. Your Pa loves me and I care for him. And I have nowhere to go.'

'Like I had nowhere to go when I was in that place and you refused to have me back here?'

'I thought I was doing it for the best.'

'And what did you do with the money you were given when you sold this child? I suppose it's all gone, is it?'

'I'm sorry. I can't say it enough. A woman has to do what she can in these times.'

'You are disgusting. Just stay away from my baby. That's all.'

That evening, after supper, Emily sat in the chair that had been pulled nearer to the range beside her Pa. He was smiling at her as she fed her little Billy with a bottle. 'It really is so good to have you home, Emily,' he said.

'I'm glad to be here, Pa. I can't thank you enough. And I am so happy now I have my baby. Life will be good from now on, I'm sure.'

'I'm sure it will too. When am I going to meet this young man of yours?'

'Soon, Pa. And you must meet Mrs. Berry, his Ma. They are going to come and visit as soon as they can.'

Kate sat in her Ma's old chair on the other side of the range. She seemed uncomfortable as she watched Emily with her baby. Looking across at her Emily included her in the conversation, saying, 'We are planning our wedding at the church in the village. We want to start our new life in Droxford as soon as possible. I can't help thinking, that if Joe hadn't been from Droxford, I may never have found my child. My life could have been so different.'

Soon it was time for bed. Emily had settled Billy in the cradle that Pa had placed beside the bed. Laying there, listening to the sounds of the baby as he slept Emily's thoughts went over the past months.

She'd had it in her head and now it was gone. No sign

of the madness that had sowed its seed all that time ago. Just a tiny seed that you didn't even know it was there but it grew into something beyond control. It was strange how things could get so bad and how a person could feel so useless, so unable to smile, to move through each day without purpose, and then again, how it was possible to move through it, beyond it, and leave so much behind.

She felt the weight lift from her soul, bounce on her shoulders and drift into the air. She remembered the cabbages that were her way out of that black place. They were the start of her healing. It seemed strange now, thinking about it, but it was the truth. Without the fields of cabbages she may never have got beyond the four walls and the pain and the hopelessness that seemed to follow her around wherever she was.

She saw Joe's face in her mind's eye, staring at her that first day. She'd felt fear then when he looked at her. It reminded her that she was loved once, and she had loved in return. It reminded her of losing her sweetheart Billy, losing all she'd loved before and she didn't want to go there again. So she'd bowed her head against his stare, against the sun, and let her hands do their work, pulling the weeds from the earth, allowing the sunshine and the nourishment of the earth feed the cabbages, so beautiful and so green. Suddenly, she'd been able to see colour again, the grey of the world had slipped out of her eyes, but the sun was too bright at first, so she'd kept her head down, looked away from him and when it was time to return to the safety of the ward, she went and did feel safe. When the key turned in the lock behind her she'd breathed a sigh of relief, knowing that he could not follow her into the building.

Sometimes, she'd looked out of the window at night, looked up at the stars and had wondered if he was seeing the same stars, wherever he was. She'd dreamed of walking with him and often shook it all away, afraid to dream of anything good. Sometimes the wind was so strong it blew all the stars from the sky and she'd thought that he would have been blown away too, just another wonderful thing in her life to be taken from her.

On days when the rain fell, bouncing off the green leaves, she'd loved it even more outside, felt the cold water run into her eyes, down her neck, cleansing her. Raindrops were like emeralds glistening on a necklace that she would never afford. Better than emeralds as these were all hers fleetingly and no one else's. She'd laughed sometimes and when she'd looked, he was laughing too. She'd felt an invisible ribbon of laughter spun between them and her heart had warmed alive again as she'd recognised the kindness in his eyes.

Chapter Seventy-three

Joe

The path to the church was crowded. Many of his friends and neighbours from the village had turned out and were watching as they approached from the lych-gate. There was Joe's own dear Ma smiling, holding little Billy in her arms, and Mrs. Simpson, Marjorie as she insisted they call her, standing beside her with Emily's friends Mabel, the nurse Maud, and May with her handsome husband in Naval officer's uniform. Annie and Johnny were there both grinning. Old Fred looking so smart in his best Sunday suit, standing to attention as they passed was beside Emily's own Pa and his wife Kate. They were both smiling as well and with them was young Percy, grinning widely. They stopped in front of the little group and Emily stepped towards her Pa and took his arm.

'You will walk me down the aisle, won't you, Pa?' She smiled up at him.

'I'd be more than proud to,' was his answer. Joe noticed the smile slip slightly from Kate's face, which was swiftly replaced when Emily's Pa turned to look at her. 'Kate, you can sit with Percy.'

Kate sniffed then nodded and Percy took her arm.

There was Jack, his pal from the asylum farm, which was now called the Portsmouth Mental Hospital. 'You'd best get in the church, Joe,' he said. 'You've already broken the rules and seen your bride before the wedding. It's bad luck you know.'

Joe laughed at that. 'We've used up all the bad luck, mate. Come on then, let's get in there. Have you got the ring?'

'What do you think? You didn't ask me to be your best man for nothing.'

The two men waited at the altar and when all the others had filed in and the music began, Joe turned and watched Emily and her Pa walking down the aisle towards him. She had a tear in her eye but she was smiling and as she walked he saw the light shining in her hair, just like he had that first day he'd seen her in the fields.

His heart was fit to burst when he saw behind her two figures in khaki uniforms slip into the back row of the church. Recognising them from the photograph Emily had shown him of her two eldest brothers, he realised that her best wedding present had arrived.

Emily saw the look on his face and stopped walking, looking back for a moment. When she turned to face Joe again, it was as though she'd walked through a rainbow, with all the love in the world shining from her eyes.

Ingram Content Group UK Ltd.
Milton Keynes UK
UKHW021934260723
425832UK00013B/577